AT SOMERTON

SECRETS &
SAPPHIRES

AT SOMERTON

SECRETS & SAPPHIRES

LEILA RASHEED

HOT
KEY
BOOKS

First published in Great Britain in 2013 by Hot Key Books
Northburgh House, 10 Northburgh Street, London EC1V 0AT

First published in the US in 2013 by Hyperion

A CIP catalogue record for this book is available from the British Library.

ISBN: 978-1-4714-0086-5

1

Typeset by Palimpsest Book Production Limited, Falkirk, Stirlingshire
This book is set in 10.5pt Berling LT Std

Printed and bound by Clays Ltd, St Ives Plc

Hot Key Books supports the Forest Stewardship Council (FSC),
the leading international forest certification organisation, and is committed
to printing only on Greenpeace-approved FSC-certified paper.

www.hotkeybooks.com

Prologue

At Sea in Summer, 1912

Lady Ada Averley leaned on the rail of the steamboat *Moldavia*, feeling the hum of the ship's huge engines through the steel, a rhythmic shudder like a giant's breathing. The black sea glittered with the reflection of the stars above her, and the wind tugged at her hat and loosened the dark curls that framed her pale face. Her features were a perfect mirror of her late mother's, but the gray eyes and the proudly lifted chin were pure Averley.

This steamboat had carried many young Englishwomen to India in its time, just as it would have carried any other commodity that was in short supply in the colonies. Less frequently did it bring them back again. Even less frequently was the Englishwoman in question as attractive and eligible as Lady Ada, eldest child of the Earl of Westlake.

The wild romantic shores of Italy lay behind them; tonight they were passing through the Straits of Gibraltar. Before Ada lay England, and the prospect of her first season this coming spring. But she was not looking forward to the dances and the attention of young men.

Her mind was as restless as the sea. She knew what her late mother's friends said about her. "Quite beautiful," they agreed, "but too serious." It was understandable, they said, with the tragedy of her mother's death and the responsibility she had inherited for her delicate younger sister.

That was not all. The news about her father's resignation from the post of lieutenant-governor only added to her worries. Georgiana was too young and too naturally light-hearted to understand the severity of the rumors that circled like kites, but Ada understood what they meant for her, on the eve of her first season. At least the other debutantes would be relieved: another contender out of the race meant more chances for them. It seemed her parents' efforts to bring up a perfect lady would be wasted. She knew quite well that it was wrong to be on the first-class deck at midnight with no hat, no gloves, and no chaperone. But she could not sleep. After days at sea even the luxurious stateroom felt like a prison, but it was not just that, nor the scent of the sea wind, that had brought her up to the deck. It was the sense that the ship carrying her to England was also carrying her ever closer to adulthood. This homecoming meant freedom from the *Moldavia*, but it might also mean an even more stifling prison. So much depended on the next few months, and whether she could persuade her father to take her dreams of university seriously.

In her ungloved hand was a piece of paper torn from *The Times*, an article about women's suffrage written by the Liberal peer Lord Fintan. She'd meant to read it in the bright moonlight, but she had quite forgotten it. Now the wind whisked the paper out of her grip. It fluttered away across the deck. Ada exclaimed and ran after it.

It blew toward the shadows by the lifeboats. A red star gleamed there in the darkness above the rail. The paper twitched up into the air. Ada grabbed for it.

She smelled the cheroot first, and then the darkness

became solid, and she gasped as she bumped into the soft warmth of a man's body. She hadn't seen him there, hidden by the shadow of the lifeboat, until she ran straight into him.

He stepped forward into the moonlight. She saw the handsome, strongly carved face of a dark-skinned boy, his teeth gleaming in a smile. In one hand he held her paper. With the other, he steadied her. From his looks he was not much older than she, but his movements were not awkward and boyish, they were confident—almost, she would have said, arrogant.

He removed the cheroot from his mouth and flicked it overboard, its red tip glowing. "Do you throw yourself into the arms of every man you meet?" he said, with a deep, soft laugh. "Or am I particularly honored?" His eyes shone like moonlit water and she felt very unsteady in their gaze.

"I—I beg your pardon. I—I didn't see you." She was breathless, and her face grew hot with shock and embarrassment. To have run across the deck like that, straight at him! He must have thought her insane. Her hand went to her hatless hair, until she remembered she had no gloves on either, and let it fall. She flushed again at the thought of her appearance. Willing her heartbeat to slow down, she said as coldly as she could manage: "I would like my paper back, please."

He glanced at the paper, and with a bow, offered it to her.

"'The Suffrage Question.' An unusual choice for a young lady's reading."

His ironic smile annoyed Ada. She was no stranger to being mocked for her desire to learn. But this young man's knowing expression somehow irked her more than others', and with the worry about her father fresh in her mind, she felt especially stung. "Not all young ladies are quite as lacking in intelligence as certain young men would like them to be," she said, taking the paper from his hand. Her fingers grazed his as she did so, and the burning returned to her face.

She turned, her heart thumping, and walked quickly away. She was trembling. With rage? Or something else? Already she was regretting her sharp words. It was unladylike. It was undignified. But it got very tiresome, being treated like a brainless doll. Sometimes she dreamed she was shut up in a glass case in a museum, screaming silently, thumping her fists against the invisible walls, while the world strolled past without noticing her.

"Lady Ada!"

He was following her. Of course he would think he had the right to be familiar now. How did he even know her name? She turned around, prepared to put him in his place, but he spoke too quickly.

"I must apologize," he said. He sounded serious. "That was not a gentlemanly comment, and I deserved what you said."

His expression was so sincere that Ada was at a complete loss for what to do next.

"I don't think we have been introduced," she said.

"Excuse me, you are quite right." He bowed quickly; the movement was particularly Indian and Ada felt a sudden stab of homesickness. "I have seen you in the first-class dining hall. My name is Ravi Sundaresan. I am traveling with Mr. Douglas Varley, to study at Oxford University."

"Oh!" Ada's frown disappeared. Douglas Varley was an old friend of her father's and a very influential politician. The two men had become reacquainted on the voyage and spent long hours in the smoking saloon together. His wispy gray mustache made her think of a dead mouse. But she did not

4

care what he looked like; he was the most welcome person in the world to her, because he was still speaking to her father, and that had kept the rumors at bay onboard ship.

Still, it was not a formal introduction, and she knew she should walk away. But the boy stood there, his hands in his pockets, looking at her intently. There was something both gentle and fierce about him and she could not make herself leave.

"I'm sorry," the boy said. "I realize that this means I've forced my acquaintance upon you. I quite forgot that we had not been formally introduced."

Ada found herself blushing again and she was grateful for the darkness. "I—I appreciate your rescue, Mr. Sundaresan." She made a half nod, half curtsy, and at once felt like a fool. "Of the article, I mean. I thought the moonlight would be strong enough to read . . ." She stumbled to a halt. How stupid to remind him of the article.

"I came out here to see the stars," Ravi said, acting as if she had said nothing silly at all. "Did you know they had names, Lady Ada?"

"Of course I . . ." she started to say, but trailed off when he placed a hand on her arm and guided her toward the rail. For a few moments Ada's world contracted to the warm pressure of his hand on her elbow. She felt a shiver of excitement that had nothing to do with the cool sea breeze. *This is terribly improper*, she scolded herself. But it was also the most interesting thing that had happened during the entire voyage.

Ravi pointed up into the sky. Ada followed his finger with her eyes, to a line of three bright stars, as perfectly aligned as guardsmen. "Orion," he said. His finger traced the outline of a great man in stars, leaning upon his club. "The great hunter."

Ada remembered being in her father's library in Kolkata, sitting curled under the desk reading translations of Aesop and Ovid, while outside the monkeys chattered in the trees and the long hot afternoon went by, marked by the swish of the punkah pulled by a servant.

"After his death the gods placed him in the sky to honor his skill," she said.

"Yes, that is the ancient Greeks' story," he agreed. "But we know these stars as the Stag, Mriga."

"I didn't know the constellations had Indian names."

"The ancient Indians were great astronomers."

His finger traced another shape, and Ada stared as the constellation of Orion seemed to reshape itself into the form of a silver stag. "Mriga is pursuing his own daughter, the beautiful Rohini—this star, here, which Western astronomers call Aldebaran. But the gods were angry at this transgression, and shot him through with Isus Trikanda, the three-jointed arrow—which you call Orion's belt."

Ada was silent, gazing up at the stars. They shone like distant diamonds. She had never guessed that there was so much more to learn even about the constellations. This boy knew so much more than she ever would.

"It must be nice to be a boy," she found herself saying.

Ravi raised an eyebrow.

"In *your* case, I don't think it would have been an improvement."

Ada shook her head, though she couldn't help but smile at the compliment. "If I were a boy, I would have been educated. There's so much I don't know."

"That's an odd thing for a young lady to complain about," he said. The ironic note was back in his voice. "Most are quite happy in their ignorance."

6

Ada's skin bristled, and before she could stop herself, she said, "As it happens, I want to go to Oxford too." She caught his eye; he looked startled.

What did she care? She wouldn't see him again. The freedom of saying her deepest wish felt so wonderful. And his face, though shocked, looked almost admiring. He was very handsome. The conversation had begun to excite her.

"Well, I hope it doesn't sound selfish if I say that I wish you success." Ada had barely time to understand the flattery before he hurried on: "I must admit to being surprised, though. I understood from your father you were to come out this year, and I suppose I thought your mind would be full of dresses and dances."

"Well, it isn't. It's full of Socrates and Euclid."

He laughed. "When we met, I took you for the perfect young lady. I see you are anything but." Seeing her expression, his face broke into a mischievous smile. "Don't misunderstand me. I think there are real ladies and perfect ladies. Perfect ladies are all gloves and fan-cases. Real ladies are . . ."

"Are what?"

"Are like you."

She had never been looked at this way by a young man, and she felt both exhilarated and frightened. She pressed her hands against the cold rail and then against her cheeks. As she did so, he moved a bit closer, and she noticed his jacket had a faint perfume of spice, and underneath it, the smell of his skin. She was aware of his closeness.

"See there, Lady Ada." He stood behind her and spoke softly, near her ear. "Your Ursa Major, the Great Bear."

"I see it." Ada gazed at the familiar constellation. "When I look up at the stars, they remind me that even those things that seem impossible can come to pass."

Ada realized something. Looking up into the depth of the night and the countless stars, she felt somehow as if she were standing on the brink of a precipice, and that if she had the courage to step forward, she might find that she could fly. She shivered—half with cold, half with excitement.

"Please." He handed her his jacket. Ada was about to refuse, but the expression in his eyes made her falter. While she was trying to collect herself, he placed the jacket around her shoulders.

"They're so beautiful," she said, looking up at the stars again.

"Yes," said Ravi. "Yes, they are. And that's the most important thing. Whoever we are, whatever we call them, we look at the stars firstly because they are beautiful. Names, stories—all that comes later."

She sensed that he was looking at her as he spoke.

"Since the dawn of time, men have loved to gaze upon beautiful things from afar."

Ada turned her head, startled, toward him.

"I mustn't—" She was breathless. He was too close to her, she should do something, she should say something, she should . . . and instead their lips were coming together, and his warm arms were around her, and all she could think was: So *this* is it, finally, *this* is what it feels like.

ACT ONE

SOMERTON

Chapter One

The clock in the housekeeper's parlor had been there since before Mrs. Cliffe had come to Somerton Court. It had a solid, squat oak casing, with brass workings and a face that had to be polished daily by the second housemaid. The numbers were inscribed in the old-fashioned script of the early years of Victoria, and its slow, heavy pulse never missed a beat. The years passed and people came and went, but the ticking of the clock was always there, behind the clash of the pans and the rattle of the tea things and the shrill summons of the servants' bells. The clock stood for Somerton Court itself; eternal, unchanging. The land had been part of the estates of the Earl of Westlake for five hundred years; there had been a house on this spot for four hundred, though the current building with its Adam ballroom and neoclassical frontage dated only from 1815. The lineage of the family they served was a source of great pride for Mrs. Cliffe and, she felt, the entire household staff.

Now, as she went over the estate accounts, it seemed the tick of the clock stood for something sinister. Time running out.

Sir William could talk all he wanted about investments. She knew it was gambling and speculation that made the money escape like water from a leaky bucket. It was a good thing Lord Westlake was coming home—for the estate, at least. Of course, it might also cause problems.

Her thoughts turned to Rose, and she got to her feet abruptly, walking over to the mantelpiece. In the mirror above it she surveyed her own face closely. How many of those lines had been there ten years ago? It was hard to remember. At least her eyes were still clear and large, and as deep a blue as a summer evening. Like Rose's eyes.

She had always encouraged Rose to wear her hair in such a way as to show those vivid blue eyes off. Any wise mother would do the same, especially now that Rose was sixteen. But the rest of Rose's face . . . her full mouth, the way she smiled . . . if anyone looked too closely, those could give away the secret.

None of the servants she oversaw would have believed her capable of such an emotion . . . but today Mrs. Cliffe, head housekeeper, was frightened.

"I don't know how we'll ever get it all done in time!"

It was Cook who said it, but they were all thinking it. Rose had been thinking it since she stumbled out of bed that morning before light, shivering as she swept out the grates and lit the fire in the breakfast room, polished the brass, and ran downstairs to get the hot water for the family's baths. Lord Westlake was due back tomorrow and although the master bedroom was in order, the young ladies' rooms were still only half ready. It didn't help that they were understaffed. The hall-boy had just been sacked for being drunk when he opened the door to the Marquis of Sunderland's eldest son, no less, and the nursemaid had given notice, to no one's surprise. Sir William and Lady Edith's son, Augustus, was generally considered below stairs to be a small demon sent from hell two years ago specifically to torture the inhabitants of Somerton. So the parlormaid had been sent up to the nursery, and she was in a fury about the insult to her dignity, and of course all her work had fallen onto the other housemaids, including Rose.

Mary, the second housemaid, passed her as she went down the servants' stairs with the last empty can of water. Rose caught her arm.

"Mary! Have you finished Lady Ada's room yet?"

"Lady Ada?" Mary shook her off. "Have a heart, I've been scrubbing the steps all morning. My knees are killing me. Then there's the drawing room to get ready—" She headed off down the stairs, her cap askew and her mousy hair escaping.

"Then I'll begin on Lady Ada's room, is that all right, Mrs. Cliffe?" Rose called after her mother as she hurried along the passage.

"Yes, Rose, and after you've done that you need to—" She broke off as Martha, the scullery maid, came bursting through the back door, practically shouting. "The luggage is here. And they've brought a tiger!"

Rose and her mother exchanged a glance and ran back along the passage to the back door. Rose burst out onto the cobbles, not sure whether to believe Martha. She was the greatest gossip in the world, but on the other hand the noise outside seemed to warrant a tiger at the very least.

In the courtyard, the station horse was pulling at his reins madly while the driver tried to calm him. Bandboxes and trunks were piled high upon the wagon. Tobias, the stable boy, looking sweaty and nervous, was handing the luggage down to James.

"Oh, Martha, that's a rug!" Rose said with relief, as she saw the tiger, rolled up with its tail between its legs. But there

13

was still something in the dead, glaring glass eyes that made her flatten herself against the wall while James carried it in. It *smelled* of India. She reached her hand out to touch the fur, half expecting the fiery colors to burn her.

If colors were music, she thought, this would be a wild dance. She could almost hear its rhythms in her head. Her fingers itched to try it out on the piano. But there was no time for that; instead she sang under her breath so she would remember the tune. If only she could have a quiet evening to herself to write the music down. But then she would have to steal a pencil and some paper, and there would be all the trouble of hiding it from everyone. Maybe it was better this way.

"You wouldn't believe how much luggage they've sent," James was saying as he unloaded. "And there's more coming up from the station!"

The servants were clustered in the passage around the unloaded luggage.

"Look at all them hatboxes! How many heads have they got between them?" Martha exclaimed. "And what's that?" She made a face as she looked at a thing like a huge metal flower fixed to a wooden base, which teetered on the top of the pile.

Rose gasped. "It's a gramophone." She couldn't believe what she was looking at. Sir William and Lady Edith didn't care for music, and they had never troubled to get one.

"A what? A grampus?" Martha said.

"No, a gramophone. It plays music," Rose replied.

"How?"

"Oh, don't ask me. Maybe that electricity does it." Rose looked at it longingly. Of course she would never be allowed to touch it, probably not even to dust it. It was far too expensive to be entrusted to a mere housemaid. But how wonderful it would be if she could carry music around with her, to listen to any time she pleased.

"Have you felt the weight of Lady Ada's trunk?" Martha was round-eyed. "Must be packed with sapphires and rubies at least. I've heard some of them Indian jewels are cursed—"

"Martha!" Rose's mother's reproving voice silenced them all. "That's none of your business. Back to work." Martha scurried off to the kitchen. "James, Roderick, get Lord Westlake's luggage up to his room."

"What about the unpacking?" James asked. "Is his lordship traveling with a valet?"

"I'm not sure. Communication has been very difficult." She looked at the butler. "Mr. Cooper—perhaps you would be kind enough to unpack just this once? You used to valet for his lordship. You'll know how he wants things."

Mr. Cooper nodded his bald head, saying, "As this is an emergency, Mrs. Cliffe, I am glad to be of service."

"Thank you." Rose's mother looked around at the luggage. "Annie and Rose, you'll have to take care of the young ladies' luggage. The footmen will carry it up when they're done with Lord Westlake's."

Rose bent down to inspect the nearest trunk. She wanted to see what kind of unpacking lay ahead. On the brass clasps there was a monogram picked out in brass studs: *FT.*

"Who's FT?" she said. "Those aren't family initials." She scanned the luggage. "And, look, those bandboxes. They've got the same mark on them. Whose are they?"

"You're right. Blow it!" Roderick said. "They've sent the wrong luggage."

Rose immediately ran to the door. "Tobias, don't let the man go!" she called. "He'll have to take it all back—" She fell silent as the station wagon rattled away, to reveal a girl with very fair hair and neat, almost doll-like features, carrying a small leather suitcase. She glanced around at the courtyard, with a careful, assessing gaze and began picking her way across the cobbles toward the door.

"Who's *she*?" Rose whispered to Annie, who was peering round the door with her.

The girl wore a pale green traveling gown and primrose-yellow gloves, and the feathers in her hat nodded as she crossed the threshold. The dress was not in the latest style, but to Rose, whose own wardrobe consisted of two uniforms, flannel petticoats, and a spare apron for best, it was an elegant dress. She couldn't be a lady, though. A lady would have entered through the front door, not the servants' entrance.

With her chin lifted delicately the girl examined the open-mouthed servants as if she were a duchess considering a selection of unpromising scullery maids.

"Why was no one at the station to meet me?" she demanded.

The servants looked at each other blankly.

"Miss—excuse me—who are you?" Mr. Cooper said.

The girl frowned.

"My goodness! I understood that things would be slow in the countryside, but I did not expect quite such ignorance." She handed Mr. Cooper her parasol and went on down the servants' passage.

Rose's mother recovered herself first.

"She can't go that way! The master will see her." She darted after her, and Rose followed, just in time to see the girl rustling up the steps into the main house. Cook came out of the kitchen as she passed, and stared after her in astonishment.

Rose caught the door on the back swing, and she and Martha and James and even Mr. Cooper pressed themselves to the gap, watching and listening. The girl had stopped in the center of the hall, right under the chandelier, looking up and around her. Portraits of Lords Westlake from centuries past lined the walls, and statues brought back from the grand tour of Italy and Greece loomed in the corners like naked guests turned to stone by the basilisk gaze of the house's former masters. Rose half expected the girl to be turned to stone too for her presumption, but she remained stubbornly flesh and blood.

"Show me to Mrs. Templeton's rooms at once," she commanded. "Why do I see no evidence of preparation for the wedding? Please tell me you have at least begun the cake!"

Mrs. Cliffe folded her arms. "You have made a mistake. This is Somerton Court, home of the Earls of Westlake. We expect Lord Westlake any day now, from India. There is no wedding, and we know nothing of any Mrs. Templeton."

The girl's mouth twitched with a slight, disbelieving smile.

"You mean," she said, "you did not receive the telegram?"

"Telegram?"

"Lord Westlake will be followed by his betrothed, Mrs. Fiona Templeton, and her children. I am Stella Ward, Mrs. Templeton's lady's maid. Lord Westlake and my mistress intend to marry as soon as possible after they reach Somerton."

"Marry?" echoed a man's furious voice from above them.

Rose gasped and looked up. On the main stairs, one hand upon the polished oak banister, below the painting of Cupid and Psyche, stood a young man with red, curling hair and a sizeable belly. It was Sir William, Lord Westlake's nephew, and until Miss Ward's announcement, his undisputed heir.

Chapter Two

"Hey, I've just come from the breakfast room. Sir William's in a right temper!" James was grinning as he came down the steps carrying the empty tray. Rose, who had heard about the master's ludicrous tantrums, couldn't help grinning back. "He threw the deviled kidneys across the room. That little dog of Lady Edith's was eating 'em when I came out."

"Glad you can laugh." Cook clattered the plates back into the sink. "A waste of good food, I call it. Annie, where have you got to with that salt?"

"That Miss Ward's something, isn't she?" Annie came running back in with the salt. "Here, do you think her hair's all natural? It's *that* blond!"

"And have you seen her waist? It's tiny, like a lady's." Martha brought her hands out of the washing-up to show her.

"Will you stop splashing everywhere and get on with the work?" Cook demanded. "I don't care about Miss Ward's waist, all I care about is she's brought a lot of hard work and trouble with her."

"Why is it trouble?" Rose asked.

"Don't be dim, Rose! Fancy London folk like that, they're going to want to make changes. If we're not up to scratch, Her ladyship'll have us out on our ears. And I don't want to try and find another position at my time of life!" She thumped the bread dough down on the table.

"You think they'd sack us?" Rose was shocked. She had lived at Somerton ever since she was seven and her mother had moved from the village to take up the post of house-keeper. It was impossible to imagine being forced to leave. Even though she knew she had no right to it, really, she had come to think of the great house as her home.

"Yes, so you'd better get a move on, hadn't you? You should be up there helping your mother get the rooms ready, not dawdling down here gossiping!"

Rose ran upstairs to begin the mountain of work ahead of her. So there were big changes ahead! It was exciting, and a little frightening, too. Usually life at Somerton ticked along quietly enough. Sir William and Lady Edith were mostly in London, and so long as Cooper made sure that the income from the Somerton estate went to their London address, they were happy. But now there would be new people, and perhaps some of them would play music, or bring musicians to play for balls. She longed to learn the piano properly more than anything. But her mother would never hear of it; lessons were far too expensive and it would be what she called "getting above her station." Rose sighed. Sometimes it seemed as though everything she wanted to do, everything she found fascinating, was somehow "above her station."

Rose came running up the servants' stairs with hatboxes piled high in her arms, to the sound of bumps and thumps as the footmen maneuvered the trunks into the bedrooms. With no hand free, she backed out through the servants' door into the east wing. Doors had been thrown open on rooms that had not been used for ten years, and the quarters seemed to blink in the sudden sunlight. She could smell polish and hear the swish and slap of Annie sweeping the carpets in the white rooms. She glanced into the music room as she hurried past. The piano had been uncovered and James and Roderick were unrolling the carpet. The house had never been so noisy.

"That's the last of Miss Charlotte's luggage," Rose announced, as she carried the boxes into the blue boudoir.

"Finally!" Annie looked up from making the bed.

"That's enough cheek, Annie." Rose's mother surged in, a crease between her eyebrows the only sign of the stress she was under. "Help her with the bed, Rose, and then go and see if Miss Ward needs any help with Mrs. Templeton's room."

"This trunk for Lady Ada's room?" James demanded, pushing open the door. "Oh, excuse me, Mrs. Cliffe, didn't see you there."

"Yes, take it to Lady Ada's room, and the other one to Lady Georgiana's. Is the gramophone Master Sebastian's? Take it up to the Chinese bedroom. That thing, too, whatever it is." She nodded at a slender vase decorated with Arab-looking gilding, from which a long, snakelike pipe coiled.

"It's a Turkish pipe," James said with some pride.

"Yes, well, don't break it." Mrs. Cliffe did not look impressed.

"I think it's going to be exciting to have young men in the house," Annie announced, plumping the pillows. "Don't you, Rose?"

"If you've any sense, you'll stay well away from that kind of excitement." Her mother's voice was sharp. "And you, Rose, hear me?"

"I wasn't *thinking* of—"

"Well, don't." She added, "We're here to work for the

gentry, not become familiar with them. They're different to us, and if you forget it, you'll be sorry indeed."

"They're not that different to us," Annie pouted. "If Rose put on a fancy dress and a nice hat, she could pass for a lady, I'd bet."

Rose was not prepared for her mother's reaction. Mrs. Cliffe turned on Annie angrily.

"Listen, Annie, we all have a place. We're born to it, and we need to stick to it. You step out of your place, and you'll regret it. The gentry can be as friendly as they like, but if you make a mistake, it's you who'll be out on your ear—not them."

"What's up with her?" Annie scowled after Mrs. Cliffe as she left. "She's scratchy as a cat."

"She's just worried we won't get it all done in time," Rose said. But as she ran off to the blue boudoir, she wondered if that was the whole truth. Her mother had been on edge since the news of Lord Westlake's return.

She found Miss Ward by the window, holding up a diaphanous beaded dress. A half-open monogrammed trunk stood nearby, clouds of tissue paper rising from it.

Rose couldn't think of anything to say. The whole house had been speaking of nothing but Miss Ward ever since she had arrived. How small her waist was, whether the color of her hair was all natural, the elegant cut of her gloves, her London way of speaking. If her maid was so impressive, Rose found herself wondering, what must Mrs. Templeton be like?

"Er . . . Mrs. Cliffe sent me to see if you need any help," she said.

"About time! These belong to Miss Charlotte. Hang them up." Miss Ward thrust an armful of satin at Rose, who staggered

21

to the mahogany wardrobe and hung the dresses carefully inside, adding sachets of lavender and violet to the hangers as Miss Ward passed them to her. She glanced around the bedroom. It had been transformed. A huge cheval glass had been set up to catch the best light, and a pretty chintz armchair was next to it. The trunks, standing here and there, half unpacked, gleamed in the afternoon sun, and the studded brass initials *CT* burned like gold. Silver-backed brushes and combs, ivory jewelry cases, and cut-glass perfume bottles stood on the dressing table. Dazzling light blazed from them as if the room were coated with precious stones.

Rose guessed by the size and style of the dresses that Miss Charlotte was around her age. "Is Miss Charlotte out yet?" she asked shyly.

Miss Ward took her time before replying, arranging a pearl-encrusted fan in its velvet-lined case.

"Not officially, but she has been attending balls and parties with her mother for a couple of months now. She's a great hit with the gentlemen. Lord Fintan was quite taken with her, and the Duke of Brentfordshire's youngest son danced with her three times at the last hunt ball." She glanced out of the window. "But I suppose there will be a change of pace now. What is the society like here? What do you do for amusement?"

"Well . . . we have a little piano in the servants' hall, and we sometimes have dances and there's always the village . . ." Rose trailed off, feeling for the first time that her life lacked something. "I suppose it must seem quiet to you, after London. It must be so exciting there." Rose had forgotten the dresses she was clutching.

"Of course it is." Miss Ward nodded. "The countryside is all very well for Saturday to Monday, but London is the

22

center of fashion and society. There's the theater, and balls and parties every night."

"With music?" Rose's eyes shone.

"Of course, how would the ladies and gentlemen dance otherwise? Then Mrs. Templeton belongs to one of the new ladies' clubs, so she often lunches there. I really don't know how we shall accustom ourselves to living here." She tucked a strand of her hair over her ear and practiced pouting in the mirror. Rose watched, wide-eyed. If she had ever primped in the mirror like that, her mother would have given her a strict lecture on vanity.

"It must be wonderful being a lady's maid," she found herself saying. "I mean . . . you're like a lady yourself."

Miss Ward caught her eye in the mirror and smiled.

"It's hard work, but worth it. And a lady's maid always attracts more followers than a housemaid. We live close to St. James's, so there are always handsome young guardsmen to walk out with."

"You're allowed followers?"

"Well, not officially. But a girl has to amuse herself somehow." She winked, and Rose found herself smiling.

"Well, I hope you won't be homesick," she said warmly. "Just tell me if you need help finding things."

Miss Ward finally turned from the mirror and smiled at her. It was a warm enough smile, but her eyes remained assessing.

"That's so nice of you. I'm sure we're going to be great friends."

She lifted the last hat out of the box and to Rose's shock set it on her own head, tilting it and glancing up under the brim of flowers.

"Are you—are you allowed to do that? Doesn't Miss Templeton mind?"

23

"What she doesn't know won't hurt her." She tilted her chin, admiring herself in the mirror. "It'll be mine soon enough, anyway. Miss Charlotte never wears a hat more than once or twice. Truth be told, she hasn't the face for a fashionable shape like this, but she keeps on trying."

Rose came to the mirror, arranging the hat until it framed Miss Ward's face perfectly. "Very elegant! You may make a lady's maid yourself one day," said Miss Ward with a laugh.

"I couldn't. I'd never know how to do things." Rose was a little frightened by the idea; lady's maids always seemed so grand to her.

"Oh, you'll learn. I did." She tilted her head in the mirror, looking up under the brim of the hat.

The door flew open, and Rose's mother came in.

"Rose? You're needed in the music room. It seems Lady Georgiana plays the piano, and she wants it all set up for when she gets here."

Rose was already scurrying away when her mother called her back. The corridor was empty, and she placed a hand under her chin and looked at her blue eyes.

"Don't forgot to wear your hair back, Rose, so people can see your eyes," she said in a whisper. She stroked Rose's hair away from her face, something she hadn't done since Rose was a little girl. "And keep your chin down, and try not to smile."

Rose stared. "Er—yes, Mother."

"I do love you, you know that."

Rose knew her mother loved her, but she very rarely said it. "What's wrong?" Rose asked in a low voice.

But her mother was back to her brisk self. "What's wrong is that we only have one more day to really get the house in order and organize the wedding. Now go and make sure the tower bedroom is ready for Lady Ada. I quite forgot her, what with the Templetons arriving."

Lady Ada's room was up a twisty staircase. Rose had begun the process of readying her room for the big homecoming, but as she pushed open the door and saw the trunk lying in the middle of the floor, she thought the room looked bare and cold compared with Miss Charlotte's accommodation. She began by making the fire, then the bed. Once the shutters were opened and the room cleaned she turned to the unpacking. She felt more confident now that she had seen how Miss Ward had arranged Miss Charlotte's room. She unstrapped the trunk and looked in, wondering if Martha's idea of cursed jewels was right.

Books!

She stared at them in astonishment. Greek books, Latin books, histories, and works of politics and philosophy . . . Where on earth was she going to put them all? In the end, she stacked them inside the wardrobe and hung the few dresses above them. It was hard not to draw a comparison between Lady Ada's sensible cotton and muslin dresses and Miss Charlotte's delicate embroidered gowns. She looked around. Perhaps Lady Ada cared more for books than for clothes and trinkets, but it still seemed a shame not to make the room more welcoming.

On the corridor below, a huge arrangement of roses had been placed under a window. Somerton was famed for its roses and especially this one, the Averley Pearl, first bred by Lord Westlake's great-grandmother. They had a powerful, sweet scent and a dewy sheen to the white petals that gardeners everywhere had tried and failed to reproduce. Rose carefully plucked a single bloom and carried it upstairs. She put it in a silver bowl, fetched some water, and placed it on the dressing table.

"There," she said aloud. "I hope she likes it."

She stood for a moment, looking at the rose thoughtfully. She knew she ought to go downstairs and help, but she was suddenly overcome by memories of her childhood, when she and Lady Ada and Lady Georgiana had played together in the gardens. They hadn't really been allowed to, but they hadn't thought of being mistress and maid. They had just been three little girls, making up stories about fairies in the orchard. How strange it was that now she no longer knew what Lady Ada liked and didn't.

Did she dare remind them of those days? Her mother would be angry if she did, and she was probably right. It was important to know your place, and none of them were children anymore. Rose sighed, and went downstairs to arrange Lady Georgiana's room.

Chapter Three

The train chuffed into Somerton Halt. Green boughs changed from a blur into the dappled mixture of sunlight and shadow, and Lord Westlake, leaning forward eagerly, exclaimed, "Well, we're here!"

"Already?" Ada jerked out of her thoughts, startled.

"What are you talking about, Ada? We've been on the train for hours." Georgiana was laughing at her. Ada smiled back, glad her sister was in such high spirits. She linked her arm into Georgiana's, and they went together down the train corridor. Their father's valet helped them down, and Lord Westlake followed.

"Isn't it green!" Georgiana was looking around eagerly. "I mean, of course India was green too, but this is a different kind of green somehow. The light's different—did you notice?"

Ada murmured something. Georgie was right—the light was different, it was somehow more distant, damp and cool. But then, *everything* was different.

She had thought she was coming home. But all she could think, as she looked around, was how foreign everything seemed.

She let the groom hand her into the carriage. Her fingers, imprisoned in kid gloves, were locked together in her lap. As the horses set off, harness jingling and hooves clip-clopping up the lane, she sank back into her thoughts. They were as turbulent as they had been ever since that night on the *Moldavia*.

How had it happened? She had always imagined that if a man tried to force himself on her, she would have screamed, fought, run away—killed herself or him, anything rather than allow her honor to be compromised. But it had not been like that. She could not bring herself to lie, not even to herself. Ravi had not forced himself on her. He had kissed her, and she had kissed him back just as passionately.

She could feel the color flushing into her face as she thought of it. If only the pink had all been from shame and regret. But the horrifying truth was that it wasn't. She had kissed a stranger—an Indian boy—and she had *enjoyed* it.

"Ada, are you quite well?" Her father leaned toward her. "Your color is very high. Do you feel feverish?"

Ada managed a smile and shake of her head.

"I'm just tired," she said. Her father was so good to her. To have let him down like this, to be deceiving him, was unforgivable. She could feel the sting in her eyes, and she clenched her fingers together tightly to try and stop the tears from falling.

She had hardly dared to leave the stateroom since that night. The thought of having to meet his eyes across the dining room had made her face burn. It was not hard to fake seasickness when her stomach was churning. What if he boasted of his conquest? What if Douglas Varley found out and told her father? What had come over her?

You will doubtless never see him again, she told herself. Oddly enough, it was not a comforting thought.

She stared out at the gentle green fields. It was not exactly raining, but the sky was gray, the boughs dripped with water, and damp hung in the air like dust. She found herself longing for the release of a monsoon storm. Something—anything—to break the tension.

There was a sudden hooting, and a roaring like a dragon. Ada sat up, startled. The horses whinnied and she heard the driver's warning voice. A cloud of dust surged up by the window, and looking out, she had a sudden impression of speed, a strong smell of burning oil, and the glimpse of a man, his eyes covered in insectlike goggles.

"A motorcar!" Georgiana exclaimed, leaning forward. "Papa, look!"

"Thank you, Georgiana, I could hardly miss it!" Lord Westlake said with great disapproval.

Ada exchanged an amused glance with Georgiana before turning to her father with a teasing smile. "You will have to get one of those, Papa. Everyone has them now, you know— like electric light."

"Electric nonsense!"

Ada couldn't help laughing at her father's expression. She looked out of the window again, just as the high hedgerow gave way to a smooth, grassy slope running down toward the distant hills and valleys. And there, nestled in the folds of the hills, was a mansion built of honey-colored stone, with more chimneys and windows than she could count.

"Somerton!" she exclaimed. "We're . . . home."

Chapter Four

Rose hurried into the hall, smoothing down her black dress. She thought it was clean, but she hoped she hadn't missed a stain by mistake. It was hard to keep the uniforms spotless when you were working all day in them, often on your hands and knees. And she didn't want to make a bad impression—that would really let her mother down.

Mr. Cooper indicated that she should join the line with the other servants in the hall, waiting for the family to arrive. Rose nervously did so. The hall always made her feel tiny and overawed. The high dome with its Grecian friezes echoed to the sound of feet on the marble floor, and to the side, in a recess, stood the priceless Westlake Vase, a huge, ornate Roman urn that Lord Westlake's father had collected in Paestum on his grand tour. Rose lived in terror of breaking it, even though there was no chance of that—only Cooper was allowed to dust it. "I hope they won't want to eat all that foreign muck like they do in India," Rose heard Martha's voice say, farther down the line. "So hot it blows your head right off, that's what I've heard."

"Martha!" Mr. Cooper snapped, and Martha held her tongue, turning pink under her freckles.

The next moment, the drawing room doors swung open and Sir William and Lady Edith came in. Master Philip,

Sir William's younger brother, followed, looking sulky and miserable in his stiff collar and best suit. Their stately entrance was slightly impeded by the fact that Master Augustus was clinging to Lady Edith's skirts, and howling at the top of his voice.

"Oh dear, Gussie!" Lady Edith sighed. "You seem dreadfully distressed today . . . Would you like something nice to eat? Just please behave for your great-uncle's return. Please, dear."

Philip rolled his eyes, and Rose stifled a smile. She felt sorry for Master Philip—everyone knew that he had a hard time from his older brother.

The clatter of the carriage's wheels and the horses' hooves grew closer and closer until the harness jingled to a halt outside the door. Rose heard the bright, excited voices of young women. Her heart swooped. Lady Ada and Lady Georgiana!

Mr. Cooper gave Martha a last warning glare and then moved to the door, as stately as an ocean liner. James and Roderick, the two footmen, drew themselves up to their full six feet, chests almost bursting through their striped waistcoats. Rose suddenly felt a horrible desire to giggle bubble up inside her. She bit her cheeks.

The door swung open, and Rose heard a muffled male voice outside.

"Good morning, sir," Mr. Cooper replied. Rose, gazing decorously at the ground, saw Sir William's shadow move forward, and heard him say, "Welcome home, Uncle."

"Thank you," replied a deep, quiet voice. "It's good to be back."

Rose sensed the hall filling, the scent of perfume, the soft voices of young ladies, the rustle of skirts.

"Philip! How you've grown. You're quite a young man now." That was one of the girls—Lady Ada, Rose guessed. She had a soft and gentle voice. Philip mumbled something shyly, but he sounded delighted to be noticed. "And this must be young Augustus!" said another girl's voice. "What a terrible noise to welcome your Aunty Georgiana with!"

Augustus stopped crying with a startled hiccup.

"The staff," murmured Mr. Cooper, "may I say on their behalf how delighted we are to welcome you home."

There were polite murmurs. Rose, still gazing demurely at the ground, was aware that Mr. Cooper was leading Lord Westlake and the others toward the drawing room. She sensed them drawing nearer. Mary beside her bobbed a curtsy, and Rose did the same. As she rose, she risked a glance up through her lashes.

She saw two young ladies, still in their hats and veils. One was dark-haired and gray-eyed, taller and more graceful than the other. That had to be Lady Ada. The other was Lady Georgiana, of course. She did not have such fine features, but her expression was so full of good humor that it was hardly noticeable. Rose thought she looked pale and tired, and though she rattled on to Augustus, it seemed almost feverish, as if she were forcing herself to be bright and cheerful.

Rose barely had time to be disappointed that they did not recognize her, because behind them was a tall, handsome gray-haired man with deeply tanned skin. It was Lord Westlake, and he was staring straight at her, with a strange, half-troubled expression in his eyes.

Rose's heart thumped and she looked down, her face burning. There was no reason for him to be staring at her. Had she done something wrong? Somehow she did not think so. What shocked her was the emotion in his eyes.

She could not find a name for it. Certainly not one that made sense. If she had not known it was impossible, she might have thought it was . . . tenderness.

She kept her head bowed until the family had disappeared into the drawing room and the doors had swung shut.

It was hours before Ada was at last alone in her room, and by that time she felt exhausted. She had never been close to her cousin William, but he seemed to have grown even more obnoxious, and Lady Edith even more irritating, in the ten years they had been apart. To make matters worse, her father was clearly angry with him, though she was not sure why. The atmosphere had seethed and bubbled over stilted conversation in the drawing room. It was a horrid situation. William was the steward and the heir, and Lord Westlake had been like a father to him and twelve-year-old Philip since their parents had died. For them to be at odds cast a shadow over her family's return.

She sighed as she sat down in the chair before the window. It was a small room, but it had the best view, across the lawn to the ha-ha and the deer park. The fire warmed it up quickly, and Ada found herself aware of a sweet, familiar scent in the room. It brought back memories of being a child and playing in the rose garden, with Georgiana and another little girl—what had her name been?

She looked around for the source of the scent, and spotted it at once. On the dressing table, she saw, someone had placed a white rose in a silver bowl. It was simple but beautiful. All the light in the room seemed to be drawn into it, making it more luminous and larger, glowing like a pearl. Ada felt grateful to whoever had placed it there. It reminded her of the flowers placed at Hindu shrines.

There was a knock at the door.

"Come in!" Ada jumped up happily. Georgiana had found her, then. But the door opened to reveal a stern-faced woman in a black dress. It took Ada a moment to remember who she was: the housekeeper.

"Yes, Mrs. Cliffe?"

"I have a letter for you, my lady. It arrived this morning." She offered Ada a silver tray, on which lay the envelope.

"For me!" Ada was startled. There was no one who would write to her—perhaps a few friends from India, but none who would be likely to write so soon. She took the envelope. "Thank you." She smiled, and noticed that though Mrs. Cliffe looked stern, she had very handsome blue eyes. At some point she must have been beautiful.

As soon as Mrs. Cliffe had gone, Ada took her paper knife and opened the letter. She did not recognize the hand; it was firm and masculine. She scanned the single sheet of paper, and a line leaped out at her: *I have the honor of requesting your hand in marriage.*

"What!" she exclaimed aloud.

She dropped into her chair. The words blurred in front of her eyes. The first person she thought of was Ravi, and she had to read the name at the bottom three times before it sank in. Douglas Varley.

"Douglas Varley?" She still didn't understand, and she turned the paper over, as if there might be some explanation on the back of it. Perhaps Varley was writing on behalf of his protégé. But no: how could she have expected that? Men didn't marry girls they kissed. The thought was like a knife in her heart. She reminded herself that it would be impossible anyway, even if he hadn't doubtless lost all respect for her the moment she allowed herself to give in to him. They were far too

34

different in every way. She forced herself to read the letter through properly.

My dear Lady Ada,
You may be surprised to receive such a letter from one who you no doubt consider a stranger. However, I claim a connection through my long-standing friendship with your father. I shall come straight to the point: I have the honor of requesting your hand in marriage. I shall be at your father's wedding and shall expect to hear your answer then.

I hope that my boundless affection and respect will encourage you to accept my proposal and become my wife, so that the ties between our families may become ever closer.

Just a few lines, businesslike and brusque. As if he was offering to buy a horse, she thought, and crumpled the paper in her fist.

She got to her feet and paced up and down, not seeing the room around her. It was inexplicable. Douglas Varley did not even know her. He had not exchanged three words with her. But—she stopped pacing—he knew her father.

She uncrumpled the paper and read it through again. This time she understood the meaning behind the letter. Yes, it was like offering to buy a horse—or a seat in Parliament. So this was what he was offering: to help restore her father's reputation, in return for a wife.

She stood, deep in thought, the breeze through the open window caressing her hair and the sunlight setting it glowing like bronze. The whispers about her father that she had heard in India—cowardice, dishonor—came back to her, and she felt sick at heart. All her life she had looked up to her father and

35

been proud of him. She had thought him the perfect gentleman: straight and true; and when he'd had to resign as lieutenant-governor, it was as if something she had thought eternal and entirely English, like the Houses of Parliament or the Tower of London, had come crashing down. She knew the whispers were lies, but they still cut deep. She would do anything to set her father right again in the eyes of the world.

But Douglas Varley! She did not know whether to laugh or cry. He was at least forty. Could she love such a man? Could she bring herself to try? It was impossible to imagine kissing him—she realized she was thinking about Ravi again, and tears suddenly came into her eyes.

She turned from the window, wiping the tears away. That decided it. The Indian boy clearly had some terrible influence over her heart, and that frightened her. It was wrong of her to have kissed him, but now she had a chance to put things right, to do what was expected of her, to fulfill her duty toward her father and her family. All she had to do was accept Douglas Varley's proposal and forget about her one shameful lapse.

Varley will never allow you to go to Oxford, whispered a voice inside her. But after her shocking behavior, did she truly deserve to go? And . . . could she trust herself there, near Ravi? Color flushed into her face as she thought of seeing him again. "I won't think about it a moment longer!" she exclaimed aloud. She jumped to her feet and ran to the door. She needed company, she needed someone bright and happy to chatter to, to drive this chaos of thoughts and feelings out of her mind. She needed Georgiana.

Ada found Georgiana in the music room, halfway through playing a waltz on the piano. Her cheeks were pink, and Ada smiled to see how happy she looked.

"Oh, Ada!" Georgiana saw her and brought the waltz to a crashing halt that rattled the busts of the great composers in their alcoves. She jumped up from the piano stool. "How wonderful it is to play on something in tune, at last. Have you explored the house?"

"I thought you might come with me," Ada replied. "I need some fresh air and I want to see how the gardens look." And she did not want to sit alone and fret over the proposal. She was in two minds about whether to tell Georgiana about it. Though she longed to confide in her sister, there was too much that she could not tell her. Maybe it was better to say nothing at all. It hurt to think that she now had a secret from Georgiana. Never before had she had something to hide.

They went down the main stairs. Ada was aware of all her ancestors' faces looking down at her from the family portraits. How could she put her own dreams before the honor of the Earls of Westlake? And yet . . . how could she spend a lifetime with Varley, and all the while be remembering stars, and the sea wind, and a boy who moved like a sphinx?

Desperate to escape her rebellious thoughts, she ran down the last few steps and into the drawing room. She thrust open the French windows and took a grateful breath of the fresh country air. A charming, shady terrace stretched out before her, with ferns in pots and steps that led down to the green lawn.

"I can't believe we're finally home!" Georgiana gave a little skip as they walked along the terrace. Her face shone with happiness. She brushed a strand of hair from her eyes, and smiled at her sister. "And did you see that maid in the hall? You must have recognized her! It was Rose. You remember

Rose, don't you? We used to play together all the time. Hasn't she grown up pretty and elegant-looking? I wonder if I dare ask her if she remembers that we used to play together. Would that be proper?"

Ada laughed. They walked down the steps of the terrace and onto the lawn.

"You have to remember that we are not children anymore. Don't go making her feel uncomfortable."

"I suppose you're right." Georgiana half sighed. "We all have our places and must stick to them."

"Yes . . . like pieces on a chess board," Ada said, a little sadly.

"Some of us are pawns, and some are queens." Georgiana looked up as rooks flew over, cawing. "I wonder how we all look to the birds—perhaps they can't tell the difference from above."

They walked on, Ada wrapped in her own thoughts as she looked out toward the gently curving hills and the shadowy woods. Georgiana broke the silence.

"I sometimes thought we'd never come home. After Mama died, it seemed impossible to imagine returning without her." She sighed. "I suppose Papa must be very much in love with Mrs. Templeton." Her voice had lost its enthusiasm.

"Of course he is," said Ada, mirroring her sister's tone. Her father had met his betrothed on his last trip to England. Ada saw how his face lit up when a lavender-colored envelope appeared with the post at breakfast. Unlike her sister, she had not been surprised when her father announced their engagement.

"Hmm. You wouldn't think it, at his age."

Ada's eyes lit up as a real smile broke through.

"Georgie, you sound like an old lady!"

"Oh, I adore romance! But . . . I wish we didn't have to live with strangers. I can't bear the idea of it."

Ada caught her sister's eyes. "We have been over this, Georgie. We have no choice but to live with them so we may as well make the best of it."

"I know," Georgiana sighed. "It's just such a strange home-coming. I never imagined Papa getting married. Least of all to someone with three children of her own. We'll never have Papa to ourselves."

"They might be delightful."

"And they might be dreadful." She went on, "But you have nothing to worry about. Sooner or later one of your many admirers will propose, and then you'll be a married lady and I'll be left here, alone, with the Templetons!" Georgiana laughed, and then coughed, putting a handkerchief to her mouth.

Ada could not bring herself to smile.

Georgiana looked curiously into her sister's face, but Ada did not meet her eyes. Her thoughts had returned to Ravi, to her own shame.

They walked in silence across the lawn, their shoes leaving impressions in the grass, which was silvery with dew.

"It is a terrible thing the way Papa's appointment in India ended," Georgiana said in a low voice. "Oh, Ada, do you think he really has done something wrong? I don't want to think it, but . . ."

Ada shook her head. It was almost a relief to put Ravi out of her mind for a moment. "I don't believe he has done anything, any of the things they accuse him of. I won't believe it. It would be too disgraceful. There has to be more to it than there seems."

"He has said nothing to you?"

"No, nothing. But I can only think the best of him."

"Of course," said Georgiana. She sighed. "I do wish someone loveable would fall in love with me, or you, though, and there would be a real wedding." She half laughed.

"You sound tired." Ada looked at her keenly. "You've walked too far—and in this cold and damp, you're not used to it."

"Oh, I'm perfectly well!" Georgiana protested, though her face looked drawn. "I can walk as far as the trees, I'm sure."

"No, absolutely not. Come on, now, if you want romance you will have to conserve your strength and not do yourself in! Back to the house, I insist."

As they turned round, Ada looked up at the great stone bulk of Somerton Court, massive as a pyramid. They had been walking in its shadow all this time, she realized. Dark windows gazed back at her like secret eyes, and she thought she glimpsed a figure at one of them, dressed in the black and white of a maid. But it was gone the next moment she looked.

"Yes, back to the house," Georgiana said with a sigh. "We must get used to our new home—and our new family."

Chapter Five

Dinner was finally over, and the housemaids had filed off to bed in the attic. The footmen were snoring in the hall. Only Mrs. Cliffe was still awake.

She walked from room to dark room, the gas lamp in her hand. Its light and the faint jingle of keys at her belt marked her path through the house. She paused by each ground-floor window to try it. Satisfied that they were fastened, she moved on, toward the main stairs.

Though there was little light, she did not hesitate. With her eyes closed she could have told you where the outbuildings and the stables lay, she could have told you on which of the four floors and in which of the two hundred rooms she stood. Placed blindfolded in the attic or the cellar, she could have made her way unerringly back to the servants' passage, taking her clues from the line of the wainscoting, the height of the ceilings above her, the creak of a floorboard, the pattern of echoes. She could feel Somerton around her even when she was not aware of doing so, sensing her place in the house, as familiar and secure as the stays she had put on every day since she was fourteen. For better or worse, her life was here.

On her way back to the parlor, she paused. A faint sound echoed down the stairs. It was music, the halting notes of a piano.

Mrs. Cliffe stood, thoughtful. Perhaps she should go upstairs and check that the music room was secure. On the other hand, if the young ladies wished to practice at this time of night, it was not her place to complain.

She walked on to the parlor. As she entered it, the clock was just striking eleven, and as she set the lamp down, there was a knock at her door.

Mrs. Cliffe hesitated only a second before turning back and opening the door.

"Good evening, Lord Westlake," she said, her voice perfectly calm, despite the fact that there was no good reason for the master of the house to be in the servants' quarters at this time of night. She stepped back to let him in and, with a glance up and down the servants' passage, closed the door behind them. Then she turned to face her master, who stood awkwardly in the center of the room.

"Won't you sit down, sir?"

Lord Westlake grimaced. "Rosaline," he began. He hesitated. "Mrs. Cliffe. You must be surprised to see me here at this time."

Mrs. Cliffe startled herself by wanting to smile. He was the same as always—oblivious. "Not really," she said.

"I came to—well, I came to apologize."

"Please, do sit down. It wouldn't be proper for me to sit in your presence unless you do, and my feet are tired."

Lord Westlake sat, hurriedly, in one of the easy chairs near the dying fire. Mrs. Cliffe lowered herself into the housekeeper's chair.

"I cannot imagine what you have to apologize to me for," she said.

"For this marriage, of course. It must be—I know it must be a shock to you."

Rosaline stared into the fire. The embers were nearly cold.

"It has meant a lot of extra work for the staff, but that cannot be helped. It was the fault of the telegraph service."

"You know what I mean," he answered.

Rosaline considered denying it. But they had known each other too long to be anything other than honest.

"I think I know what you mean," she said. There was a dull ache in her feet and she wanted nothing more than to be asleep in bed. It had been a long day. "But I assure you there is no need for apology. I understand the necessity for the marriage."

"You better than anyone, I think. The estate accounts—"

"They are worrying."

"They are bloody awful." He leaned forward, scowling. "William has made a mess of things. I had no idea he was this incapable with money. If this goes on the estate will be bankrupt in a year."

Mrs. Cliffe looked at her hands.

"I understand the late Mr. Templeton's money was made in finance."

Lord Westlake got to his feet abruptly.

"You must think me a cad. It isn't like that. Fiona is a dear thing, and I think she has a real affection for me."

"I am sure she has."

"Besides, the girls need a mother. They will come out this year or next, and I feel I have not done right by them, keeping them in India all this time. I just hope I haven't spoiled their chances. Ada at least has the looks and the charm to marry really well, with a force like Fiona behind her." He frowned at the floor, then looked up to her. "Do you think I've done the right thing, Rosaline? Tell me honestly, as a friend."

Mrs. Cliffe took a moment to find the right words.

"I think you have done exactly the right thing," she said. "Somerton cannot be lost because of one man's foolish spending. I never expected, nor hoped for anything more from you. You know that." The look of gratitude in his eyes was overwhelming. "But I hope you will be able to do something for Rose."

Lord Westlake sat down again. "Yes, Rose," he murmured, looking at the floor. "I saw her in the hall. You can't mistake her. She has turned out very well, it seems."

"Yes, she has." Mrs. Cliffe tried not to sound too eager but could not resist leaning forward. "She is intelligent, and good, and hard working. Everyone remarks how well-bred she is. Your lordship"—she wanted to call him Edward, but she felt it would somehow not be fair—"if you could do something for her, give her a chance of advancement, perhaps an education, something that would help her improve herself—"

"But how can I do that, Rosaline?" Lord Westlake interrupted. "Can you imagine the questions that would be asked, the comments that would be made if I paid special attention to her? If the gossips didn't leap to the right conclusion, they would certainly draw an even more unpleasant one— I am sorry, I've shocked you."

"Not at all," said Mrs. Cliffe through tight lips. She should have known better than to expect anything from him, she thought. And yet he was right, she knew it. She would never be free from the curse of her one great mistake, though the result meant she could never regret it.

She got to her feet. If she had learned one thing in her life it was that a servant could not afford love.

"Well, sir, it is late, and I don't think we have anything

more to discuss. It will be a long day tomorrow—may I ask if there is anything else you wanted to speak of?"

Lord Westlake shook his head as he got to his feet. As the door opened, he turned suddenly back to Mrs. Cliffe.

"Rosaline—don't let us part like this." There was a tenderness in his voice that nearly brought tears to her eyes. "I very much want to do something for Rose. But it is a delicate matter. Listen: Ada and Georgiana will need a lady's maid. How would it be if Rose took that post?"

Rosaline smiled. It was an advance in status, without doubt. "I know she would give satisfaction, sir."

"Then that's settled. Good night, Mrs. Cliffe." He bowed, and she dropped a curtsy.

"Good night, sir."

She watched him walk down the corridor, the circle of gaslight going with him. She was exhausted, she realized, heavy in body and mind. *I must go to bed*, she thought.

Just before she closed the door, there was a small click in the darkness, like another door closing. But Mrs. Cliffe was so tired and her mind so full of troubled thoughts that she did not give it any notice.

Chapter Six

"Well, Rose, congratulations!" Cook exclaimed as Rose came nervously into the kitchen the next morning.

"Thank you!" Rose still wasn't sure if she was more frightened or more excited by the news of her promotion. "I just hope I can do it."

"'Course you can," Mary said, patting her on the arm. "You've always done our hair and our dresses when we go out. Even Lady Edith's maid says how nice we look when you've been at work. And she's French!"

"Now you'll have a room to yourself, you lucky thing," Martha sniffed. "Well, I wish I had a mother to put in a good word for me, that's all."

"Martha!" Cook rounded on her. "Rose deserves her new post and you know it."

The bell jangled in the passage.

"That's the hall. You'll be wanted to help Miss Ward decorate the place. Off you go, both of you!"

Rose and Annie ran up the servants' stairs and came out into the hall. Miss Ward was standing on a chair, pinning up wreaths of roses and honeysuckle. The hall smelled sweetly of flowers.

"Rose!" Miss Ward stepped down from the chair and came

toward her, smiling. "I'm so delighted. I've heard of your promotion."

She took Rose's hands and pressed them warmly. Rose blushed and smiled, but Miss Ward's expression changed and she looked down at Rose's hands. "Oh dear, these are housemaid's hands, aren't they? I don't know how the young ladies will feel about that."

Rose snatched her hands back. They were red and rough, as all the housemaids' hands were. She had never thought of it before. "Do you think they will mind?" she said, frightened. "I don't know what to do about it."

"Oh, nonsense, Rose, your hands are fine, and you'll wear gloves anyway," Annie said, giving Miss Ward a look of annoyance.

"Annie, you mustn't call her Rose now that she's been promoted," Miss Ward said, sweetly. "You must call her Miss Cliffe, just as you call me Miss Ward. Rose, you may call me Stella."

"Oh, I don't think—" said Rose, horrified.

"No, she's right," Annie said, though she looked angry. "There's rules, aren't there, and you're a lady's maid now."

"But I—" Rose trailed off, realizing it would do no good.

They climbed onto chairs and worked silently to pin the wreaths of flowers along and over the arch of the hallway. At the other end, Mary ran in and out, carrying plants from the hothouses to decorate the orangery, where the wedding ceremony was to be performed. Footmen came in and out, carrying chairs to set in rows for the guests, and an oak lectern for the priest to read from.

"Why aren't they getting married in church?" Annie asked, pinning up a garland of white roses and pink ribbons.

47

"It's not done for a second marriage," Stella replied.

"Why not?"

"It just isn't." She looked down her nose at Annie. "But I wouldn't expect you to understand the etiquette."

Rose caught Annie's eye and made a wry face. Then Annie's expression changed.

"And who's he?"

Rose followed her gaze. James and Roderick were not alone; helping them set up the chairs was a handsome young man with black curly hair. When he spoke to James, Rose was struck by his educated accent.

"Oh, that must be Mr. Templeton's valet," she said, remembering that her mother had mentioned him to her. "Oliver Campbell, I think his name is."

"He's ever so elegant," Annie said, smoothing her hair back as if unconsciously. "Maybe I should go over and introduce myself."

"If you want to make a fool of yourself, go ahead," said Stella with a smile that Rose found hard to make out.

"You'd better not, Annie," she said. "Think how cross Mrs. Cliffe would be." Hoping to take Annie's mind off the handsome new arrival, she jumped down from her chair and looked up at the wreaths. The hall now looked like a bower of flowers.

"Doesn't it look beautiful?" she said, feeling proud of their work.

Annie and Stella climbed down, and Rose could tell that, even though they didn't say much, they were pleased.

Before she could finish, there was a rumble and a roar that came closer and closer.

"They're here!" James hissed across the room. "Make yourselves scarce!"

Rose hastily gathered up her things and ran for the door, followed by Annie and Stella. She couldn't resist slowing to peek through the French windows. A huge, majestically gleaming motorcar was drawing into the courtyard. The man at the wheel looked up, caught her eye and winked. Rose gasped and backed away. Annie caught her arm.

"Come on, Miss Cliffe," she said with a twinkle in her eye.

"You don't have to call me that!" Rose ran up the stairs after her, leaving Stella behind.

"I do, though. And Miss Ward likes it, I'm sure." Annie added: "Don't get too high and mighty, though, will you?"

"Of course I won't. You're my friend." Rose had shared a room with Annie since they were twelve, and she had a lump in her throat at the thought of that ending. "I'll miss you."

"Huh!" Annie sounded pleased, though. "You'll soon forget us and make friends with Miss Ward, I'm sure."

Rose glanced behind her. Stella was nowhere in sight.

"I hope I'm friendly, but I couldn't be friends with her. She's much older than me."

"Nonsense, she's no more than eighteen."

"She can't be!"

"She is." Annie nodded knowingly.

"But she's so sophisticated and confident, and . . . she looks twenty-five at least!"

Annie dropped her voice to a whisper: "She wears makeup."

"She doesn't!"

"She does. You're *that* innocent, Rose!" Annie giggled, and that set Rose off.

"What are you two giggling about?" Stella caught up with

them, looking annoyed. "Come on, they've gone into the drawing room and there's still a lot to be done before the hall looks ready."

"They're here!" Georgiana rushed from the drawing room window, back to Ada. "Is my dress all right?"

"Yes, of course." Ada sounded soothing, but her heart was beating fast too. This was it, the moment they met the people who would share their lives from now on. She wondered whether she should stand or sit. Which would look more dignified and casual—but welcoming too? But it was too late. She could hear footsteps outside, her father's voice and a woman's—and other voices too.

Cooper thrust the door open, bowed, and stood back. Ada smiled nervously as her father came in, followed by a tall, very handsome woman wearing a well-cut burgundy motoring dress that showed off her elegant figure. The furs of what looked like an entire den of foxes were wound around her neck, and despite the long drive her gloves were spotless.

"Mrs. Fiona Templeton," Cooper announced in his most sepulchral tones.

Ada was startled. She had not expected her new stepmother to be so stylish—or so young looking. Was she young enough to give birth to another son? she wondered for the first time. No wonder William's nose was out of joint.

Before she could gather her thoughts, Cooper went on: "Miss Charlotte Templeton."

Into the room came a girl of Ada's age. She had all of her mother's style and did a good impression of having her beauty. Her hair was dressed with mischievous golden curls escaping from under her hat, and she wore sapphires around her neck that brought out the glint of her eyes. Ada smiled and moved forward, but Charlotte did not echo her smile.

"Master Sebastian Templeton," Cooper went on.

Charlotte was followed by a young man in motoring clothes. He looked more like his mother than his sister did. He had her height and her strong, aristocratic features. Ada knew just enough about men's clothes to see at once that his were of the best tailoring—better, perhaps, than his sister's. There was genuine taste there, as well as the same sense of fashion.

Cooper glanced out into the corridor as if he were expecting another person, then backed out with a bow.

"I am delighted to bring my future wife to Somerton," Lord Westlake said, with a warm smile at Mrs. Templeton. Ada could see that he genuinely cared for her. "This is Sir William and Lady Edith."

Mrs. Templeton smiled politely. William growled under his breath, and Edith looked away. Mrs. Templeton seemed not at all concerned by their lack of enthusiasm. But Ada cringed at their lack of manners. She swallowed and stepped forward.

She had agonized over the greeting she would give her father's new bride. She supposed it had to be warm and welcoming, to make Mrs. Templeton feel at home, without being overly familiar. They were, after all, strangers. "We are very happy to welcome you to Somerton, Mrs. Templeton," she said, looking up at her. "And above all, to thank you for making Papa so happy. We wondered what you would like us to call you. Mother, or Mrs. Templeton, or—"

Mrs. Templeton laughed. "Lady Westlake, dear—after all that is my title, or will be in just a few days." She patted Ada's head absently and her eyes passed over Georgiana

51

before she turned back to her betrothed. "They *are* a young-looking pair, aren't they! One would never think they were nearly ready to come out." She took Lord Westlake's arm and drew him away toward the windows. "You must show me all the grounds, Edward. I've been so looking forward to it."

Ada stood speechless. Sebastian looked about him with a faintly cynical smile.

"So this is Somerton!" he drawled. "I must say it's a very stately pile. I'm not surprised Mother fell so very much in love with Lord Westlake."

"Very nice, for the countryside," sighed Charlotte, moving toward her mother. She seated herself in an armchair, where the light played flatteringly on her features, and toyed with her necklace, her lips parted prettily as she gazed out of the window. Edith's expression turned even sourer, and she turned away, cooing to one of her pug dogs, which was sprawled, panting, on the hearth rug.

Sebastian curled his lip as he looked at his sister. "Charlotte, that pose is so well rehearsed," he said. "You'd make a delightful statue. Much nicer than the live version."

He turned to Ada, who had turned quite pink, and bowed gracefully over her hand. "Whatever my mother's preferences, I hope you'll consider me your brother. I'm certainly in need of a new and improved sister."

Charlotte frowned. "Oh, Seb, how ridiculous you are."

Ada felt completely at a loss. Sebastian meant to be kind, she was sure, but she couldn't imagine what she would do if he treated her with the easy insolence with which he treated Charlotte. She struggled for a way to break the awkward silence, but it was done for her.

"Hello, Mother!" came an annoyed shout from outside. "Where are you?"

Startled, Ada turned toward the door just as Cooper, looking harassed, thrust it open.

"Master—" he began, but he was forced to stand aside as a defiant-looking boy came through the door.

"Michael. Michael Templeton," the boy finished. He strode over to fling himself down on the sofa, removing the motoring goggles still pushed up in his blond hair. He nodded roughly at Ada and Georgiana "Michael Templeton. Is there anything to eat? I'm starving."

Ada did not know whether to laugh or cry, especially when she caught the expression on Cooper's face as he shut the door behind him.

"I—er—I'll ring for some tea," she said quickly. She pressed the bell, and secretly caught Georgiana's eye. Georgiana made a slight, horrified face. They didn't need to speak. It was clear that the Templetons were going to take some getting used to.

Chapter Seven

Rose hurried after Stella, up the winding stairs toward Lady Ada's room. Stella had only been here a few days and yet she already seemed to know her way around better than Rose did. But all this was new to Rose. She had never before been allowed to walk freely through the family's part of the house. She had always been a downstairs maid. It was Annie who lit the fires in the family's bedrooms in the morning. It was like finding herself in a whole new Somerton.

There was something in Stella's assured smile as she pushed open Lady Ada's door that made Rose nervous. She told herself she was being silly. Stella and she were equals, Stella had said so herself. She just needed to believe it. She looked around at the room. It seemed more lived in now. A discarded dress was strewn across the bed, and there were books lying open on the windowsill.

"Now, it's true that there's a lot to learn and you are in no way prepared, but you mustn't feel daunted," Stella said. "We all had to start somewhere."

"I'm very grateful," Rose said, and she meant it. Looking at this room through the eyes of someone who had seen how London ladies live, she felt the full responsibility of what lay ahead.

Stella wrinkled her nose as she looked around the room. "I'm not sure if the fact that these girls are truly countrified makes your job easier or more difficult, Rose. You will certainly have trouble turning them out stylishly. You'll have to convince them to buy some more gowns—those drab old muslins are no good to anyone. I wouldn't wear them myself."

Rose found herself wanting to defend Lady Ada.

"I think Lady Ada always looks nice. I know her dresses aren't as"—she searched for a word—"fashionable as Miss Charlotte's, but they seem to suit her."

"I hope you're not comparing Miss Charlotte to Lady Ada!" Stella sounded quite scandalized. "Everyone knows Miss Charlotte is one of the most elegant debutantes in London. Now . . ." She looked thoughtful. Rose waited, listening carefully. Stella would be able to teach her so much—if she wanted to.

"I expect you have previous experience of dressing ladies?" Stella went on. As she spoke, she moved around the room, picking up a kid glove here, a silk stocking here, and placing them into drawers or setting them on one side for mending or washing.

Rose followed her, trying to take note of everything that she did. "I've done my mother's hair and dresses for years." But as Rose looked at the huge wardrobes in front of her, she had to admit that it was much like comparing sailing a dinghy to captaining an ocean liner.

"Oh dear, that's hardly the same thing." Stella smoothed a glove into a drawer. "Let me explain. Your main duty is to make sure the young ladies look their best. You must prepare their clothes and do their hair." She plucked a stray hair from the pillow. "Keep the dressing table in order, make sure they have cologne and cosmetics—" She arranged the items on the dressing table as she spoke, placing a silver-and-amber brooch into the jewel case, and folding a fan and putting it away.

"Dressing table, cologne, cosmetics . . ." Rose repeated, wondering how on earth she would remember all this.

"That's not all there is to the job, of course . . . Miss Charlotte often doesn't finish a ball until three in the morning. Lady Ada seems a bit quiet for that, but you must always wait up until she comes home, to undress her. There will be plenty to wash and mend while you wait."

"I can wash and mend," Rose said eagerly. "But how shall I know what to give her to wear?"

"She will tell you what she intends to do that day, and you make your selection accordingly, of course. From her wardrobe." Stella threw open the wardrobe doors.

Rose looked in horror at the rails of clothes. They had seemed sparse when she compared them to Miss Charlotte's, but now that she was in charge of them, they seemed overwhelming.

"But I don't know which are right for riding and walking and visiting . . ."

Stella looked at Rose pityingly. "You have more to learn than I thought. Just concentrate on well-cut tweeds and some really presentable evening dresses, a number of tea gowns, and so on."

"Tea gowns," Rose repeated, wondering again in panic how she would remember.

"But the most important thing is not to forget your new status. You are a lady's maid. This means you won't eat in the servants' hall. One of the housemaids will bring you a tray. It's very important that you set yourself apart."

Rose had always eaten in the warm servants' hall. She felt a lump in her throat at the thought of Annie bringing her a tray. She was aware of Stella's eyes on her.

"How on earth *did* you get this post, Rose? I am dying to know who you impressed."

Rose, taken aback by the abrupt question, answered automatically: "It was Lord Westlake who suggested it. I think he must be a very kind man."

"He must be," said Miss Ward lightly, "to have taken your mother in."

Rose looked at her in surprise.

"What do you mean?"

"Oh, only that few households of this consequence would take on a maid with a child," said Miss Ward. Her blue eyes glinted with an expression Rose couldn't decipher. "Let alone promote her to housekeeper."

Rose felt herself turning pink. She knew her father was dead. She didn't remember him, and her mother didn't speak of him, but that didn't mean . . . "My mother's a widow," she said as calmly as she could. "You surely don't mean to imply—"

Miss Ward's eyes grew round. "Of course not! I simply meant to say that it is unusual, isn't it, to take on a servant with a child in tow."

"My mother gives very good satisfaction, and I hope I do too," Rose said, her voice trembling slightly.

"I can see that is the case. It's not me you have to convince. And indeed, it needn't make the slightest bit of difference," Miss Ward said warmly. "What will matter is how well you perform your work. The first thing is to make sure Lady Ada has something suitable for dinner tonight." She ran a critical hand over the dresses. "This eau-de-Nil tulle may do, if she has some pearls to wear with it. Just a strand or two . . . Have you quite considered whether you're right to accept this post, Rose? I wouldn't want you to be embarrassed, you see. I'm only thinking of your own good."

Are you? thought Rose. Out loud, she said, "You're very kind. But I think it's my duty to give it a try."

Stella smiled tightly. "Well, if you're determined, I'm glad. We must be very good friends, then, mustn't we?"

"I suppose we must," said Rose.

Stella turned back to the wardrobe, running a thoughtful finger down a satin dress. "I'll give you a word of advice," she said in a voice as smooth as the cloth. "There are a lot of opportunities for a lady's maid, if you're wise enough to know how to take them."

Rose stayed silent. Stella clearly meant much more than she was saying.

"The trick is to find ways inside your mistress's defenses," Stella went on. "Once you know what she's afraid of, you can wrap her round your little finger." She looked at Rose and when Rose did not answer, scowled. She left the wardrobe and moved closer to Rose. "Do you think they're in charge, just because they pay your wages? They *need* us. They couldn't live a day without us. It is up to us to show them how indispensable we are—how much they need our loyalty. After all, a lady's maid often hears and sees things that have a certain . . . value to them."

Rose stared at her, speechless. She could hardly believe what Stella was implying.

"I think I understand you," she said, her face hot, her voice tense. "And you've made a mistake. That is not me."

Stella stepped away from her as if she had burned herself.

"You never know what you'll do until you have to, *Miss Cliffe*." Her voice was icy, but there was color in her cheeks, and Rose noticed something like fear in her eyes. "Those who ride on high horses have a long way to fall."

Chapter Eight

Dinner was served, and the candlelight was reflected in the crystal and the silver, a shimmering, glimmering display of ice and fire. The shadowy old masters looked down from the walls, and in the center of the table a carved ice swan melted slowly into a silver tray.

Ada, not used to such luxury, felt all fingers and thumbs. The Templetons seemed more at home. Michael tore pieces of bread and rolled them into balls, his face set in a moody reverie. He was certainly handsome, like his older brother, Ada thought, but too sulky to be likeable. Georgiana was making a fine attempt of talking to him, but he answered in monosyllables.

"Fine motor, that, Mrs. Templeton. We've ordered a Rolls," William said at the other end of the table. "Chauffeur, though—wouldn't want to drive it myself."

"Ordered a motorcar?" Lord Westlake raised his eyebrows. "How much did that cost?"

"Everyone has them nowadays," William said, raising his glass for the footman.

"So I'm told." Lord Westlake watched the wine filling William's glass. "The chauffeur will cost more than he's worth—they're not good servants."

William took a generous swig and wiped his mouth.

"So, Uncle, why the hurry to return? India lose its charm?"

"Your sincerity is overwhelming," Lord Westlake said dryly.

"We're obviously delighted to see you back," William said gruffly. "I'm sure you understand that we found the sudden homecoming and subsequent marriage announcement a bit jarring, that's all."

"Did you?" Lord Westlake laid down his knife and fork. "Because I found what happened with the fields above Redlands Copse a bit jarring as well, William."

"They were going to rot. I saw opportunity in the sale. No need for them, so we sold them at a profit."

"Those fields had been in the estate since the seventeen hundreds. I left you here as steward, not to try and turn a profit to your own account."

"I think you're very hard on a fellow," said William. He buried his nose in his wineglass, his eyes darting here and there as if looking for an escape. "And it's not as if I'm the only sinner in the room, either."

Ada's food had turned to a lump in her throat. William had always been pigheaded, but he surely couldn't be foolish and rude enough to bring up the matter of Papa's resignation over dinner. Not with the Templetons listening avidly. Sebastian's eyes were dancing with curiosity.

"I'm going to pretend, William, that you did not say that."

William, eyeing the dangerous expression on his uncle's face, muttered, "Right, sir."

Georgiana clattered her fork, and all eyes turned to her.

"I'm so looking forward to our first season—I mean, Ada's first season," she said, looking at her sister pleadingly. The message was clear: *Change the subject!*

"Yes—yes, I can't wait!" Ada forgave herself for lying.

61

It was in a good cause. "I can hardly believe there are only six months to go."

"Neither can I," Charlotte said, looking Ada up and down. "But don't worry, I'm sure we shall get you ready somehow."

Ada and Georgiana looked at each other. Ada had never considered that she might not be ready. The "season" was a round of social visits, balls, parties. She had imagined enduring it, laughing at its frivolity under her breath. She had never imagined that she might not live up to its standards.

"It really was a little much for your father to expect you to go directly from the jungle to the ballroom," Charlotte went on in a lower voice. Ada glanced up toward Lord Westlake, but he was scowling at William and did not hear them. "I do pity you. I suppose you have never been at a really smart gathering before."

"There is society in India too, you know," Georgiana said.

"People, no doubt. But not society." Charlotte smiled sweetly.

Fiona raised her lorgnette and examined Ada across the table.

"Yes, there isn't much time to prepare you," she said. "Our first goal must be to secure a sponsor for your presentations at court this spring. Unfortunately I myself cannot perform that duty. I never had the honor of being presented to the monarch. However, I hope to persuade Mrs. Verulam to be kind enough."

"That will be such an awful bore," said Charlotte. "It's so strange that we have to wear plain white dresses, and no jewels at all."

"I thought debutantes were allowed a string of pearls?" Sebastian said.

"I don't call pearls *jewels*," said Charlotte scornfully.

Ada, who was wearing her mother's pearls, blushed and looked at the table. Charlotte could not have meant it unkindly, she told herself.

"It was an absolute shame to ruin your complexion by exposing it to the sun," Mrs. Templeton announced, examining Ada through her lorgnette. "And your clothes are quite out of style, but then what can one expect from India? A visit to Worth before the season begins is in order, don't you think, dear?"

Charlotte pouted. "Not Worth, Mama, he's *démodé*. Poiret is the place to be dressed now. And it isn't just Ada. I shall need a whole new wardrobe. My ball dresses are very much last season."

"Right as always, my dear." Fiona examined Ada again. "I have been observing you move, and it really will not do. You shall have to have dancing lessons."

Ada colored even more. "I can dance," she protested.

"Not to the standard required for a state ball. Your movement shows that—there is a certain lack of grace, an energy that men find very unattractive."

"Nothing worse than an energetic woman," murmured Sebastian, giving Ada a sympathetic glance. Ada smiled gratefully. She was beginning to appreciate Sebastian's presence very much.

"Oh dear, then I don't think I shall ever manage to find a husband," said Georgiana in horror.

Ada couldn't help but laugh. "Nonsense, of course you will," she said.

"Yes, *someone* will be prepared to take you off Lord Westlake's hands eventually," said Charlotte.

Ada's laugh disappeared, and she was suddenly furious. No one should talk to her beloved sister like that!

"As it happens, I have always thought a cultivated mind more important than a cultivated wardrobe," she retorted.

"Oh goodness, you don't mean to tell me you're one of those suffragettes?" Charlotte recoiled.

"I believe in women's right to vote, if that's what you mean." Ada looked firmly back at her.

Fiona looked down her nose at Ada. "Well, may I beg you not to admit to anything so vulgar when we are in company, my dear?" she said. "No man likes a bluestocking."

"Bluestocking, you say?" William brayed from the other end of the table. He was swaying slightly and he had spilled red wine on the tablecloth. "I remember that of you, Ada. Always with your beak in a book."

Ada did not know where to look—not because she was embarrassed about being a reader, but because she was ashamed of William's obvious drunkenness. He did not seem to have noticed her father's expression of anger and contempt or Sebastian's sarcastic smile. Ada cringed. Whatever William's faults, he was an Averley, and his behavior reflected badly on her and Georgiana also.

Lady Edith did not seem to feel the embarrassment. She had lifted her pug dog onto her lap and was cooing over it. She glanced up to say, "I don't read myself. It tires the brain."

"It would, in your case," Ada said, under her breath. Sebastian subtly raised his glass to her across the table, a smile creasing the corner of his eyes. But Ada could not smile back. Suddenly the season seemed a daunting prospect. The possibility of letting her family down glared at her. How could she not have known her clothes were out of style, her complexion not quite the thing, and her movements as elegant as a cart horse's?

64

As they rose from the table, Charlotte spoke to Ada. "You must be feeling terribly homesick for India," she said.

Ada wondered if she was trying to make up for her earlier bad temper. They were to be sisters after all—they had to stay on good terms. She decided to give her the benefit of the doubt.

"I am," she said sincerely. "I miss the sounds and the sights and even the smells—"

"Well, don't worry." They were passing through the door now toward the drawing room, while the men lit up cigars behind them. Charlotte dropped her voice as the passageway squeezed them close together. "You may be back there sooner than you think."

"I don't know what you mean."

"Why, what do you think girls do when their season fails—when no one wants them? They go to India and see who will have them out there." She gave Ada one of her dazzling smiles and swept ahead into the drawing room, triumph radiating from her straight back and glimmering in the sequins on her dress. Ada pressed her lips together in a brave effort not to make a very unladylike retort.

As Rose walked down the servants' passage, she could hear Martha and Tobias gossiping in the kitchen as Martha tidied up.

"So there's something fishy about the master's resignation? Who would have thought it? I'll bear that in mind next time he's reading prayers," Martha said.

"Pretty clear from the way they were talking about it, I'd say." Tobias answered her. "Sounds like he's done something disgraceful. Wonder if Mrs. Templeton knows?"

Rose quickened her step. Martha had a hard job, but she

was spiteful too. Trying not to think about what she had heard, she ran up the servants' stairs and opened the door onto the second floor. She jumped as she came face to face with an Indian girl dressed in a maid's uniform. The girl gasped and curtsied.

Rose laughed. "You don't have to curtsy to me!"

"I'm sorry, miss. I'm not sure—I didn't know—I'm lost." The girl was the most dark-skinned person Rose had ever seen, and her eyes gleamed like the polished mahogany furniture in the drawing room. Rose tried not to stare.

"Who are you? Did you come with the family from India?" she asked.

"Yes. My name's Priya. I'm the nursemaid—only I can't find the nursery." She half laughed, and her voice wobbled. "Everything's so new here. And I don't know who I'm allowed to talk to."

"You poor thing. Never mind, I'll show you the way." Rose tucked Priya's hand under her arm and set off toward the nursery. "I'm Rose. You can talk to me, anyway—I'm the young ladies' maid."

Priya looked around, awestruck, as they went along the corridor. "I don't know how I'll ever find my way around here . . . Tell me, is young Augustus always this naughty?"

"Yes! I don't envy you your job," Rose said with feeling. "But hasn't anyone shown you around?"

Priya sighed. "I tried to ask them in the kitchen, but the cook screamed when she saw me, so I thought I had better go away." She caught Rose's eye, and they both started giggling.

"I'm sorry, I shouldn't laugh," Rose managed. "Only I can just imagine Cook doing that. Did she drop anything?"

"Yes, the chickens!" Priya put a hand to her mouth. "And they went onto the dinner table, I'm sure of it!"

"Oh well, what they don't know won't hurt them."

Rose left Priya at the door to the nursery. The girl smiled gratefully at her. "Thank you. I hope we see each other again."

"So do I," said Rose. She wondered if they would. Both of them were going to be so busy, and there was little opportunity to meet and have friends. She missed Annie more than ever.

On a whim, she took the main stairs, down into the east wing. She was allowed to do this now, she reminded herself. She no longer had to scuttle like a mouse behind the wainscot. But she also knew she was not really at home. She had no right to do what she was about to do. And even though she had done it hundreds of times, her heart still skipped a beat as she pushed open the door of the music room.

Now that the young ladies slept in the rooms along this corridor, there would not be another chance to come here. It was not the way it used to be, when the piano was shrouded in a dust sheet and the carpet rolled back. It was not hers anymore.

Sheets of music were scattered across the piano, and a chair was drawn up cozily to a music stand. Someone had adjusted the stool too; it did not fit her anymore. The lid was up. Like her, the room had changed.

She had never had any real right to be here, she knew that, but still it hurt to know that she would never be able to come back. It was only now that she realized what they had meant to her, those stolen moments when she escaped into music, her hesitant fingers searching out half-remembered folk tunes from her childhood on the piano. It felt as if she were weaving a magical web of color and light, an escape ladder from the daily drudgery.

She had only meant to look, but she could not resist pressing one key down, very gently and slowly. Deep inside the piano, she felt an answering thrum.

"Good-bye," she whispered.

Chapter Nine

They came by special railway carriage and motorcar. The men wore top hats and the women satin and lace veils, their spotless gloves offered daintily to the footman who helped them squeeze their vast hats, decorated with the plumes of birds of paradise and ostriches, into the carriage sent to collect them from the station. They came from the House of Lords and from the great country estates, from the Foreign Office and the Home Office and the salons of London society. They stepped down before Somerton, looked up at the colonnades, and smiled. "Exquisite," they murmured, "simply charming," as they entered the great main doors and smelled the orange blossoms Rose had pinned to the arches, and saw the huge bouquets of orchids and lilies Mrs. Templeton had ordered from London and arranged in the great crystal vases Lord Westlake's father had collected in Rome. They passed James and Roderick, motionless and mighty as Greek gods carved in stone, if such gods had worn knee-breeches and an expression James himself had described as "constipated pig," and were ushered through the house into the conservatory, following the sound of treble voices singing and the scent of roses and lilies. Although all had been to countless society weddings before, not one of them could repress a gasp of admiration as they saw the way the conservatory had been transformed. The autumn sun poured through the glass, and bathed the ropes and loops of wreathed roses and foliage that festooned the columns. At the far end, a bower decorated solely with Averley Pearl roses had been created. The priest stood there, with a lectern before him upon which the family Bible, which dated from the reign of King James, rested. The piano, strewn with flowers, was set up and ready, and a choir of small boys sang "O Perfect Love" as the footmen ushered the guests to their seats.

Ada, seated in the front row, fanned herself. She was filled with a mixture of dread, nervousness, and excitement. She knew Douglas Varley would be attending the wedding, expecting an answer to his proposal. But would Ravi be accompanying him? Did he know of Mr. Varley's proposal? Ada's fingers went unconsciously to her lips and she colored as she remembered their kiss. Again.

At least she thought she was looking attractive. Fiona had chosen matching dresses for her, Georgiana, and Charlotte, though it was not usual for a second-time bride to have official bridesmaids. They wore tunics of rose-pink chiffon, richly beaded with real diamond dewdrops and draped elegantly over sheaths of ivory silk. The effect was breathtaking. Fiona might dislike her, Ada thought, but she would not suffer anything at her wedding to be in bad taste.

The guests murmured as Lord Westlake approached.

Georgiana took her seat at the piano, looking nervous. As Fiona appeared at the end of the aisle, smiling, with Sebastian by her side, Georgiana struck up the "Nuptial Chorus" from *Lohengrin*.

Ada had to admit that Fiona had made a great success of herself. She looked beautiful and hardly a day over thirty, and showed no signs of nerves. She walked up to the priest as demurely as befitted a widow, in mauve French lace by Worth and a cream toque, and knelt with her groom upon the satin cushions provided for them, smiling as she said the vows that turned her into the Countess of Westlake. Ada smiled bravely, trying to conquer her nerves, and was glad to see how happy her father looked as he slid the ring of Welsh gold onto her stepmother's finger.

After the wedding, Lord and Lady Westlake stood before the open doors to the ballroom, smiling with their children as they formally received their guests. Ada smiled until her face hurt, all the time wondering when and if she would see Ravi. She did not know if she feared it or longed for it.

"Lord Sandringham! How delightful to see you," Lady Westlake said, and she sank into a deep curtsy.

There were so many people in the hall, it was hard to see who was coming next, but Ada heard a familiar voice say to Charlotte, "Ladies, your beauty puts the three Graces above you to shame." It was Douglas Varley. He had glanced up at the frieze that ran around the dome.

Ada felt a stab of annoyance. The classical women in the frieze were not the three Graces; they were three Greek goddesses, Hera, Aphrodite, and Athena. It was a scene from the story of the Trojan War: the judgment of Paris. Asked to judge the most beautiful among the three, he had chosen Aphrodite. In return she promised him the love of the most beautiful woman in the world, Helen of Troy—and so the bitter ten-year war began.

"In fact," she began, "the women portrayed are . . ." but no one was listening. Varley's eyes were on her, but his attention was taken up by Lady Westlake.

"As Lady Ada was saying," said a familiar voice, "I believe the frieze shows the judgment of Paris."

Ada felt a thrill. It was Ravi. Of course he would have known what the frieze showed. She met Ravi's eyes and her heart flew up like a bird bursting out of a cage. The memory of their night together washed over her and she was helpless.

"It isn't the most promising allusion for a wedding day," she found herself saying. "I mean, Paris and Helen—the ten-year war . . ." Fiona was staring at her coldly, and she swallowed and blushed.

Douglas Varley bent over her hand, and Ada's heart sank as readily as it had soared a moment before.

"How delightful to see you," she managed. As he bent over her hand, she was left looking full into Ravi's eyes. There was nothing between them but a foot of air, air that she could not draw into her lungs because he was smiling at her. It barely touched his lips, but the smile was in his eyes like reflected stars. And once again she had the feeling that she was standing on the brink of the whole universe, and nothing held her back. Then Douglas Varley straightened up, and came between them again. He pressed her hand and smiled, too—but a very different smile. This one had the calm self-satisfaction of one who knows a by-election is in the bag. He leaned in closely to her.

"There's no need to reply now. I can see you are over-whelmed. I hope to hear your answer after the wedding," he said in her ear, and passed on to Charlotte, who was staring with open curiosity at them. To Ada's relief, she had to look away as Mr. Varley greeted her. Then Ravi took her hand and drove all thought out of her mind.

"I didn't know you would be coming," Ada said. Her voice

felt as if it came from far away. She became aware that something was pressing into the palm of her hand. A slip of folded paper.

"Nothing could have kept me away," he replied, just above a whisper. It could have been a compliment to the occasion, but Ada knew he meant it specially for her.

Douglas Varley had moved on, and then Charlotte was smiling at Ravi. He let go of Ada's hand and she let it fall to her side, the folded paper in it. She turned aside as if to adjust her gloves, and slipped the paper inside one of them. Then she turned back, her heart pounding so loudly she worried it would echo around the dome above her, and smiled with the courage of an Averley at the next elderly gentleman who bowed above her hand.

Chapter Ten

The ballroom was hot, crowded, and noisy. Ada moved through the crowd, attending to the needs of the guests, summoning footmen with more champagne and petits fours. All the time, Ravi's note felt like a burning promise on her wrist. She tried to distract herself by watching the way Charlotte flitted from man to man like a hummingbird, industrious and efficient. She had a way of throwing back her head to laugh that showed off her alabaster-white throat and a little too much of her décolletage, in the valley of which a diamond hung, as tempting as the fly on a fishing line. And some of these gentlemen were very fat fish indeed, covered in titles and estates like scales.

Georgiana wove her way through the crowds. Her cheeks were flushed and her eyes bright. "Isn't Michael such fun?" she exclaimed. "I hope he doesn't get packed off to school again. It would be so much more amusing to have him here."

"Amusing?" Ada looked at her in astonishment. "I wouldn't have chosen that word to describe his company."

Georgiana shrugged with some defiance.

"You simply have to get to know him . . ."

"Well, from what his mother says, there's no school left that will have him, so you may get your wish."

"Oh yes, I know it looks bad to be expelled, but it sounds

like Rugby was so stuffy and boring. I can't believe they made all that fuss about a mere fire. It didn't even spread. And it was a dare, after all. Of course he had to do it if it was a dare." She craned to see through the crowd. There was a look on her face, and her lips were parted in a way that frightened Ada. She saw something in the look that she had felt herself—and what kind of example was she to her younger sister?

"Georgie, please don't make a fool of yourself over that boy." The words were out before Ada had thought them through. As soon as she saw the hurt on Georgiana's face, she wished them unsaid.

"I don't see why you have to be so cruel. I might not be making a fool of myself. People can love people even if they're not beautiful."

Then she was gone, threading through the crowd. Ada started after her, but the Duke of Brentford blocked her way, offering her congratulations on her new family.

"Delighted to see so many here," he went on, surveying the room.

Ada nodded and smiled. The meaning of his words hit her only after he had walked away, and Lady Fairfax had replaced him. She was less tactful.

"I was so sorry to hear of your father's trouble," she said, her eyes flashing with eagerness for gossip. "But it doesn't seem to have affected the attendance, does it?"

Of course, Ada realized. Half the conversations in the room were likely revolving around her father's resignation.

"He has done nothing to be ashamed of," she said firmly.

"Certainly not! But it is dreadful, isn't it, how rumors spread? We heard he had simply gone native, assisted the rebels in Bengal . . . ?" She trailed off hopefully, but Ada was not prepared to give anything away.

"I must find my sister," she said, excusing herself.

But as she made her way through the crowd, only half her mind was on Georgiana. The rest was given to listening to the conversations around her. The words *shocking* and *shameful* and *resignation* buzzed around her like mosquitoes. And a number of people fell hastily silent as she passed by.

Ada held her head high and continued across the room. She had nothing to be ashamed of and she would not let them make her blush—and then she saw William, part of a group of men that included Ravi and Douglas Varley. He was talking loudly, red-faced, gesturing with his glass of sherry so the liquid spilled out.

"I know the old fox has been up to something," he went on. "And then he comes here to moralize at me. Well, we'll see about that."

Ada closed her eyes in horrified embarrassment. The expression of contempt on Ravi's face burned into her mind. What a fool William was! Couldn't he see he was exposing not only her father but himself? She opened them again just as Douglas Varley cleared his throat and interrupted William.

"I think Lord Westlake has been badly misrepresented," he said.

A rush of gratitude overwhelmed Ada, and she smiled at Varley as he looked up and caught her eye. She wanted to go up and join the conversation, but at the next moment the dressing gong sounded.

Ada ran up the stairs, her dress flying around her like a cloud, and out of breath, put her back against the door and ripped off her gloves. She unfolded the note and read it as it trembled before her eyes.

I have to see you. I looked for you everywhere on the Moldavia. I don't wish to embarrass you but I must see you.

And then, in a passionate, almost angry scrawl—

Nothing in my life has meant more to me than that evening.
R.S.

She read the note over and over again before it sank in. She pressed it to her chest. He didn't despise her. It was quite the opposite. A smile spread over her face. The note clasped in her two hands, she moved across the room. "'Nothing in my life has meant more to me than that evening.'" She whispered the words to herself, gazing into her mirror. He wanted to see her . . . and her smile faded. But it was impossible.

It had been unforgiveable of her to let herself go so far with a stranger, a foreigner no less. Meeting him again would only compound the offence. What could they say to each other, anyway? This was not the *Moldavia*; this was Somerton, the heart of respectability, of her family. His patron had proposed to her. If they were caught meeting clandestinely it would be catastrophic for them both. The proper thing to do was to burn the note and pretend it had never existed.

The fire crackled behind its guard. Ada folded and refolded the note in her hands. She gazed into the mirror but she didn't see her own reflection, her intense dark eyes or the heightened color in her cheeks.

She ought not to meet him. But wasn't it her duty to explain to him exactly how impossible things were? Somerton was a big house; no one could watch every corner of it all the time. It might be possible, but she would need help. But who would help her? Georgiana could not know, she could never drag her sister into something this shameful. Charlotte Templeton—everything about her revolted from the idea of Charlotte knowing her secrets. She did not even consider her stepmother. But she had to decide soon. Rose would be here in a moment to help her dress, and . . . She hesitated.

Rose. A lot had changed since they had been little girls playing in the gardens, but perhaps she could trust her. But that meant telling her—telling her what was going on. Ada felt sick with fear at the thought.

It was a huge risk. Did she dare to take it?

There was a knock at the door. Ada started. But of course, it was time to dress for dinner.

She folded the note from Ravi in her fingers, but instead of putting it on the fire, she slid it into her jewel case.

"Come in," she called, her voice trembling.

Rose paused to catch her breath and smooth her hair before pushing open Lady Ada's door. The evening light was flooding in through the sash window, and for a moment she thought that one of the pink-and-gold clouds had come in through the window and was lying across the chair. Then her eyes grew used to the light and she saw it was Lady Ada's evening dress.

Lady Ada herself stood before the long mirror, twisting her sash over and over in her hands. The silk tightened and pulled between her slim fingers, but she didn't seem to notice it.

Wordlessly, Rose began undressing her. Her heart thumped with nervousness. This was the first time she had dressed a lady in an evening gown, and she was afraid in case she did it wrong. But Lady Ada didn't seem to be paying much attention, and that relaxed her. She deftly unlaced the corset strings and settled the petticoat correctly around Lady Ada's waist and hips. She smoothed the fabric down, kneeling to arrange it correctly, and looked up to see her reaction. But the question "Are you comfortable, my lady?" died on her lips as she caught Lady Ada's eye. It was filled with pleading.

Rose dropped her gaze instinctively and went on smoothing the petticoat. Her hands trembled slightly. She did not know what to say. Lady Ada's expression had been so desperate. As if Rose—of all people—were her last hope.

I must act as if I haven't noticed anything, she thought. It would be an unpardonable liberty to ask her what the matter was. Servants did not comment on what ladies and gentlemen felt or said. They developed eyes, ears, and speech only when instructed to do so.

But Lady Ada was different from the other ladies and gentlemen. They'd been friends once, long ago.

She looked up. Lady Ada's lips were pressed hard together as if she were trying not to cry.

Rose dropped the hem of the petticoat, stood up quickly and placed a hand on Lady Ada's shoulder. She found herself saying, "My lady, can I—can I help?"

Ada visibly swallowed and Rose could see her forcing herself to breathe calmly. Whatever Lady Ada was about to say, it was important.

Ada blushed and could not meet Rose's gaze as she said, "If I were to—" she began. "If we were— If I needed to meet someone, Rose, and no one was to know, and he was in this house, and . . ."

"He?" It escaped before Rose could stop it. Lady Ada wanted to meet a man?

The startled expression on Ada's face made Rose realize that she had never before interrupted a lady. It was a terrible breach of etiquette. But Lady Ada did not seem to take offense, instead she pressed on. "I wondered if you could tell me, how I could meet Mr. Sundaresan—privately?" Ada's voice curled up at the end of the sentence.

Rose was speechless for a second.

Oh dear, she realized. Lady Ada was in love—and with, of all people, that Indian gentleman. She could not help feeling sorry for her. It was so clearly impossible and improper.

"You see, I—we—" Lady Ada stumbled.

Rose realized that her mistress was about to blurt out her feelings. Instinct told her that, for her own sake, she could not be allowed to do that. If she did, she would regret forever that she had allowed her maid to know her vulnerability, and the consciousness of it would come between them. No, they would have to play charades.

Rose darted behind Lady Ada's back, to hide the shock on her face, and began lacing up the corset. Lady Ada, the back of her neck still pink with blushes, began to speak again, and Rose quickly jerked the strings of the corset. Lady Ada gasped.

"Oh—sorry, my lady—if you'll just breathe in now." Rose pulled the whalebone tighter, the laces biting into her fingers. Her mind worked rapidly. All she needed to do was prattle on, as Martha did. How hard could it be? If Lady Ada had any sense she would play along.

"I do the gentlemen's rooms." She wished her voice didn't sound so shrill. She went on, sewing the laces in and out of the eyelets: "I'm in and out of there all day. If anything were to slip out of my pocket, I'm sure someone would—would find it." *Was that too obvious?* she wondered.

There was a brief pause. When Lady Ada spoke again, she was slightly breathless from the pressure of the corset, but she had grasped the game perfectly. "Yes, of course."

"I daresay I'll be popping into the rooms during dinner, to just . . . tidy some things up." *I'm sure I'll think of something to tidy,* Rose thought. *Gentlemen are always needing buttons sewn on and suchlike.* She tied the strings in a double bow and stepped back. Lady Ada's silhouette was perfect.

Ada's eyes went to the scented notepaper on the dressing table. Rose turned away, and as she busied herself over arranging the dress, she heard the rustle of petticoats and the scratch of a pen.

"I'm ready for my dress now, Rose," she heard Lady Ada say.

"Yes, miss." Rose turned around. Lady Ada stood, the silk sash clenched between her hands, her eyes wide and nervous. "Allow me, my lady. You'll tear it," Rose said gently. She reached out and took the sash from Lady Ada's hands and felt the note folded behind it.

She turned away and slid the note into her pocket. Then she lifted the silky weight of the gown and stepped onto the footstool. For a moment it felt as if she were holding the sky above Lady Ada's head.

"Please raise your hands, my lady," she commanded.

Lady Ada raised her hands and Rose slipped the gown over her head. Lady Ada vanished, and then emerged like a magician's trick, her cheeks flushed. The dusky-pink and dull-gold silk fell obediently into place over the frame of the petticoat and corset, and under Rose's hands sorted itself into curves as elegant as those of a wildflower. Rose buttoned up the back.

"It's beautiful," said Lady Ada. She sounded startled.

Rose smiled and knelt to straighten the hem. As soon as she was kneeling, her smile disappeared. *You're a fool, Rose Cliffe*, she thought. If Lord Westlake found out, she would get the sack, and so would her mother, perhaps, and there would be no reference to find another place. But what could she do? Lady Ada was distraught, anyone could see that. You would need a heart of stone not to help her if you could.

She straightened and watched Lady Ada nervously adjusting her dress before the mirror, and as she did so, another thought, unwelcome as a worm in an apple, crept into her mind. Stella's proudly tilted chin, her cold voice as she said, *You never know what you'll do until you have to.*

She wished Stella had never said anything. Of course she would never use Lady Ada's secrets against her. But she did not even want the possibility of doing so.

She turned away, wanting to distract herself, and spotted a rose in the vase on the dressing table, white as the evening star. She plucked it and placed it against Lady Ada's hair and looked in the mirror to judge the effect.

Why, we're the same height, she thought with a sudden, uneasy shock. For a second she wondered what the rose would look like in her own dark hair. She quickly looked away from the mirror and concentrated on positioning the flower and securing it with hairpins.

"There," she said, standing back. "Perfect."

Lady Ada turned this way and that in front of the mirror, smiling as the silk swished across the floor.

She backed away softly to the door. As her hand closed

on the handle, she heard Lady Ada say softly, "Rose . . . thank you."

"You're welcome, my lady," she replied without looking around.

Chapter Eleven

Rose sat mending Lady Ada's stockings in her mother's parlor. Opposite her, Stella was working at the same task for Miss Charlotte. Rose was on edge, listening to the frantic noise echoing down the corridor as the kitchen staff hurried around to serve dinner. It seemed unnatural not to get up and help, but she knew that was no longer her position. They were managing perfectly well without her, she thought rather sadly.

Besides, she had a more important errand. She placed the stockings to one side and stood up.

"Where are you off to, Rose?" Stella looked up as she went to the door.

Rose turned back reluctantly. Stella watched her like a snake, and it was hard to lie to her face.

"Mr. Sundaresan asked me to starch some collars for tomorrow for him."

Stella raised her eyebrows. "As if we didn't have enough work to do. Doesn't he have a valet?"

"I don't mind," Rose said, perhaps too quickly.

"Well, you're very obliging," Stella said, with meaning, at last releasing her gaze. Rose hurried to the door and went up the stairs, trying her best to keep out of the way of the footmen and Annie, who were ferrying the second course up to the dining room. She pushed open the door to the second floor and froze as she heard voices. It was Lord Westlake and Sebastian Templeton.

Rose waited, knowing that she couldn't go out into the hall in front of his lordship.

"I say, sir, may I have a word with you in the library, later? About that little matter I mentioned." Sebastian sounded anxious.

"You may, Sebastian." Lord Westlake straightened his cuffs as he strode on. "But I'm not happy about it, I warn you. It may be your mother's money, but that doesn't mean you can waste it. You will have whatever is settled on you when you are twenty-five, those are the terms of your father's will."

Rose drew back as they passed her. A whiff of cologne reached her, and she saw Sebastian Templeton's face up close through the crack of the door. His expression startled her. A few moments ago he had been laughing loudly, debonair and devil-may-care, among the guests. But now he looked almost desperate.

"I promise you, sir. It's sure of a good return. It just needs a little time to get going, that's all."

They disappeared down the passage, their voices fading. Rose slipped out of the door and hurried on, clutching the note. She was not going to let Mr. Sebastian Templeton's money worries bother her. She had enough to think about with one person's secret in her charge. She went into Mr. Sundaresan's room, made a show of tidying the fire, placed the note in a marble bowl with his cuff links, and left before she could have second thoughts.

As the ladies went from the dining room into the drawing room, Ada placed a hand on Georgiana's arm. "I'm sorry for what I said earlier," she said quietly. "I didn't mean it harshly. Let's not quarrel."

"Oh, Ada, I could never quarrel with you," Georgiana said instantly, covering her sister's hand with her own. She sighed. "I expect you're right, though, and I am making a fool of myself. He's just so handsome."

Ada tactfully did not reply. Instead she looked across the drawing room, searching for Lady Westlake. She was dying to get out into the garden and see if Ravi had received her note. If he wasn't there . . . but she did not want to think about that.

She stood up and made her way through the occasional tables toward Lady Westlake. Augustus had been brought down from the nursery and Lady Edith was parading him before the ladies, while Priya, the Indian nursemaid, stood by, obviously waiting for him to get overexcited and need whisking away. Ada thought she was very beautiful, with her glossy, thick black hair, dark skin, and large, full-lashed eyes. As she drew near to the ladies she heard them questioning Priya.

"What a curiosity! What is your name, dear?" Lady Blandford demanded, raising her lorgnette to examine the girl.

"Priya, madam." Priya kept her eyes modestly cast down.

"Goodness!" Lady Blandford's eyes widened.

"Quite unpronounceable," Lady Fairfax agreed.

"Of course, I call her Prudence," Lady Edith announced. "She does have the most extraordinary power over Gussie. But then Indians are a very mystical people, you know."

The ladies exclaimed. One eagerly demanded, "But how do you do it? Is it some word of power?"

Priya hesitated. "It is, my lady."

There were gasps all around.

"How terribly thrilling! Can you let us into the secret? What is the word?"

"Oh, do tell us what it is!" echoed Lady Edith.

"It is *no*, my lady," said Priya.

Ada stifled a smile as she bent to speak in Lady Westlake's ear.

"I have a headache. I'd like to lie down for a little, if you'll excuse me," she said.

"Of course," said Lady Westlake, aware she was being watched in her role as a new mother, adding, "Shall I send the maid up with something?"

"Oh no! Thank you, but I just need a little rest," Ada said, horrified. There was no way that she wanted a maid going into her room and finding out that she was not there after all.

She left the room, but instead of going upstairs, she glanced left and right to check that no footmen were watching, then slipped out of the side door. She had always gone this way when she had played with Rose as a child.

Outside, Ada took a deep breath of the night air. Dew sparkled on the lawn and the box maze loomed before her like a dark sea. Feeling like a trespasser, she pushed open the wrought-iron gate—how it creaked!—and with a nervous glance behind her, stepped into the maze.

It was silent in here, and secret, and sheltered. Sound was dulled by the dark living walls on both sides. Only her footsteps crunched on the gravel, and it felt as if she were somehow outside time, outside everything she knew, as if Somerton had evaporated like a dream, leaving nothing but herself, drawn onward as if by a magnet, through the dark coils.

She reached the center. A small stone fountain played

before her, a nymph with an urn spilling water. Behind it were shadows, and out of those shadows stepped Ravi, the white of his collar gleaming in the moonlight.

"You came." His voice trembled as he approached her. He took her hands and pressed them, and she realized how cold she was. She looked up into his dark eyes and her first impulse was to kiss him again. But she drew back quickly.

"Mr. Sundaresan—it's impossible—"

"Yes, I know," he interrupted her, awkwardly and hastily. "Of course it is. I simply wanted to see you again."

"You must understand that I am not that kind of girl." She couldn't look him in the face.

"I do understand. It was my fault, I should never have let it happen. I should have thought of you—of your position." He was still holding her hands.

"You don't think badly of me?" She looked at him then.

"Of you? I could never. I should have resisted the temptation that I felt being so near to you. You are stunningly beautiful, of course, but talking to you is even more . . ." He dropped her hands at last. "It doesn't matter. What I did was as bad as theft. I had no right."

"So we can be friends?" She said it hopefully, but she felt so very disappointed, as if she had opened a Christmas parcel and found it empty. She scolded herself. He understood the impossibility of the situation completely, and he did not judge her for her behavior. What more could she have hoped for?

Ravi studied her face and after a second's hesitation he said: "I hope we can be friends. If you can forgive me."

"Of course I can," she said softly. He cleared his throat and looked away. She thought he looked almost angry.

"Let's talk of something else," he said gruffly. "How are you finding your new family?"

They strolled into the maze as they talked in low voices.

"I like Sebastian very much," she told him. "I think Charlotte will be a little more . . . difficult to get to know. I imagine she finds it quite trying to be here."

"You're very tactful," he said, his eyes dancing with humor. "In fact, I thought the judgment of Paris was a very appropriate subject for this particular wedding."

Ada caught his eye and laughed.

"Oh dear, is it so obvious that there is going to be a war?"

"It's obvious that you belong in quite a different sphere to her ladyship's and her daughter's."

"I'm afraid they think the same."

"It would be best if you could get out of their influence," he said. "Have you thought more about Oxford?"

"I never stop thinking about it. This may seem strange to you, but an education, to me, means independence."

"That does not seem at all strange. It means the same to me. And what is more important in life than independence? You must go to Oxford, Ada. Promise me you will take the exams." He stopped and took her hands again, looking into her face. "Why are you hesitating? I hope you don't think you wouldn't be capable. You are so intelligent—"

"Mr. Varley has proposed," she said.

He drew in his breath sharply and walked ahead of her. "That does not quite answer my question."

"You know it does, to an extent." Ada said, catching up to his stride.

"To an extent?" He stopped abruptly and looked at her.

"Ada, promise me you will not marry someone who forbids you from following your heart."

She thought of her father. Of her sister. Of Somerton, and the weight of all the Averleys who had come before her, and who had been held up as examples all through her childhood for doing their duty.

"It isn't that simple," she said, starting to get angry. "It's so easy for you. You're a man. You want to go to university and you just go, there is no one barring your way."

"Easy?" he said roughly. "Believe me, it has not been easy. I am no maharajah, I am the son of a clerk—what your kind of people would call middle class." He pronounced it with some bitter scorn. "My father saved for years to send me here to study. It is unheard of for an Indian of my class to go to Oxford, and it would still have been impossible without Mr. Varley's support. You once asked if I thought you ridiculous for wanting an education. I don't, but plenty of people think *me* ridiculous for wanting the same thing."

"Then they're fools," Ada said.

He took her hand, and went on, more gently.

"I didn't mean to upset you. And my story is not important. I am—let me say I am concerned about you. You *must* marry someone who will let you follow your dreams."

She pulled her hand away.

"Why should it be everyone's concern whom I marry?" she said, her eyes flashing.

"Perhaps because they care for you."

"Do *you* care for me?" she said. The words didn't feel like her own.

In answer he took her hands again and drew her close to him. His breath was warm on her face, and she felt dizzy, as

90

if it were a drug. His lips touched hers as gently as a snow-flake. She took a shuddery breath.

"Ada?" came a distant voice.

Ada jerked away, her eyes wide and frightened.

"It's your sister," Ravi whispered.

"Oh God! She can't find me in here." Ada was already tiptoeing through the maze.

As Ada reached the last turn Ravi caught her hand and pulled her back and kissed her long and fiercely. Before he let her go he held her still closer and whispered, "I don't care if it's impossible."

"But it is," she whispered back, and pulled away and hurried out into the shadows.

"Ada! Are you there?" Georgiana was on the terrace, looking in the other direction.

"Here I am," she called, trying to steady her voice. "I just went out for a breath of fresh air."

"Oh! I was worried about you. Are you sure you're all right?"

"Perfectly." She was breathing fast and she was terrified that Georgiana would sense the desire she still felt. She said as calmly as she could, "The fresh air has cleared my head. But you will catch cold and you know how it goes to your chest. Let's go inside."

"It's too terribly boring being ill all the time," Georgiana sighed.

As they went back inside Ada saw Charlotte looking out through the brightly lit window of the drawing room. She shivered.

Chapter Twelve

The next day, as the guests prepared to leave, Ada was in the hall when Cooper murmured in her ear that Douglas Varley wished to speak with her in the library.

Ada nodded, though her heart sank. She moved toward the door. There, leaning against the frame, was Ravi. She tried not to catch his eye. She could not let him influence her away from her duty. But although he stepped aside politely to let her pass, she felt his gaze burning into the back of her neck as she walked down the corridor.

"I am going to accept Douglas Varley." She said it aloud, to try and make herself believe it. Her voice came out small and trembling.

She was determined not to look back, but she could not help one glance, just as she turned the corner. Ravi was still watching her. She quickly looked away, her heart beating, and half ran the rest of the way to the library.

She paused to catch her breath and smooth down her dress before she opened the door. Of course she was going to accept him. What choice did she have? There was no future with Ravi. No matter what he said, no matter how he made her feel, it *was* impossible. At least, if she married Varley, she would see Ravi sometimes. Perhaps they could continue to meet secretly . . .

She shook her head in horror. She was actually contemplating behaving dishonestly, marrying Varley in cold blood with the intention of betraying him. What had come over her? Perhaps she was making a horrible mistake.

She could hesitate no longer. She opened the door, and with a deep breath, walked in.

Douglas Varley shook out the newspaper he had been reading and put it down. He rose from his chair, a self-satisfied expression on his face. Ada found herself staring at his wispy, dead-mouse mustache. The memory of her kiss with Ravi rushed back, the memory of his lips. Kissing Varley would repulse her. She knew this completely.

"Ada, I'm delighted to see you alone at last. I've spoken to your father."

So this was it. This was the moment of truth. How could she be so undecided, on the most important moment of her life? But she realized, as Mr. Varley went on speaking, that if she was undecided, he was anything but.

"There is nothing to stand in our way, so I suggest a summer wedding, it will be an excellent opportunity to bring many influential men together—"

"Mr. Varley, I must stop you," Ada burst out in a panic. "You have entirely the wrong impression."

"Oh?" One of his substantial eyebrows rose.

Ada swallowed; her voice seemed to have soaked away into her dry throat. But she finally found it. "I am very sorry to disappoint you," she went on, trembling. "I truly respect you and feel the honor you have done me by proposing. But I cannot accept."

There, it was out. She had done it.

Douglas Varley stared at her in silence.

"I beg your pardon?" he said.

"I cannot accept."

"Yes, that's what I thought you said. Lady Ada, I don't know if you understand that your father is entirely in favor of this match."

"I do, I do understand that." She moved forward. "But I cannot marry a man I do not love."

"Love?" he said blankly. "My dear, you will have a house in Eaton Square. Think it over."

"I *have* thought it over." She was getting annoyed.

"Clearly not. Allow me to set your ideas in order." He steepled his fingers as if preparing a speech. "All of your stepmother's money is tied to the estate of Somerton, save that which is already settled on her children. Your only fortune is your face and your title."

Ada fought to keep down her anger. She was suddenly certain she had done the right thing. Varley was not only physically repulsive to her, he was also an arrogant, high-handed man.

"I am sorry, but I am quite decided," she said. "Please spare us both further pain by accepting my reply as final."

He stepped back as if he had been slapped.

"Very well." His voice was full of resentment. "If I'd known you were such a childish little thing I would never have proposed. Your father is at fault for leading me to believe you were an intelligent girl."

"I am. That is why I am refusing you! Oh—" Ada put a hand to her mouth, a shocked, nervous giggle escaping her. "I'm terribly sorry, Mr. Varley. I didn't mean that as it sounded."

"Enough!" He had turned a shade of purple. "Westlake's a bloody fool to throw his friends over like this, God knows he needs them now more than ever."

Ada was suddenly not laughing anymore.

"Sir—"

"Good afternoon, Lady Ada!" He strode to the door and went out, shutting it with a bang that shook the dictionaries on the shelf.

Ada, left alone, put her hands to her face. She felt as if she had been left in the aftermath of an earthquake.

"Oh, what have I done?" she said aloud. She was trembling. Varley's words had frightened her.

"Ada?"

She hadn't heard the library door open. Her father was already halfway across the room toward her. "What has happened? What's the matter? I saw Mr. Varley storm past without a word . . ."

At the concern in his voice, Ada almost burst into tears.

"Papa—I'm so sorry—Mr. Varley asked me to marry him, and I refused him."

"You refused him?" Her father's brow creased, and Ada knew he was startled and upset.

"Yes. I'm sorry!"

"Oh, Ada!" he exclaimed. He took a few angry paces.

"I'm sorry, Papa. I wanted to accept for your sake, but I just couldn't. I couldn't! I don't love him. Our marriage would have been a lie."

She put her face in her hands again and sobbed. The worst thing was the guilt. Not only had she ruined her father's chances of returning to politics, but she had met Ravi without his knowledge, and she hadn't ended the relationship. If her father knew the things she had done . . .

She felt him take her hands gently.

"There, there. Don't cry. It's done now, and can't be helped."

"You're not angry with me?"

"No, no." He was silent. "It's true it would have been . . . helpful, if you had felt differently, but you mustn't think I want you to be unhappy. Fiona led me to think that you liked him, and when I saw you greet him this morning you seemed quite overcome . . . I confess I thought it would work."

Ada was at first embarrassed that her father had noticed her reaction to Ravi's arrival and confused it for passion for Mr. Varley, and then angry at the thought of her stepmother meddling in her life. Already.

"Mrs. Templeton—I mean, Lady Westlake said that?"

"Yes, but she was clearly wrong. It doesn't matter, anyway. You have plenty of time to make a brilliant match. Your first season is still ahead of you. It's a good thing that Charlotte is here; she will be able to bring you out of yourself. I keep telling you, sweetheart. You're too bookish for a young girl, it isn't healthy."

Ada swallowed. Perhaps this was as good a moment as any to test the water.

"Some girls do read books and still marry, Papa. Some even—even go to university."

Her father laughed. "University! It's quite useless—what do they imagine they're going to do with a degree? You would do better to spend three years studying how to run a household under Mrs. Cliffe."

Ada managed a halfhearted smile. Her father stroked her hair.

"No, your first season should be all gaiety. No doubt by the end of it you'll be settled and off my hands." He smiled. "Being married gives you all kinds of opportunities to support your husband in his career. You will be busy hosting benefit galas, putting a word in the ear of the most important people . . . an intelligent wife can be a real help to an ambitious man."

"I see," said Ada quietly. She knew her father loved her, but he didn't seem to want to understand her. She did not want to be a man's helper. She wanted her own life.

"I'm glad." He patted her shoulder. "Now I must get back to Fiona. This is the first day of our married life, you'll remember. Dry your eyes and come back downstairs as soon as you can."

The door closed behind him, and he left Ada alone in the library.

The storm of emotion had passed, and she felt she was looking at a clear view, even if it was not the one she had wanted to see. She had never expected her father to support her in her desire to go to Oxford. But now she knew what he did want. He wanted her to marry well—brilliantly, in fact. Perhaps if she did that, going to Oxford would be possible. Perhaps.

She did not regret refusing Varley. But if she were not to be forced by her stepmother into a marriage with someone little better, she had to make a success of the season and find a husband who her father and society would entirely approve of. And an Indian student with no prospects was not such a husband.

There was no choice in the matter. She had to forget Ravi.

Chapter Thirteen

"Sir, I really think you should slow down!" Oliver shouted above the roar of the engine. The dirt and dust of the road rattled by and the hedgerows passed in a blur of green.

Sebastian glanced at him, an exhilarated grin on his face. He looked like a Greek god in his chariot, golden and vengeful.

"Ah, come on, Oliver. Don't you like to live dangerously?" he shouted back.

He held Oliver's eyes for just a second longer than was necessary before the De Dion–Bouton reached the next bend and he had to look back at the road. It was just long enough for Oliver's heartbeat to speed up in response. He looked away, pressing his lips together to stifle an answering, unvalet-like smile. *You don't know the half of it*, he thought.

"Where are we going, sir?" He glanced back at the picnic hamper in the back.

Sebastian pulled the car to the side of the road, slammed on the brakes, and brought them to a shuddering halt. The silence was like a thunderclap. Oliver blinked at the blue sky. Small noises like the birds in the trees and the creaking noise of the car's metal became audible in the sudden stillness.

They had stopped on a patch of grass surrounded by willows

and small shrubs. Oliver climbed down, aware of his dusty face and the hot sun making him sweat inside his uniform. Sebastian got down, too. He brushed his blond fringe from his sweaty forehead and, with another provocative—at least, Oliver thought it was provocative—glance at Oliver, strode toward the trees.

Oliver hesitated before following. He went to the car and lifted out the picnic basket. One thing was for sure, he was not going to make the same mistake as last time. Caution was everything.

He followed Sebastian down through the trees, trying not to slip as he carried the picnic basket down the narrow, muddy path. He was so busy looking at his feet that when he looked up he was startled to find himself on the shores of a small lake. The water was calm and blue as the sky; a jetty led out into the water, a rowing boat moored to it. In the distance was Somerton, small as a doll's house, and Sebastian stood at the end of the jetty, stripping his shirt from his muscular, clean-cut chest.

Oliver found himself breathless. He was glad Sebastian was not looking in his direction. He turned away and looked for a dry spot for the picnic basket.

When he turned back, Sebastian was in the water, and his clothes were tossed aside on the jetty.

Oliver went to collect them. Sebastian, treading water at the end of the jetty, looked up.

"I hope you like this spot. It seemed the best place to go to get away from all that rot."

He nodded toward the house. A month had passed since Lord and Lady Westlake's wedding, but the stream of guests arriving to congratulate the new couple seemed endless.

Distantly, the sound of shots cracked the air.

"The shooting season, sir?"

"Yes. I fail to see why humans find their amusement in destroying life."

He swam a few slow, strong strokes out into the lake. Oliver watched the water ripple from his shoulder muscles.

"I must say I agree, sir."

Sebastian turned in the water, smiling up at him. It was a devilish smile, which Oliver knew very well by now. He suspected that Sebastian also knew its effects.

"Why don't you come in too? It seems a shame to have you stand there hot and sweaty when you could be cooling off." He paused. "Especially when there is no one here to see us."

So I was right, thought Oliver. He said, "I'm not sure it would be appropriate, sir," and turned away with the clothes, to hide the broad smile on his face. Caution, Oliver, he told himself. No one who involved himself with a Greek god ever came out of it happily. The immortals flew away in their chariots of fire, but Phaeton crashed to earth.

"It wouldn't be appropriate for a master and a valet to swim together," Sebastian said lazily behind him, "but you're not an ordinary valet, are you, Oliver?"

Oliver almost froze. He managed to keep walking, but his heart was beating fast now, and not with pleasure. *What does he know?* he thought. He pretended not to have heard, and Sebastian did not call him back.

Behind the screen of the trees, he placed the clothes safely with the picnic basket. As he did so, a letter fell from the pocket. Oliver picked it up. The hand was uneducated; it was addressed *Master Sebastian*.

The temptation to open it lasted for only a second, but it was very strong. Oliver placed the letter back in its pocket and walked back to the jetty. Perhaps his reply would be treated as insolence, but in such circumstances, a fair employer would excuse a little insolence.

"Maybe," he said, as if their conversation had not been interrupted. "But perhaps none of us are exactly what we seem, are we, Master Sebastian?"

Sebastian smiled up at him from the water. It was a thoughtful smile, hard to read. Beneath the surface of the water his body seemed white and liquid. Distantly, the guns of the shooting party echoed. Oliver made himself meet Sebastian's eyes with an equally firm gaze. He found himself, to his surprise, liking Master Sebastian. Yes, he liked him a lot.

"Perhaps not," said Sebastian quietly.

He broke the moment, splashing away from the jetty. Then he turned again in the water.

"I say, Oliver, would it be a bore if I asked you to move the picnic into the boat? We might eat in the center of the lake. That would be amusing, don't you think? And less chance of being taken for a duck and slaughtered."

"Certainly, sir." Oliver, a little relieved and a little disappointed that nothing had happened, went to collect the picnic basket and lugged it to the rowing boat. Cook had packed it well. Champagne bottles clinked against silver, and the boat sank perceptibly in the water when he loaded it in.

He got in the boat and rowed with smooth, fast strokes into the middle of the lake. He had not rowed for a long time, but it was a pleasure to get back into it. Sebastian swam after him. Oliver stopped the boat. They were in the dead center of the lake.

Sebastian reached him and propped his elbows on the gunwale. His skin was golden.

"You row very well for a valet, Oliver," he said

101

thoughtfully. "I can't think where you learned such a classic stroke."

Damn, thought Oliver. Before he could cover his confusion, Sebastian was hoisting himself over the wale of the boat. Oliver dropped an oar, which fortunately caught itself in the rowlock.

"Sir, I—your clothes are still on the bank," he stammered.

Sebastian gave him another of his devastating grins.

"Well, isn't that inconvenient?"

Chapter Fourteen

Ada put her hands over her ears as the guns broke out again in a crackle of shots. Dogs barked and the birds tumbled out of the sky, as if a jealous god had turned them into stones.

"I wish we hadn't come now," she said under her breath to Georgiana.

"Oh, I think it's quite exciting," Georgiana said. "Have you seen how many Michael's bagged?"

Ada made a face. She didn't know what Georgiana saw in the boy. He was moody and sulky, a spoiled little puppy. But perhaps, she thought, she was being unfair. The smell of smoke and blood and wet dog was stifling her. Behind her, the footmen were piling limp, feathered bodies in a pyramid.

"How are we going to eat all these? It'll take forever."

"We don't have to. They'll get distributed in the village. That's what Papa said . . . Oh, jolly well done!" she exclaimed, as another two ducks fell from the sky in quick succession.

Ada backed away from the guns.

"Where are you going?" Georgiana turned back to her.

"Back to the house."

"My lady, may I suggest that one of the footmen accompany you?" Cooper loomed gently forward.

"No, thank you, Cooper—I just want to be alone." Ada almost stumbled in her haste to get away. She hurried on through the woods, following the path they had come down. As the noise of the guns receded and the smell of the hunt lessened, she relaxed.

But alone in the wood, there was nothing to distract her from the thoughts she'd been trying to suppress for days.

She was taking a huge risk, she knew it. Her reputation would be ruined if it were known that Ravi had written to her, and that she had replied. But it was so innocent, she told herself. She had made it quite clear they could only be friends—and, on impulse, she had enclosed an article on Indian life she planned to send off to *The Spectator.* After all, he was the perfect person to advise her on it.

Now, though, she almost wished she hadn't replied. What if he did not write back? What if he did not like her article? What if he was critical, or worse, dismissive? When she thought of him reading it, she felt ready to sink into the ground with embarrassment. Yet she knew it was a good piece of writing—at least, she thought she did. And if she could make a success as a journalist, she would have an independent income. There were so few things that a woman could do to earn money, but this was one of them. Then she would not be so completely dependent on her father—and her stepmother. She would be free. She told herself that that was the only reason she could not sleep for wondering if tomorrow was the day that his letter would reach her.

A shot rang out, almost in her ear, and at the same moment a shout of alarm. Ada instinctively flung up her hands to defend herself. Something black hurtled past her, and thumped to her feet. A splash of blood flew up and soaked her tweed.

There was a crashing in the undergrowth, and a young man came running toward her, his face pale.

"My God! Are you hurt? An inch lower and I might have—"

"Hurt? No! I—it was my own fault. How foolish of me!" Ada gasped out.

"What the devil were you doing walking around in front of the guns?" The man's color had returned and he was angry now. His blue eyes snapped fire.

"I was trying to get back to the house, but I was—distracted. I must have taken a wrong turn." The world was turning dizzyingly black and white; dots swam in front of her eyes.

"You're hurt. Lean on me." His voice came from far away, and as if he were under the sea she heard him say, "Marston, stop the shoot."

"No!" She struggled to stand. "I'm not hurt, I'm only shocked, and turned a little faint. Please, don't stop on my account." She dropped her head and slowly the world stopped spinning. The man looked into her face with concern. He had well-chiseled, handsome features, the eyes a little pale and very shrewd. A moment later she recognized him from the morning papers. It was Lord Fintan, the Liberal peer who spoke so warmly in favor of women's suffrage.

"Very well, but you must allow me to escort you to the house." He hesitated. "It is Lady Ada, isn't it? I don't think we were introduced, but I recognize you from Miss Templeton's description." He helped her to her feet. "I am Lord Fintan."

"Of course," she said warmly. "I owe you a great debt, all Englishwomen do."

He raised his eyebrows and smiled. "Ah, you follow the news then? Good. I'm glad to see women involving themselves in the life of the nation."

They strolled along through the woods, away from the noise of the guns and toward the house. Ada was flattered by the way he spoke to her, as if he took her seriously.

"I think we all have a responsibility to involve ourselves," she went on, "especially in these troubled times. The strikes this year and the problems in Europe . . . sometimes it seems as if the world is coming to an end."

He laughed. "This is weighty talk for a shooting party."

She smiled. "Don't pretend you came here simply to have your revenge on our duck population. I know that after dinner the real work is done."

"You're correct," he agreed. "And very insightful."

She laughed, and, suddenly conscious of his eyes on her, speeded up her pace. As they left the woods and stepped onto the lawn, a golden-brown leaf fluttered down from above and she caught it and twirled it in her fingers.

"They say that's good luck," she said, turning to him. But he was not looking at her anymore. He was looking up to the house, and the terrace, where the dresses of the ladies blossomed like flowers.

"Yes, you're correct," he went on, as if he had not heard her last words. "I don't care for shooting much. I came here to work. But I'm glad to have found pleasure, also."

Ada followed his gaze and saw Charlotte. She was laughing as she clung to her hat with one hand, and with the other raised a glass of champagne that glittered in the sun.

"How do you know Charlotte?" she said, surprised to find a prick of jealousy in her tone.

"Oh, we danced together a good deal last season," he replied. Offering her his arm, he escorted her up the terrace steps to the waiting eagle eyes of the ladies.

"I wish that man would do something to help or get out of our way!" Annie snapped, winding through the kitchen to the pantry. Rose, who was helping out by decorating the cakes for tea with candied violets and spun sugar, looked up. The man in question was handsome, but there was something brutal about his heavy features, and his eyes were cold. He was loitering in the passage, a cigarette behind his ear.

"That's Simon Croker, Lord Fintan's valet," she said. "I suppose he's waiting to attend his master."

"Well, I wish he would wait somewhere else!" Annie went to the door. "Here, you, if you're not doing anything, you can take these game pies up to the terrace."

Simon scowled. "I don't work for you."

"You don't seem to work at all," Annie retorted.

Simon smiled without humor and lowered his voice. "Here, I'll tell you what. You do me a favor and I'll do you one."

Annie and Rose looked at each other.

"You've got the wrong kind of girl," Rose said with a laugh.

Simon's lip curled. "Not that sort of favor. I just want to know if it's true that Sebastian Templeton's staying here."

"What's it to you?" Annie raised her eyebrow at Rose.

"Just curious."

Rose frowned. It seemed an innocent enough question—but odd. As she was hesitating, the front doorbell rang. Annie started.

"Dear life! Who's that at this time? Mr. Cooper's out with the guns and I can't go, I'm all over flour. You'll have to, Rose."

"Me?" Rose was scandalized. "But they don't like maids answering the door—"

"It'll have to do for once. Go on, hurry up!"

Rose wiped her hands on her apron, hastily tidied her hair, and ran up the stairs two at a time. By the time she had crossed the marble expanse of the hall to the front door, she had more or less got her breath back. Shyly, she pulled the bolts back and opened the door.

"Rose!" Sebastian Templeton was flushed and swaying slightly on his feet. His eyes sparkled. Behind him was the motorcar, hissing and creaking. His valet, Oliver, his dark curls messed up and his cheeks also red, was unloading a picnic hamper from the car.

"Mr. Templeton!" Rose was confused and then amused. She backed away as Sebastian came striding in, smelling of cologne and champagne. He was not really drunk, she realized, just tipsy. But she could not allow him to go into the drawing room in that state.

"Don't worry, Rose, I've no intention of disturbing my mother and her guests." Sebastian's eyes twinkled as he pulled off his gloves and motoring hat and flung them down on the hall table. "We've had a simply glorious drive, and we're in high spirits—isn't that right, Oliver?"

"It is, sir." Oliver came after him, laden down with the picnic basket. Rose caught his eye and pressed her lips together to keep from smiling. Then his expression changed, and a shocked look came over his face. He put down the picnic basket and leaped past her, exclaiming, "Sebastian! Are you all right?"

Sebastian? Rose was shocked to hear Oliver address his master that way. She turned, saw Mr. Templeton, and gasped. His face had turned quite white, and he stumbled as she looked at him—straight into the Westlake Vase.

Rose darted forward to try and catch it, but it was too late. The vase shattered on the floor with a noise like several chandeliers exploding.

Oliver's arm was around Mr. Templeton, supporting him.

"I'm well—I'm perfectly well," Sebastian managed to say. His lips were quivering. Oliver led him to a chair, but he shook his valet off. "No—no, I don't want to sit down."

"What happened, sir? Were you taken ill? Shall I call the doctor?" Rose, frightened, went toward him, but stepped back as glass crunched underfoot.

"No! That is—thank you. I'm quite well." He took a deep breath and steadied himself against the wall. The color was returning to his cheeks. "I—I must rest, that's all. Too much sun and champagne, no doubt."

He pulled himself up straight and went to the stairs without another word or glance behind him. Oliver, looking puzzled and pale, went after him. Rose caught his arm.

"Are you sure I shouldn't call the doctor? It wouldn't be any trouble."

"I don't think so," Oliver replied, in a low voice. "It wasn't a funny turn, I think. He was looking over there—toward the servants' door—and unless I'm wrong, he saw something that gave him a shock."

Rose followed his gaze to the shadows by the door. When she looked back, he was hurrying up the stairs after his master, his face full of concern.

Saw something, thought Rose. *Or someone?* Now she remembered it, she had not heard the door swing closed after her. She went back to the baize door and looked down the stairs. There was no one there, only a whiff of cigarette smoke.

Whatever it was he saw, she thought, it must have been a big shock. It had sobered him right up.

But there was no time to wonder about it. She had to get the ruins of the Westlake Vase tidied up—and she was not looking forward to what her mother and Mr. Cooper would say about it.

The table on the terrace was laden with the fruits of the season: game pie, ham, casseroles, stews, and curries. The men applied themselves with vigor; the ladies, conscious of their corsets, held back.

Ada listened carefully to the conversation around her.

"Women's suffrage is an imperative, not a choice." Lord Fintan leaned forward to make his point. "It will follow naturally from women's education."

"I find women's education so odd," Charlotte smiled. "I personally could not wait to get out of the schoolroom."

It was an innocent enough statement, but Charlotte somehow managed to make it not innocent at all. Lord Fintan smiled and raised his glass of red wine, studying her over the rim.

"Some women are perfect just as they are, and have no need of education to refine their minds," he answered.

"Lord Fintan, do you really think that women's education is a good thing?" Ada asked.

"I do." He added, "My sister is at Oxford, as it happens—"

Ada did not hear the rest of his sentence. Georgiana, sitting next to her, suddenly whispered. "Ada, I feel so unwell."

Ada turned to her at once. Her face was pale, and she swayed where she sat.

"Georgie!" She put an arm around her, frightened. "Lean on me, dear." She looked up. "Please, excuse us—she has these turns sometimes."

Lord Fintan half rose, asking, "Can I help?" but her father was faster. He came hurrying down from the end of the table and helped Ada steer Georgiana away from the table. They placed her in one of the wicker chairs on the terrace. Rose hurried over with a glass of water.

"So silly—I'm much better now." Georgiana's color was returning. "I just felt faint for a moment. I can't think why."

"But I can," Lord Westlake said. "You have been overdoing

110

things, as usual. Your health must come first, my dear!" He took the glass and let Georgiana sip from it.

"You should lie down for the rest of the afternoon." Ada was still frightened. The spots of color in Georgiana's cheeks, her fast breathing—it had reminded her so much of her mother before she died. They said consumption was not congenital, but a weakness of the lungs might be. "Let me take you inside."

"If I must," Georgiana sighed.

"I'll help you."

"No need, Papa. You should stay with the guests. Rose will help, won't you, Rose?"

"Of course, my lady."

Lord Westlake stood back as Rose and Ada helped Georgiana to her feet. They made their way slowly to the house.

"She can lie on a sofa for a while, rather than walk up to her room." Ada directed them into the yellow drawing room, and helped Georgiana onto a chaise longue.

"Really, I feel like such a fraud. I'm much better already—let me sit up." Georgiana struggled.

"Georgie, will you do as you're told for once? Lie down and stay quiet. Rose will fetch you more water."

"Yes, my lady—and if I could have a word with you? It's about that little matter . . ."

Ada's heart thumped.

"Of course," she said calmly. She walked to the door with Rose. Rose glanced up and down the corridor and, seeing they were alone, reached into her apron and drew out an envelope. She handed it to Ada.

"It arrived this morning," she whispered.

Ada's breath came fast.

"Thank you, Rose. Thank you so much," she replied in the same tone. She glanced back. Georgiana was lying down, breathing quietly on the sofa.

"Lady Georgiana seems better, but could you please bring another glass of water? I will sit with her."

Rose hesitated, as if she wanted to say something else, then nodded and went away down the passage.

As soon as she was gone, Ada ripped the envelope open. The words danced in front of her eyes and finally steadied:

My dear Ada,

I cannot tell you how happy I was to receive your reply. To tell you the truth, I have not been able to stop thinking about our last meeting. There was so much more I wanted to say to you, so much more I wanted to hear you say. I understand why you say we can only be friends, and believe me, I shall not betray your trust, but . . .

Here some words had been scribbled out harshly, and Ada could not make them out.

. . . I hope friendship will be enough.

Instead I shall talk about Oxford, as you ask me to. It is a beautiful city, serene and eternal. It is exhilarating to be surrounded by the past and the greatest minds of the present. I wish that everyone here appreciated it. Perhaps I appreciate it too strongly. I gather that it is a matter of style in some of the aristocratic students to look down on the university and do as little work as possible in order to scrape through. I do not think they appreciate their privileges, but I expect they would consider that a very middle-class and Indian attitude.

The women students, on the other hand, have impressed me very much with their dedication. I certainly think that you would do well to come here, and I think you would certainly pass the exams. Your article has convinced me, as if there were any doubt, that you have ability and intelligence. It is excellently written.

But I wonder—and here I hope I shall not hurt you—if you really know the true India? The picture you paint is a beautiful one, but I feel there is much else that could be said about the condition of the poor, in particular, and there are many questions to be asked about British rule in my country. And I feel an intelligent woman should ask those questions.

Forgive me if that is overstepping the bounds of our friendship. But you asked me for an honest opinion, and I respect you too much not to give it to you.

Ada's face was pink. For an instant she felt a strong urge to rip up the paper. How could he imply she did not understand India? After she had lived there, and loved it, for years! But after a moment's thought, she realized he was right to question her. She had asked him for his opinion and he had given it. She swallowed down her hurt pride, and read on.

I promised myself I would not speak of this next matter, but I cannot hold back. I am glad you have refused Douglas Varley, but please, think hard before you accept any proposal. I cannot see you sacrificed on the altar of society. I understand that we cannot be together—at least, I am trying to understand it, with all the reason at my command, which is not much when I think of you—but if I cannot be with you, I want to know that you are with a man

who will allow you to live your dreams. If you could be
persuaded that you and I—but I had better not write
anymore, or my feelings will give me away.

Only believe me, ever yours,
Ravi

Ada drew in her breath. Her first feeling was one of joy and triumph. So she was not wrong. He did still feel for her. Whatever was between them was not over.

But it had to be over. She pressed her lips together tightly, folded the letter into a tiny square, and slipped it into her jewel case.

Chapter Fifteen

By the time she reached Lady Ada's door, Rose had almost lost courage. *I should never have started this,* she thought. *She'll be angry, and I'll lose my place, and then whatever shall I do?* But there was no help for it. She knew what she was doing was dishonest. The knowledge had sat in her mind like a cold toad, refusing to move until she did something about it. She took a deep breath and knocked at the door.

"Come in!" Lady Ada sounded startled. Rose pushed the door open. Lady Ada was sitting by the window, and she had just pushed a book under the cushion. Rose could see the corner of it poking out.

"Oh Rose, it's only you." She sounded relieved, and pulled her book back from under the cushion; it was a Latin grammar. "These declensions get more perplexing by the day. What is it? You should have free time now, dressing for dinner isn't till later."

"Yes, my lady . . . but I wanted to talk to you." Rose swallowed. "It's about the letters."

Ada looked up quickly.

"Has someone found out? Is it Papa?"

"No, no. Nothing like that. I don't think anyone suspects. But I don't feel comfortable, my lady, that's what I wanted to say to you. I mean . . . Lord Westlake pays my wages. It doesn't seem quite right, to be going behind his back this way, receiving letters from Mr. Sundaresan in my name that are meant for you. I know how upset he would be if he found out. He thinks the world of you. I have a bad conscience, miss. I don't think I should do this anymore." She ran out of breath and words. Lady Ada had turned pale.

"Are you going to tell him?" she burst out in terror. She must have seen the expression on Rose's face, because she caught herself at once. "No, no, Rose, I'm sorry. Forget I said that. I know you would never betray me."

"I wouldn't, my lady." Rose stepped forward, her voice pleading. "I never would. But I don't feel right about my part in it all. If Lord Westlake knew you were receiving love letters, maybe planning, I don't know, my lady, but perhaps planning something foolish . . ."

"But it's not like that at all." Ada's voice was pleading too. "We aren't planning to elope or anything like that. We are just friends." She blushed and looked away from Rose's gaze. "It's true," she protested, though Rose had said nothing. "Our relationship is quite platonic. He is going to help me get into Oxford, that's all." She jumped up, pacing back and forth, an anguished expression on her face. "Oh, Rose, can't you see? I know it's improper, and scandalous, and every person I know and respect would turn away from me in horror if they knew what I was doing . . . but I feel as if this is the first friendship I've ever had that belonged to me, just me." She paced to the window, looking out through the rain-dappled glass. "Sometimes it feels as if every thought, every feeling, is laid out for me the night before by other people, just as my clothes are. But this . . . it feels real. More real than anything in the world ever has before. I am so tempted to find out, don't you see? I want to know what will happen if I follow my heart."

"I do see, my lady," said Rose, softly.

"But if you won't help me . . . then who will? I can't trust anyone else here." Ada turned back to her. "Rose, I don't want you to go against your conscience. But please won't you think again? I need your help, and I'm willing to help you in return. Oh—don't look that way. I don't mean money, I know you better than that, I think. But isn't there anything you want? Anything you've dreamed of? Anything I could help you achieve?"

Rose stood silent. A moment ago she had been feeling trapped, now she could think of nothing that she wanted. Nothing that Lady Ada could give, anyway. Visions of bright feathers and the sounds of the jungle flashed in her head. Then, she heard, distantly, the sounds of someone practicing their scales on the piano.

She smiled. "Well . . . there is one thing, my lady. If you think you could make it happen . . ."

"And you're sure this is all you want?" Ada looked around the music room. "Time to practice the piano?"

"That's all, my lady. I know it's presumptuous of me. I wouldn't like you to think I was giving myself airs . . ."

"No, no, Rose, of course not. I'm just surprised. My sister adores the piano but I could never wait for the lessons to end." She laughed and Rose joined in. "But we will have to handle this carefully. If I allow you to practice, people will want to know why, and that will lead to awkward questions." She pressed a finger to her lips, thinking. "I know! It's simple, of course. In the afternoons, I will pretend to be practicing, and I will say I have you in here for company, while you do some mending. But I won't be practicing. It will be you. And I will . . ."

"Do the mending, my lady?" Rose grinned.

"I don't think so!" Ada grinned back. "No, I shall be studying."

Rose looked at her half in admiration, half in surprise. "You really mean it then, my lady? To go to university?"

"I mean to take the exams, at least. As for going there . . . we'll have to wait and see." She sighed. "It depends on Papa."

"Sometimes I think I am lucky not to have one, myself," Rose said. "A father, I mean."

Ada smiled rather sadly, but did not reply. It hurt her conscience, to deceive her father. He and Georgie were the only people that she loved in the world, without complication or fear or deceit. But now it seemed that she wanted things of which he would never approve.

Rose sat at the piano, and played a few notes, then broke into a melody, a folk tune that Ada vaguely recognized.

"You have never had a lesson?" Ada said wonderingly after a few moments. "But who taught you to play chords?"

"No one, my lady. I worked it out myself—and I took a correspondence course to learn to read music. My mother has Irish blood and there was always music when I was little." She sighed and stopped playing.

"You must miss your childhood village," Ada said gently.

Rose shrugged. "It seems so long ago, my lady. Like a different country."

Ada opened her mouth to say, *That's just how I feel too*. But before she could speak, there was a huge smash, and the window seemed to explode. Rose shrieked and jumped up from the piano. Ada ducked. When she looked up, there was a huge hole in the window, and shards of broken glass

118

spattered the piano. In the center of the piano lid lay a cricket ball.

"What happened?" Rose was looking around wildly. "What on earth—?"

"It must be the boys," Ada picked her way across the broken glass and looked out of the hole in the window. Rose joined her. Three horrified-looking figures stared back up at her: Philip, Michael, and . . .

"Georgiana!" Ada exclaimed.

Georgiana covered her mouth with the hand that was not holding the cricket bat.

"Oh, I'm so, so sorry!" she moaned.

"Georgiana," said Ada, putting her head around the door of the drawing room, "may I speak to you for a moment?"

Georgiana put down the book she had been reading. "Is this about the window? Because Papa has given me a lecture already. He said that I should be grateful he didn't swish me because if he did I would get it as well as the boys for being such a hoyden." Her voice trembled miserably.

"No, you goose. I don't care about the window, although I think you should stick to what you're good at." Ada laughed as she closed the door behind her. "Cricket! What on earth possessed you?" Georgiana opened her mouth and Ada added, "Don't answer that. I know the answer begins with an M. Just look at this, please, and tell me what you think of it."

She walked over and handed Georgiana a sheet of foolscap covered with penciled staves and marks. Georgiana looked at it, puzzled, then began humming along under her breath, reading it by sight. "It's delightful!" she exclaimed at the end of it. "Did you write this yourself? I knew you were practicing seriously, but I had no idea you were composing—"

"I'm not!" Ada glanced around to check they were alone, then lowered her voice. "Will you keep this secret if I tell you? Even from Michael?"

Georgiana, eyes wide, nodded.

"It's not me playing the piano. It's Rose."

"Rose? . . . Rose, the maid?"

"Yes. We have an . . . arrangement." She had thought long and hard about how to say this. "You know how much I want to go to Oxford, don't you?"

"Ye-es . . ."

"You see, Rose wants to play the piano. She's had no lessons, only a correspondence course, and of course she has no chance to practice." She quickly explained their arrangement, leaving out all mention of Ravi. "And she makes up her own tunes, and this is one she wrote down," she finished. "I wanted to know what you thought, because you're so much more musical than I am."

"I think it's marvelous!" Georgiana jumped to her feet. "Ada, this is so exciting, we have a real genius downstairs!" She walked about the room, humming the tune again under her breath. "May I play this? Would she mind, do you think?"

"I hoped you would say that," Ada answered. "She isn't strong enough on the piano yet to play her own inventions, I think, but if you could play it, she could hear what it sounds like, and that would be so useful for her."

"I'll do it now." Georgiana hurried to the door. Ada followed her. They went up the great flights of stairs, past the Reynolds and Turners, to the music room. Georgiana sat down at the piano, her long, pale fingers ready, and after a moment's thought, began to play.

Upstairs, Rose was in Ada's room, picking through stockings for mending. Her head was full of music, full of tunes.

It was as if, as soon as she had been allowed to touch the piano, they had been born, like seeds drifting from a shaken dandelion clock. The old scraps of melodies she had known in her childhood came back to her, and as she stitched she sang under her breath. Music painted itself across her mind. It was as if she could really hear it . . .

She grew still, gazing into the air, her eyes startled and wide. Was she imagining things? A moment of fear caught her. She stood up, a pair of stockings slipping unheeded to the floor, and opened the door.

The notes of the piano, her music made real, came up the stairs like a beloved friend running to meet her.

"Oh . . ." Rose whispered, a smile spreading over her face. "Oh . . . thank you."

Chapter Sixteen

"Ada," Lord Westlake said, raising his voice so that she could hear him along the breakfast table, "your piano playing has improved immensely since you began regular practice. Sebastian and I were passing the music room the other day and we were very impressed."

Ada blushed and managed a thank you.

"No, but really," Sebastian added, his intelligent green eyes fixed on her. "You deserve congratulations. And what was that delightful little tune you were playing called? It had real spirit to it."

"Oh . . . I forget. I think it was a folk tune." She glanced guiltily at Georgiana.

"Well, it was very pretty," Sebastian said, returning to his toast. "I wish you'd play it for me some time. I'd love to hear it properly."

Thankfully, Ada was spared answering by the entrance of Charlotte and Fiona, Fiona dressed in the most elegant tweeds and Charlotte in a very daring peacock-blue and terracotta tunic dress. Both wore long strands of pearls and Ada could not help admiring their style—though she did wonder how long their clothes would stay spotless if they decided to walk outside.

"*So* sorry we're late," Fiona said, dropping a kiss on Lord

Westlake's head before swooping to sit next to him. The footman approached with a dish of cold meat, but she waved him away. "Just a little coffee for me, thank you."

"We had trays brought to our rooms," Charlotte said. "Family is all very well but you hardly want to see them over breakfast." She yawned. "So what plans have you for today?" Glancing at Georgiana's riding habit, she added, "Please don't tell me you are being let loose with a horse?"

"Yes, Michael's taking me out," Georgiana said, excitedly reaching up to touch the feather in her hat.

Charlotte raised an eyebrow. "Do you think that's wise? Between the two of you, you might bring down the stables."

Georgiana's lip trembled and she glanced nervously toward her father, who was watching them.

"I'm sure everything will be fine," Ada said. "Georgie's a good rider, and Beauty is a quiet old thing."

"I have more trust in Ada's good sense than I do in yours, Georgiana, so I shall let you go on her recommendation," Lord Westlake said.

Georgiana smiled. As she rose to leave, she whispered, "Thank you, dear sister!" in Ada's ear.

Chapter Seventeen

Georgiana followed Michael up the long drive, Beauty clopping along as placidly as a cart horse. Prince, Michael's tall bay, was more challenging, shying and sidestepping and shaking his head. Georgiana hardly noticed; her eyes were fixed on Michael's handsome, taut face. He pressed his lips together, concentrating on managing the horse. Georgiana was dying to tell him about Rose, but she had promised not to, and besides, perhaps he would not be very interested. He didn't seem to care for music much; he was always outside, playing cricket, or riding, or shooting. It was very wearying, but it was worth it to stay by his side. Sooner or later, she was sure, he would notice her. He would have to. She was not going to give up until he did. And then . . . well, she had never been kissed, but she was sure it would be dizzying, swooping, somehow more wonderful than anything she had ever experienced before. Her imagination usually went blank at this point, because the simple bringing together of two sets of lips—she was fairly certain that was how it went—did not seem at all exciting, certainly not to the extent that everyone said it was. But just looking at Michael made her heart beat faster, and her hands clutch tighter on the reins.

"I can't hold Prince to this pace," he flung over his shoulder. "I'll have to canter."

He was off in a kick of flying gravel, Prince bounding away like a deer.

"Oh, come on, Beauty!" Georgiana clicked her tongue and urged Beauty forward. Beauty ambled into a startled trot and eventually a reluctant canter. The wind whipped by and brought the color into Georgiana's cheeks. She loved going fast, it was like her fingers flying over the piano keyboard, when she went into a world of her own.

Michael didn't look back until he reached the gate in the hedge.

"Here I am!" Georgiana cantered up, eyes bright and cheeks pink.

"Finally," was all Michael said. Georgiana wilted.

"Shall we ride down to the village?" she suggested as he dismounted to open the gate. "I've a little money, we could get chocolate and sit by the river." Riverbanks were the kind of places where one might get kissed, she thought.

"Trust a girl to think of something that boring," he muttered, holding the gate open for her.

Georgiana turned pink. Once she had ridden through the gate she drew rein and looked around. "I think you're very rude," she said firmly. "I don't see you suggesting anything so exciting."

Michael looked startled and a little remorseful. He closed the gate and remounted. They rode on side by side. "I suppose you're right," he said, with such honesty that Georgiana was disarmed. "I have a rotten temper, I'm sorry. I'm just . . . well, if I'm honest, I'm wishing I hadn't got expelled."

Georgiana's eyes widened. "But you said you didn't care. You said—"

"Well, maybe I was bluffing." He looked embarrassed, and ran a hand through his blond hair so it stood up. "The thing

125

is, I hate school. I want to go into the army. But Mother won't let me, and now that I'm at home she spends all her time nagging me and babying me. I can't stand it, I tell you." He slapped the air crossly with his riding crop. "Even Eton would be better than this."

"Oh . . ." Georgiana understood, and forgave him at once. "But why won't she let you go into the army?"

"Says it's dangerous, of all things. I just want to get out and see the world."

"I know what you mean," Georgiana said. She smiled. "Well, at least we can see as far as the road. Race you!"

She urged the startled Beauty into a canter and rode to the fence that separated Somerton land from the road. Michael followed. At the fence they drew rein and stood, the horses panting, while they looked back over the park toward the house. The road curved past them, and as they sat there a carriage came along it. Inside, Georgiana glimpsed Edith and the nursemaid, Priya, a fractious Augustus squirming on her knee. Georgiana raised her riding crop to wave. Edith smiled graciously.

"Who was that?"

Michael's tone startled her. She turned toward him. He was staring after the carriage as if thunderstruck.

"Lady Edith, of course. Probably going to the village to call on Lady Fairfax."

"Not her! The . . . other one."

Georgiana felt a shock of anxiety go through her. She wasn't quite sure why, but she disliked the way he was looking after the carriage so intensely.

"Just the—the nursemaid," she said reluctantly. "I believe her name is Priya."

"Priya," murmured Michael, gazing after the carriage.

126

Georgiana thought he looked like a prince under a spell—the spell of a mysterious fairy.

She panicked. She had to draw his attention back to her somehow. "Let's gallop!" she burst out, wheeling Beauty around. "Come on—into the woods!"

She set Beauty off at a fast pace down the hill. Behind her she heard him shout after her, but she ignored him. The slope was much steeper than she was used to, and inside the woods it would be dangerous. But she had to distract him. She had to break the spell.

"Come on, Beauty!"

She reached the woods and guided Beauty away from the branches and onto the track. Beauty, who had not galloped in years, tossed her head in protest, but Georgiana spurred her on.

Wanting to show Michael what she was made of, she did not slow her pace, but urged Beauty down the track, clods of mud spattering from her hooves thudding on the ground.

"Georgiana, stop!" she heard Michael shouting behind her. She turned round to grin at him, and when she looked back, she saw was a fallen tree trunk blocking the way.

Georgiana bit her lip and urged Beauty forward. The old horse heaved herself over the trunk—and the ground on the other side wasn't there. There was a sudden drop, Beauty neighed in fear, and stumbled. Georgiana barely had time to gasp before she was flying over the horse's head, the world was green and fast, and in the long, almost luxuriously stretched-out second before she hit the ground, she had time to think: *This will hurt*.

She was swimming in darkness, a roaring pain in her head. The pain became words.

"Georgie! Georgiana! Can you hear me?"

It sounded like Michael, but it couldn't be. Michael never sounded like that: terrified, on the brink of tears.

"Georgiana, wake up! Say something!"

She tried to say, "Stop shouting," but she couldn't drag her voice up, it was like fishing a heavy weight from deep water. She tried again, and managed a groan.

"Oh, thank God. You're not dead." He really was sobbing now. This was too intriguing to miss. She forced her eyes open and the glare of the weak sunshine hit her like a sledgehammer.

"O-o-o-oh . . . my head!" she gasped.

Michael was crouching next to her. In fact, she was in his arms. She did not have time to enjoy this quite as much as she would have liked, for she was too busy being sick in the bushes. Even at the time this struck her as unjust.

"What happened?" The memory of the tree trunk, like a black barrier across her path, rose up.

"You came a cropper. What a jump you took! I thought you would go round."

"Beauty?" She struggled to sit up. Beauty stood not far away, an I-told-you-so expression on her face.

"She's all right. Bit of a graze on her hock, but she was clever—picked herself up. You landed right on your head, though. I thought you were dead, Georgie. Never do that to me again!"

Georgiana beamed at the concern in his voice, and winced as pain shot through her skull. It forced her to say, "Perhaps we ought to go home now."

"You shouldn't move. I'll ride back and fetch someone, if you're all right alone for a few moments." He stood up and caught Prince's reins. He looked down at her again and said,

"I'm so glad you're not badly hurt. I'd have felt—well, never mind."

Georgiana smiled weakly. *I must do this more often*, she thought.

Chapter Eighteen

Everyone in Oxford knew which Sebastian Templeton's rooms were. They were the ones with the windows always open, from which the loudest laughter and gramophone music spilled, the ones where the sunshine seemed to linger longest, the ones out of which undergraduates leaned, calling raucously and drunkenly down to the passing students. They were the ones outside which the motorcars drew up day and night with a screech of brakes, to offload boys with glossy toppers and the most ringingly aristocratic accents, who raced upstairs talking and laughing so loud that dons asleep half a mile away sat up groaning and vowing to send Sebastian down the very next day. Only somehow Sebastian never was sent down. Oxford would just not have been the same without him.

"So we just left the motorcar there, in the haystack, and simply swam the rest of the way home!" Lord Evelyn Spencer said, finishing his anecdote. There was a roar of laughter from the rest of "the Set," as fashionable young men and women of means were known. Lord Evelyn held out his glass vaguely. "Sebastian, where is that valet of yours with the champagne?"

Oliver heard him from inside the kitchen and hurried out with the fresh champagne. He kept his head down and bowed, and hoped no one could see how nervous he was. Sebastian lolled on the couch, between Archie Ffoulkes and Prince Alexander Tatenov, and winked at Oliver as he poured the champagne. Oliver allowed himself a brief smile in return.

But his heart was not in it. He retreated to the kitchen and went on with setting out the small porcelain dishes that Sebastian had picked up in an antiques shop on their drive down. It was hard to see Sebastian so at ease, so careless, and not be able to join in the laughter, to have to keep a poker face and stay in the background. After the days they had shared together, it felt like a betrayal.

He scolded himself as he carefully placed a silver spoonful of caviar in each dish. Sebastian couldn't be expected to change his life completely, just because of Oliver. If he did, everyone would get suspicious. And he had known that this was what Sebastian was like. Truth be told, it was why he liked him so much.

The doorbell rang just as he came out with the caviar.

"Oh!" Evelyn exclaimed. "Is this your new find arriving, Sebastian?"

Oliver thought for a second he meant himself, and turned pale. But Sebastian answered, "I hope so! He's quite fascinating—dark and handsome, and so intense."

The words rang in Oliver's ears as he went to the door and opened it. Joke or not, it wasn't funny of Sebastian to flirt in front of him. He opened the door. Outside stood two men—a tall, handsome Indian boy who looked as if he would rather not be there. And the Honorable Peregrine Winchester.

Oliver half gasped, and his hand jerked automatically to hide his face. He managed to turn the gesture into brushing his hair from his eyes, and hastily stood back. Of all people, Perry—here. Of course, he *would* have been going to Oxford. If he recognized him . . .

But Perry Winchester just thrust his coat at him and strode in, saying in his booming voice, "Sorry I'm late, everyone. I've brought my friend—Ravi Sundaresan."

Sebastian jumped to his feet, smiling broadly.

"Ravi, my dear chap—I'm so glad you could come. Sit down, have a drink. Campbell, fetch him a drink." He ushered Ravi to a chair. Ravi sat down, managing a smile. "I said, Campbell, fetch him a drink!" Sebastian threw impatiently over his shoulder.

Oliver started, Perry's coat still in his arms. He had been so thrown back into the past by thinking Perry was sure to recognize him that he had forgotten that Campbell was the surname that he had given when he became a valet. "Right away, sir."

He was angry, at his own lapse, and at Sebastian's rudeness. He was glad to retreat to the kitchen to hide his anger. So this was what it was to be a servant: not to dare to speak back or to defend yourself, but to put up with humiliation. *Well, you were a bloody fool to expect anything else*, he thought, but he couldn't stop the spots of color coming into his cheeks, or the ache of rejected disappointment that opened in his heart. He was a servant now, he had to remember that. It had been his own decision to throw his life away, and by God he had made a good job of it. There was no sense in expecting a gentleman like Sebastian to take what they had together seriously.

He came out with the champagne and handed it around. He trembled as he handed Perry his glass, but Perry didn't even look at him. Oliver was half annoyed, but relieved also.

132

It seemed that as a valet he was invisible even to his old friends from Harrow.

He noticed that Ravi did not seem impressed with the Set. He sat silently, giving the barest minimum of answers as the others rattled on, exchanging gossip about society figures and plans for country house parties. Oliver wondered why he had come, and why he did not leave, if the company was so little to his taste.

It was not until much later, when some of the Set had left, and others had lounged over to the pianola to play records, that Sebastian was left alone with Ravi on the sofa. Oliver came out of the kitchen to collect the empty glasses. Ravi sat, frowning into his glass. Sebastian watched him thoughtfully. He paid no attention to Oliver.

Ravi broke the silence. He said, abruptly. "How is . . . everyone at Somerton, Sebastian? I hope you left them all well."

"Quite well." Sebastian looked surprised.

"Good," Ravi muttered. He half frowned, and Oliver could see that he was trying to think of a way to continue the conversation.

Sebastian cleared his throat. "You don't like me, do you?"

His tone was flirtatious. Oliver hastily snatched up the last glass and returned to the kitchen to hide his feelings. But once there, he could not resist moving to the crack between the door and the wall, and watching and listening to the conversation unfold.

Ravi's reply was cool and distant. "On the contrary. I like you very much."

"Really? I would have said you almost despise me. Why is that?"

Ravi hesitated. "Perhaps because I dislike waste."

"Waste? What do you mean?"

Ravi paused again before answering. The sun sparked golden flecks from his brown eyes. "You are an intelligent man. That's clear. You could make a difference to society." He dropped his voice discreetly. "Yet you choose to waste your time and your intelligence talking inanities with these . . . butterflies." He nodded toward Archie Ffoulkes and Perry Winchester, who were laughing by the pianola.

Sebastian gave a small, thoughtful "Hmmph." He twirled the stem of the champagne glass between his fingers as if thinking of a reply.

Oliver's heart beat hard. They were sitting so close together on the sofa. And he was stuck here, marooned in the kitchen, behind a wall of propriety.

"Society. Yes. You see, I don't consider myself a part of society."

"I don't mean polite society," Ravi said with some contempt. "I mean people. All people, everywhere."

"I know you do. But I still don't belong."

Oliver shivered. He knew what Sebastian meant. He was talking about the love that could get them both arrested, that could make friends and family turn away from them in disgust. He knew. He had lost both friends and family already, and his name and his station had followed.

"How can you say that? You're one of the human race, after all."

"I don't think much of the human race." Sebastian kept his tone light and witty, but Oliver could hear a hardness underneath.

"Really? What has made you so cynical?"

Sebastian smiled. "Betrayal."

"How dramatic."

"Not really. I expect everyone lives through it at some point. You learn not to trust people. Not to let yourself be hurt."

"But if you don't let yourself be open to pain, how can you be open to . . ."

"What?"

"I was going to say love, but I wouldn't want you to get the wrong impression."

Sebastian laughed. "No fear of that. I don't think much of love, either. I don't believe in it."

Oliver stepped back, feeling as if he had been punched. *What did you expect?* he asked himself again. But it seemed his heart was not as sensible as his head. His heart had expected more.

"I used not to believe in love either," said Ravi. "But I think you will change your mind. I have."

He stood abruptly, placing his glass down. Sebastian rose too, and Ravi held out his hand.

"It has been interesting to talk to you, Sebastian. It has been interesting to observe English society at close quarters."

Sebastian took his hand and shook it firmly. "Are you sure you must go?"

"Yes. I have a letter to write."

Sebastian followed him to the door. Oliver remained in the kitchen. He realized he still had a glass and a cloth in his hand. He put them down as gently as he could.

Sebastian came back into the room, a thoughtful, rather sad look on his face.

"Oliver . . ." he began. Then he hesitated, and shook his head. He raised his voice, calling to his friends. "Come on, let's go down to the river before the sun sets."

They went out, laughing and talking. Oliver stood in the kitchen, listening as the door slammed behind them. He heard their voices fade down the stairs and reappear in the street. He ran into the main room and looked down into the street. Sebastian, arm-in-arm with Perry, was laughing and joking as he strode across the quad toward his motorcar. The door of the motorcar slammed behind them, and it was as if it had slammed onto Oliver's heart.

Sebastian did not return that evening. Oliver knew this, because he lay awake waiting for him long after he knew it was stupid to hope.

Ada was walking toward the dining room, following the sound of the dinner gong, when Rose darted out from the servants' passage. With a quick glance up and down the empty corridor, she pressed an envelope into Ada's hand. Ada clutched it tightly: she didn't have to look at the handwriting to know it was Ravi's reply to her last letter.

"Thank you!" she whispered. Rose gave her a quick smile and was gone at once.

Ada looked up and down the corridor. No one was coming. She tore open the envelope and read the letter hastily.

My dear Ada,

I was so pleased to receive your last letter and know that I had not given offense. I think I admire you more with every day that passes. Sometimes I wish I did not, it would make it easier to be here, away from you.

You ask me about India, and accuse me of being unjust to men like your father, who have worked hard to improve matters there. I do not deny that he has done much, but he has done it in the interests of the British. How can the representatives of an invading force, who have exploited the riches of India for their own gain, be considered our benefactors?

I know it is hard for a patriot to see the actions of their country as criminal, but if, let us say, France invaded England and took over its administration, managing and directing it and diverting its economic wealth to the glory of the French Empire, would you feel that they had a right to do so? India is an ancient nation, a great nation—as great as Great Britain. We were promised equality by Queen Victoria herself. Yet under British rule wealth is being drained from the country, leaving Indians impoverished and starving. Curzon made things all the worse with his Partition of Bengal.

Oxford has also opened my eyes to some unpleasant facts. This is where the sons of those who will inherit the rule and administration of India study. Some are dedicated, but many others are not. Many are interested only in pleasure and decadence. They are able to be here only because of their birth and wealth, not because of their merit. Yet they will have much political power and determine the fate of my people, just because of who their fathers are. This is unjust. I cannot respect them. What right do they have to rule us?

Things are beginning to change, however. The Indian National Congress has finally brought together both Hindus and Muslims against the British. Even from his cell in Burma, Tilak is making sure that its voice is heard. This gives me hope. The meetings I have attended have been inspiring, and I feel now that I am a part of a great force for change. We shall rid India of the British by one means or another.

I know that your own sense of justice is so strong that you will come around to my point of view. For now, though, I must close this letter in order to catch the post. I wish I were able to see you and speak to you face to face. But perhaps I had better say no more.

Ever and faithfully yours,

Ravi

Ada jumped as she heard footsteps at the end of the corridor. William was heading toward her. He looked more sullen than ever as he strode past without a greeting. She hastily tucked the letter into her sleeve and followed him toward the dining hall. She was shocked by Ravi's letter, she couldn't deny it. It was almost sedition, to speak like that about the Empire. And he had as good as called her father a criminal! The argument about France was persuasive . . . and yet India was so different. It was not a well-ordered, peaceful country like Britain. Surely it needed good administrators, people who could think rationally and stop the Hindus and Muslims from killing each other. What he had said scared her.

She hurried in and took her seat at the table, between Michael and Edith. As she did so, she noticed a satisfied glance pass between Charlotte and Fiona.

Now what's that about? she thought as the footman handed around the lobster. It worried her. She wished Sebastian had not gone back to Oxford; he would have had some explanation. But his place was empty, as was Georgiana's, who was confined to bed following her fall. She glanced toward her father. Perhaps she could ask him what the Indian National Congress was. But his attention was entirely on Fiona, who was flirting and laughing with him.

Suddenly she felt someone's breath on her cheek. "Ada—I'm sorry." It was Michael, whispering urgently in her ear. She looked at him, startled. He had been quite meek and silent since Georgiana's accident, and Ada suddenly understood why.

She turned to face him. "If I thought it was you urging her on to take that jump . . ." She left the sentence unfinished. "But I know Georgiana is headstrong. I expect it was her own fault—and no lasting harm done, the doctor says," she added in a gentler voice. He really did look anguished.

"I know how much you care about her though," he said. "You must be angry with me."

"A little," Ada admitted. "Georgie and I, we only have each other, you see."

"I wish I cared about my brother and sister the way you care about yours," Michael said. He looked down the table, to where Charlotte, devoid of anyone to flirt with, was chatting to her mother about the latest Fortuny gowns. "Sebastian's a decent chap but we don't have anything in common. And Charlotte . . . well, I just wish Georgie was my sister instead of her, that's all."

Ada hesitated. Her first impulse was to agree heartily, but she felt that would be unkind. After all, what could she really say against Charlotte? That she had a cold manner, that she was more interested in dresses and flirting than in reading and art?

"But Georgie *is* your sister now," she said finally. "And so am I, Michael—and we're both very glad of it."

She smiled at him, and was touched and startled to see the look of gratitude and warmth he gave her. *Poor boy*, she thought, *he's simply lonely*. She wished she hadn't been so quick to judge him. Georgiana had seen further than she had—Ada had been wrapped up in thoughts of Ravi. But he was in London now, even farther away than Oxford.

"Papa," she said, taking advantage of a gap in the conversation. "Do you know anything about a man imprisoned in India named Tilak?"

Her father frowned. "Where did you hear about Tilak?"

She realized the whole table was looking at her.

"Oh . . . in a newspaper. It said he had something to do with the Indian National Congress." She tried to sound casual.

"Hmmph!" her father said. "Well, I advise you not to read anything more about him. Tilak leads what they call the INC's hot faction, and they won't stop at violence against us."

"Oh," Ada whispered.

"I quite like the idea of Indians taking some small role in their government, but Tilak is a dangerous man," her father continued.

"Ada's gone quite pale," remarked Charlotte. "This is why I never read the newspapers, they are dreadful for the complexion."

"Yes, you really have only yourself to blame if you find out such unpleasant things," said Fiona sternly.

Her father looked at Ada with concern. "Don't let it trouble you. He and his rabble are a very long way away, and I have no doubt that they will lose support very soon, as people see how unworkable Indian independence is." He added, smiling. "Besides, I have an announcement that will certainly take your mind off the matter." He exchanged a glance with Fiona, who smiled too.

"What's that, Uncle?" William asked.

"As soon as Christmas is over, we shall take the girls down to London. Fiona has persuaded me."

"London!" Ada exclaimed. That was close to Oxford—closer than Somerton, at least. Close to Ravi.

"Excellent. I was just about ready for a jaunt myself," William said, sitting up.

"Not you, William." Lord Westlake's voice was stern. William looked taken aback. "I think you have spent more than enough time in London lately. As the heir to Somerton, you should be learning more about the estates you will manage. You can look after Georgiana as well. I couldn't think of her traveling right now."

William scowled, and looked about to reply, but then seemed to think better of it.

"It's absolutely essential to prepare for the coming season," Fiona went on. "We need to make sure the girls are recognized by the leading hostesses in time. We will stay at my residence—Milborough House."

"And I must see Fortuny, and Madame Lucille, and get a new fan case made," Charlotte said. "One can't have these things planned too soon."

"I have some people to see too," Lord Westlake said. "So what do you think, Ada? Is it a good idea?"

Ada found the eyes of the whole table looking at her. She knew none of them could guess she was thinking of Ravi and that made her smile.

"I think it's a very good idea indeed," she said.

Chapter Nineteen

After breakfast, Ada tapped on Georgiana's door and pushed it open. Georgiana was lying in bed, her head bandaged. She looked pale and tired. The nursemaid was with her, a bottle of medicine in her hand.

"Shall I come back later?"

"Oh—no. Priya has just finished giving me my medicine. Thank you." Georgiana smiled weakly as Priya put the bottle down. She went soundlessly to the door. Ada gazed after her, fascinated for a moment by her thick, dark hair and the soft expression of her dark eyes.

"She's quite remarkable, isn't she?" Georgiana said with a small laugh. "I think every gentleman visitor we've had has turned back to look at her when she went past."

"If only her beauty can tame Augustus, we shall all be grateful." Ada went over and sat on the edge of the bed and took her sister's hand. "How are you feeling?"

"A little better." Georgiana struggled to sit up, and Ada helped her. "So tell me, what have I missed? It is such a bore being stuck up here in bed." Some color had returned to her face.

Ada hesitated, but Georgiana would have to find out soon.

"Well, for one, I've just learned we're going to London," she said. "Papa has people to see, and Fiona and Charlotte want to pay social calls and see their dressmaker in preparation for the season."

"London!" Georgiana exclaimed. "Oh, how exciting!"

Ada realized how she'd misled her sister and felt badly. "But you're not going, Georgie. I'm sorry."

"Not going?" Georgiana stared at her in shock. "But why not?"

"Papa doesn't think you're well enough to travel." She hurried on, as Georgiana's face fell. "We won't be away long."

"And Michael?"

"He's to stay behind as well. He and Papa are not seeing eye to eye right now." She pressed her sister's hand. "I am really sorry. I know how you were looking forward to it, but I agree with Papa—you're not well enough. Try to sleep now."

She left Georgiana and went straight to her room. Rose was not yet there to undress her. She walked to her writing case and took out her pen and scented paper. After a moment's thought, the note she wrote to Ravi was short and simple. It said only that his letter had frightened her, that she was going to London, that she hoped they would be able to meet so that she could persuade him he was wrong in his support for the INC's hot faction, and gave her address at Milborough House. As she sealed the envelope she hoped that she would be able to keep him out of danger.

There was nothing more soothing, Fiona thought, than having a maid brush your hair at the end of the day. It would have been better, of course, if the day could have been perfectly satisfying, with a comfortable lunch at Henri's, salted with plenty of scandalous gossip, some leisurely shopping at Garrard, a delicious evening in a box at the opera accompanied by plenty of amenable young

143

men to say exactly the right thing while her rival looked on, and then perhaps a late supper somewhere with royalty in the vicinity. But there were sacrifices to be made for being Lady Westlake, and one of them was having to pretend to like the countryside. So her day had involved inspecting the most depressing little cottages and an absolutely *horrid* amount of mud. Hardly the Strand.

Still, the day had not been entirely lost. She had finally managed to get Edward to give her a date for going to London. When she had expressed her concern about Ada not being properly prepared for the season, he had capitulated at once. It was about time Ada made herself useful.

As if reading her thoughts, Stella said, "I must congratulate your ladyship on persuading Lord Westlake to take us to London again." Her fingers worked soothingly in Fiona's hair.

"Thank you, Stella. I couldn't have borne another month of this." Fiona smiled in the mirror, her head quite still.

"Nor could I, your ladyship." She paused. "To be quite honest with you, some of the servants here are not quite the type I like to work with, if you'll pardon my saying so."

"Oh?" Fiona raised an eyebrow.

"That Rose Cliffe, for example. It's plain to see she's been spoiled by her mother. Do you know that Lady Ada has her sit in the music room with her when she practices? As for me, I like to do my mending without seeking to put myself on a level with the family." She tugged at a hairpin and Fiona winced. "I beg pardon, my lady."

"Do you think she gives herself airs?" Fiona slid the diamond bracelet from her wrist and laid it thoughtfully in its case. "I must say she's rather pretty."

"She may have looks, but can she do her work? It could make me cry sometimes, seeing what a dog's dinner she makes of the young ladies' dresses. She's never been a lady's maid in her life, whereas my sister, who lost her position through no fault of her own—"

"I don't see that as a problem," said Fiona, who had heard the story of Stella's sister before, and suspected there was more to it than Stella let on. "Rose may be too pretty for a housemaid, but Ada is certainly too pretty for a stepdaughter. I won't mind if Rose fails to make the best of her."

Stella was still trying to backpedal and adjust her approach when there was a quick rap at the door and Charlotte came in. Her cheeks were pink.

"Mama, I must have a word," she began. "Is it your intention to drag Ada around with us to *all* the best hostesses?"

"My dear, we can hardly leave her at home. She is the only reason your stepfather is so keen for us to go to London."

"Well, I think it's a wretched shame! She poaches."

"Darling, you will have to explain the slang to me."

"Don't pretend you didn't see her artfully flirting with Lord Fintan at the shooting party. Oh, she's very clever, I'll certainly give her that. Wandering in front of his gun on purpose." Charlotte stamped her foot.

"Really?" Fiona looked around in concern. "Well, we can't have that."

Stella saw a chance and pounced on it. "I wouldn't be at all surprised, miss, if her maid hadn't put her up to it. Those two are thick as thieves."

"Oh, the maid is almost as unbearable as the mistress," Charlotte said scornfully. "She has such a high and mighty way about her. It's clear as day she thinks we aren't as good as her Averleys. These country servants are as snobbish as their employers."

"Exactly what I say, miss," Stella said in relief. "And in

Rose Cliffe's case, I can tell you that though she does look as if butter wouldn't melt in her mouth, I have it on good authority that she receives an awful lot of letters that do seem to be addressed in a gentleman's hand, if you see what I mean. So she certainly has no call to go acting as if she's better than anyone else."

"Hmm." Fiona turned back to her mirror and began gently dabbing cold cream onto her face and neck. In the mirror she saw the reflection of her daughter, frowning. It was such a pity that her beauty had been wasted on Sebastian, who, as an eldest son, hardly needed it. Charlotte's charm came from her vivacity and mannerisms, and those never survived a fit of temper. Unfortunately she had many fits of temper. It was certainly not a good idea to allow Lord Fintan to compare the two at close quarters. On the various occasions when she had had to pawn her diamonds she had learned from a sympathetic dealer never to hang the false stone next to the real.

"Well, we'll just have to be clever when it comes to Lord Fintan," she said calmly. "And in the meantime, though we may be stuck with Ada, we are certainly not stuck with her maid. Stella, I'm sure you can think of something?"

Stella smiled as she slowly brushed her mistress's hair. "I'm sure I can, my lady."

ACT TWO

LONDON

Chapter Twenty

The streets of London seethed and hummed with human bodies, and the number of rattling cabs and motorcars seemed to multiply every day. The windows of Selfridges and Fortnum & Mason shone with the latest fashions straight from Paris. Ladies and gentlemen of fashion eddied and swirled, bright colors among the drab crush of the common people, sweeping from club to grand hotel to couturier and out again to the theaters and opera and gambling houses.

A select part of this elegant flotsam ended up at the doors of Paul Poiret, the couturier whose scintillating dresses in the latest colors and flowing, Eastern-inspired cuts were worn on every slim, pale shoulder this season. Out of those doors came Fiona, Charlotte, and Ada. The footman followed them, laden down with parcels and bandboxes.

"There really is absolutely no one in London out of season," Charlotte sighed as she took her place in the cab.

"No one?" Ada looked out of the window at the crowded streets. There seemed to be more motorcars every time she looked. The noise was immense, and her heart seemed to beat along with it.

Since they had arrived in London, life had been a nonstop whirl of visiting, dancing, theater, and shopping for clothes. She barely had time to catch her breath, and her head hardly touched the pillow when she was being woken by Rose with tea and the plans for the day. She could not say she disliked this life, much as she wanted to. The dress she had walked out with today was called La Vague, the Wave. It was straight and sheer from the chest to the floor, a delicate but strong shape that made her look and feel beautiful. London was like being carried on a dizzying tide, swept far out to sea. All that was needed to make it perfect was just a few minutes with Ravi. For him to see her in this dress. But she had had no reply to her last letter.

"No one at all. I haven't even seen the Sassoons, and not a single one of the Set. It's really like being in a desert." She glanced out of the window and yawned.

"Pleased with your new dress, Ada?" Fiona asked.

"Oh, yes. It's beautiful," Ada answered.

"I just hope that housemaid won't ruin it the first time she dresses you," Fiona went on.

Ada's smile faded. "Rose always makes me look my best."

"You only say that because you haven't known what it is to have the attentions of a real French-trained maid," Charlotte said.

"My sister and I are quite fond of Rose," Ada said firmly. She was tired of this constant refrain. She didn't understand why her stepmother and stepsister were so set against Rose. Somehow she suspected it was Stella who was behind it.

She turned to the window, hoping to signal that the conversation was over. Great white-faced mansions passed on one side, the park on the other.

"Finally!" Charlotte cried. The cab drew to a halt, and a footman hurried to open the door. Ada stepped down after Charlotte and Fiona and looked up at Seton House with trepidation. She had been nervous about this all day. Mrs. Verulam was the best known hostess in London, and she knew that Fiona had been working very hard to get them an invitation to one of her select teas. If Mrs. Verulam was prepared to present them to the sovereign, their entrance into society would be assured.

As the footman helped Ada from the cab, a small voice next to her made her look down. A child stood there, filthy and barefoot, but smiling with black teeth.

"Penny, miss?"

She was so thin. Ada's heart ached. She grabbed for her purse but remembered too late that she had no money. Fiona carried it all.

"Get away with you!" The footman shooed the child away.

"No—wait—" Ada began.

"Ada, do come along!" Charlotte exclaimed, pushing her forward. She stumbled and almost tripped up the steps.

"But—"

"Really, Ada, there is a time and a place for everything."

"She was so thin!" Ada had to hiss; they were inside the hall and being ushered forward on a wave of footmen.

"Do you want to help every beggar in London?" Charlotte retorted before the drawing-room doors were thrown open and the sound of conversation and laughter rushed out.

"My dear Lady Westlake!" The old woman who came forward to meet them was slim and wiry and seemingly encrusted with diamonds. She carried a huge fan and somehow contrived to look down at Fiona although Fiona was a good head taller than she was. "I must wish you joy. I hear the wedding was delightful. Charlotte," she nodded to Charlotte, who simpered in a way that Ada had never seen her do except before young men. "And you must be Lady Ada."

Ada blushed under the piercing gaze that fixed her.

"Come here, dear." Lady Verulam beckoned her forward with a crooked finger and examined her closely. "I knew your mother. You are very alike."

Ada smiled and blushed even more, not knowing what to say. She wanted to find out more about her mother, but it seemed inappropriate to ask, with Fiona standing by her side. Besides, Lady Verulam was already looking away from her. "Come along. I must introduce you to the Poet Laureate— have you met him?"

Ada sat alone by the tea table, feeling as isolated as the footman who stood statue-like in the corner. She could not stop thinking about the urchin who had begged her for money. She had come from the dark passage beside the house. Ada thought of the dress she had bought, and how much it had cost. Would Ravi really like to see her in it? She was no longer sure. How many pennies had she spent on the dress? How many did it take to feed a child properly for one day?

Charlotte was at the heart of a gaggle of girls who surrounded a famous explorer, giggling and exclaiming as he related tales of slaying elephants and tigers. Fiona and Lady Verulam were speaking quietly together with much raising of eyebrows.

"Watching those two at their dreadful work?" A voice spoke quietly by her shoulder. Ada looked up, startled, to see an elegantly dressed girl with a clever, foxy face smiling at her. "I can promise you that someone's reputation is dying as horribly as those poor beasts," she said, nodding at the explorer.

Ada clattered her teacup in confusion.

"Lady Verulam seems very kind," she said doubtfully.

"When she wants to be, certainly. May I sit here?" The girl sat without waiting for Ada to nod. "But there's something very shallow in this scene, don't you think? Shallow and bloody at the same time. Rather like our big game hero."

"I was thinking that I was a little bored," Ada confessed. She was intrigued and amused by the girl's outspokenness, and decided that she liked her.

"Of course you were. No one with the slightest intelligence could fail to be. And I know you have intelligence." She smiled. "My brother told me about you."

"Your brother . . ." Ada realized why the girl looked familiar. "Lord Fintan!"

"Yes, Laurence. I'm his *beloved* younger sister, Emily."

"Ah, yes. He spoke of you. He said you were at Oxford."

"I am. I have special dispensation to come down for a few days to see my family. Lady Verulam is my aunt," she added.

Ada had no time to be surprised that Emily spoke so cuttingly of her own relative. She put down her cup. "Will you tell me about Oxford? Please? I—I find it so interesting that women can study now."

"Study, though not take a degree. But even so, I believe it is the most important experience of my life. Hard work, but so very worth it." Her eyes sparkled. "We are doing something critical. I really believe that. We are showing that women can think. They will have to give us the vote if we can prove we are as good as them."

"That's exactly what I think," Ada exclaimed. "I want to go to Oxford too. I've wanted it for so long."

Emily looked at her seriously. "Are you sure about this? It is very hard work, and we have to live like nuns—there are no parties and balls, you know."

153

"I know, but I don't mind." Ada thought again of the little girl. "I just want to be of some use in the world, and I want to be independent."

"Have you read *Woman and Labour*? I shall send it to you. But we can't talk now."

Ada followed Emily's gaze to see Charlotte coming toward them across the room. She was shocked by the expression of anger on her face.

"Emily, dear. How lovely to see you." Charlotte smiled tightly. "I hoped we would meet in town."

"And now we have—and I'm delighted to have met your stepsister, also." Emily smiled at Ada.

"And Lord Fintan?" Charlotte said, her voice tense. "We were so glad to see him at Somerton. Is he quite well?"

"Perfectly, and in the best of spirits." Ada was not sure why Emily's eyes danced mischievously as she looked at Charlotte.

Charlotte turned abruptly to Ada. "Don't you think it is time we left? Mama looks fatigued."

"Of course . . ." Ada, startled, got to her feet.

"I will write to you, Ada," Emily said. "You are staying in town?"

"Yes, at Milborough House." Ada smiled her goodbyes and curtsied to Lady Verulam.

"So distraught you have to leave early," Lady Verulam said, not sounding at all distraught. "I wish you a pleasant stay in town."

"Thank you," Ada said. Fiona looked embarrassed.

As they turned to go, Lady Verulam added, "Ada, I never congratulated you on the elegance of that hat. Very becoming."

Ada smiled. "Thank you." She could not help adding, with

a sly glance toward Charlotte and Fiona, "My maid, Rose, trimmed it."

She almost wished she had not spoken, however—both Fiona and Charlotte had faces like thunder and sat silently all the way home.

Chapter Twenty-One

Rose drew back as she heard voices approaching along the corridor. It was Fiona and Charlotte.

"I really cannot understand what came over you. Lady Verulam is one of the most influential hostesses, you know that! To leave so abruptly after I had spent so long getting the invitation—"

"Oh, mother, we exhausted this last night. Was I really supposed to stand by and watch her weasel her way into Lady Emily Maddox's good graces?"

Rose flinched at the venom in Charlotte's voice.

"I know, I know, but—"

"Mother, do you want me to marry Lord Fintan or not?"

They passed, walking quickly toward the breakfast room. Rose looked after them. Whoever the *her* was, it sounded as if Charlotte hated her.

She went on toward Ada's room. It was strange being in a new house, but exciting too. The noise of the city was like a symphony that never ended. Even the new accents she heard sounded musical.

Ada was in her peignoir in front of her mirror when Rose walked in.

"Good morning, Rose," she said, her smile almost beaming. Rose smiled back, wondering what had made her so happy.

It could not be another letter from Ravi—none had come since they reached London.

"Good morning, my lady. Did you have a pleasant time yesterday?" she asked as she began to brush Ada's hair.

Ada hesitated. "I think so," she said. "At least I now have a beautiful new dress."

"That can't be bad, my lady." Rose went on combing. "Will you be visiting this morning or should I put out another kind of gown?"

"I think we are riding in the Row. Could you put out the new habit, please? And the new riding hat. The one with the feather."

"Certainly, my lady." Rose got up to do so, and Ada turned around.

"I had a letter this morning," she said, a smile in her voice.

Rose looked up, startled.

"Oh no—not from him . . ." Ada colored, and a little of the happiness went out of her face. "No, this was from Georgiana."

"Oh? I hope Lady Georgiana is in good health." Rose was a little puzzled.

"Excellent health. In fact, she is so well that she has been able to play the piano at a soiree held by Lady Fairfax." Ada turned back to her mirror and smiled as Rose began carefully dressing her hair.

"That's wonderful, my lady," Rose said sincerely. She missed her piano more than anything.

"Yes, and she made a very great impression on the people who were there."

"I'm not surprised. Lady Georgiana plays beautifully." She pinned up Lady Ada's hair and examined her work.

"But that's not why she made the impression, Rose. It was her choice of music."

"What did she play, my lady?"

"Oh, Rose, you goose—stop looking at my hair for a moment. Can't you guess?" Ada turned round and caught her hands. "It was your tune. Your 'Eastern Dance'!"

Rose stared at her in utter disbelief. "My—my—"

"Yes! Oh, don't worry—she remembered what you said about not telling anyone who had composed it. It sounds as if she made a great mystery of it—trust Georgiana to go to extremes." Ada laughed. "Listen to this." She opened the letter. "'Everyone adored the "Eastern Dance." I had several people ask me for the music afterward. And what is more, Mr. Vronsky praised it and asked for the name of the composer! When I said I was not able to tell him, he persisted in believing that I had written it myself. Imagine how I felt not to be able to tell him the truth. Anyway, I am sure that Rose will one day get over her modesty and we shall be able to praise her properly. You must tell her she was a triumph— even in her absence.'"

Rose felt herself turning pink, and a huge smile spread over her face. "They liked it! And this Mr. Vronsky—"

"Oh, what an idiot I am—of course you don't know him. He is a very great pianist, from Russia, who has been performing in England this season."

Rose stared at her, speechless.

"So if *he* likes it, Rose, don't you see? You have real talent!"

Rose shook her head in disbelief. A life flashed in front of her eyes like fireworks, a dream of writing music and having it played and being proud of it. Then the fireworks died.

"But please, my lady, you mustn't tell anyone. You mustn't let anyone know it was I who wrote it!"

Ada's face fell. "Of course we won't, if you don't wish it. But Rose, I wish you'd think again. People would admire you so."

Not my mother, thought Rose. If anything was beyond her station, this was. She cringed at the thought of her mother finding out—of Annie finding out, even. They might be happy for her, but she felt deep inside that they would laugh at her for putting on airs. After all, what maid wrote music?

"I'm sorry, my lady," she said quietly. "And I'm more grateful than I can say, to you and to Lady Georgiana. But I'd rather it didn't happen again."

Ada placed a hand on her arm.

"Rose! If anyone knows, it's me—you mustn't stifle that flame inside you that feels as if it is yours and yours alone. You must let it burn. You must be proud of it."

Rose felt tears prick her eyes at Ada's soft voice. She nodded. "I'll think about it, my lady. Now, would you like to wear the amber or the amethyst beads today?"

Chapter Twenty-Two

"Some post for you, Ada," said Lord Westlake, placing a letter and a parcel beside her. He took his seat next to Fiona and began opening his own post.

Ada eagerly looked at the post. But one glance told her that neither the letter nor the parcel was from Ravi. The letter was addressed in Georgiana's sprawling hand. She put that aside to enjoy reading later on in her room. The parcel was addressed in unfamiliar, ladylike handwriting. She picked up the pearl-handled letter opener and cut the string and unwrapped it.

Inside was a book: *Woman and Labour*. Ada glanced up nervously, but her father didn't seem to have seen it. He was engrossed in his own post. She opened the book and a note fell out, written on mauve paper and folded once. She opened it and read.

Dear Ada,
Here is the book I promised you. Please forgive the delay!
I also have good news—and a suggestion. I mentioned you
to Miss Gorman, the mistress of Somerville College, and
she said she would be pleased to meet you and discuss
the possibility of coming here. Now, she is a dragon, as I
am not sure I mentioned, but for her to show so much

interest in a girl she hasn't even met must mean something.
You really must take this opportunity. And that leads me
to my suggestion. Why not come and visit me? You would
surely not need a chaperone for such a short visit, and I
could show you Oxford. You need not mention to your
father that you are visiting Miss Gorman as well. Do say
yes! I am dying to show you my rooms—they are modest,
but they are my own, and I couldn't be happier in them.
   Yours affectionately,
   Emily

Ada hardly had time to feel excited when Fiona, who
had been reading through her own post, exclaimed, "At
last!"

Ada looked up, startled. Fiona was beaming, and she passed
the note she was reading to Lord Westlake. Lord Westlake
put down his knife and fork and read it. Ada caught
Charlotte's eye. For once Ada, thought, they had something
in common. Charlotte was clearly as much in the dark as
she was.

"Didn't I tell you I could arrange it?" Fiona said proudly.

"You did indeed, and you're a marvel!" Lord Westlake said,
his eyes gleaming. He put the letter down and placed his
hand on Fiona's affectionately.

"What is it?" Ada said, and Charlotte echoed her. "Mother,
what have you arranged?"

"An invitation to dinner with the Wellingboroughs, my
dear," Fiona announced smugly.

"The Wellingboroughs?" Charlotte frowned. "You don't
mean that dreadfully dull political couple, do you?"

"Sir Henry Wellingborough is the foreign secretary," Ada
said, a smile breaking over her face as she realized what this

meant for her father's career. "Papa, that's wonderful, that means you must be in line for a big appointment."

"We can only hope, my dear," said her father, although his smile betrayed that he did more than hope.

"I have every confidence that it's the beginning of great things," said Fiona. "You're too modest, Edward. The truth is that very few people are invited to the Wellingboroughs' dinners. It is a great honor."

Fiona and Lord Westlake talked of nothing else throughout breakfast. Charlotte looked bored, and Ada was as happy as she could be. An invitation to Oxford—there would certainly be a chance of seeing Ravi then. If he wanted to see her, of course. She remembered that he had not answered her last letter, and a cloud fell across her happiness.

As her father stood up, he added, "I'm glad they have also invited Douglas Varley. We have a lot to discuss, and I would be glad of the chance to meet him and sort out any"—he hesitated—"misunderstandings."

"Douglas Varley will be there?" Ada exclaimed. If he was there, then that meant that Ravi might be, too.

"Yes." He glanced at the letter. "Varley; his protégé, the Indian student; Lord Fintan; and several others. It should be an interesting gathering."

As he left the breakfast room, Ada jumped up and followed him.

"Papa—may I speak to you?"

"Of course, dear."

She hesitated, not knowing how to open the conversation. Then it came to her. She could use Lord Fintan as an excuse.

"I would very much like to go to the Wellingboroughs' dinner also, if it could be arranged."

"You?" He frowned. "I thought I told you not to trouble yourself with politics."

"It isn't that." She blushed, knowing she was about to lie. "I would very much like to have the opportunity of—of speaking with Lord Fintan. I found him very congenial at the shooting party."

Her father's eyebrows rose, but he looked pleased.

"Lord Fintan, eh? Well, I—"

"If Ada is going, I don't see why I shouldn't go too."

Charlotte's tightly controlled voice made Ada turn around. She was at the door of the breakfast room. Ada was startled. What had happened to make Charlotte suddenly want to attend this political dinner that she had professed to find so boring?

"Well, Mother?" Charlotte was angry, Ada could tell. Suddenly she remembered the glances that had passed between her and Lord Fintan at the shooting party.

Fiona stepped up behind Charlotte, placing a calming hand on her shoulder. "Very well, dear. I don't see why not. The invitation was open, after all, and they know we are here *en famille*."

Lord Westlake shrugged. "If you wish it, of course. Fiona will no doubt reply for all of us."

As Charlotte passed Ada, she shot her a glare that made Ada step back a pace. There was clearly something between Charlotte and Lord Fintan, and she was sorry that she had given the wrong impression. But she couldn't think of any way of setting it right. It was necessary to use him as an excuse in order to see Ravi again as soon as possible.

Chapter Twenty-Three

The bump on Georgiana's head had finally subsided, and she was allowed to go outside on her own for the first time. She had been looking forward to curling up on a bench and going on with *Zuleika Dobson*. But her head still ached too much for reading to be enjoyable. Instead, she strolled around the lawns, wondering how Ada was getting on in London. Somerton was just not the same without her sister.

She wandered into the apple orchard and picked a windfall from the ground. Nibbling on it, she went on toward the kitchen garden. It was closed off from her by a gate, but as she approached she saw someone hurry past inside. She stopped, startled. It looked like Michael. And he was holding a bunch of roses clearly culled from one of the gardens.

Georgiana went forward, full of curiosity. What was Michael doing here? The kitchen garden wasn't precisely forbidden to them, but it was part of the servants' territory, and it was certainly not encouraged for them to enter it. She sensed that both the gardeners and Mrs. Cliffe would have something to say if they found Michael there. She tried the gate, but it was locked.

"What are you doing?" came a voice from behind her.

She jumped and turned round, her heart beating fast. She saw Philip, his sleeves rolled up and his Eton suit grubby at the knees.

"Philip!" She relaxed. "You scared me."

"You're not meant to go in there. I got a telling off from my brother about it." He made a face. "As if he never broke any rules. I hate William."

Georgiana sighed. She agreed, but she didn't think it would do much good to say so. "Well . . . it's true that he hasn't got a very good temper."

"He's a bully. I saw him pinch Priya's arm when he thought no one was looking. And he cuffed me across the head when I told him to stop."

"That's horrible." Georgiana was shocked.

"He is horrible. Anyway, I'm going to go wherever I want. I shan't let him stop me." He scowled. "But what are you doing here? If you're looking for apples, I've had all the best ones already."

"I was just wondering what Michael was doing in the kitchen garden." Georgiana blushed, but Philip didn't notice.

"Michael? Is he here too?"

"Yes. I—I wanted to give him a surprise, so I was following him."

"That sounds like fun," Philip said, perking up. "Look, if you creep under the hedge you can get through." He got down on his hands and knees and wriggled under the hedge. "Come on!"

"Oh . . ." Georgiana thought of her dress and then dismissed it. How dirty could a dress get anyway? And it

165

was far too tempting to find out what Michael was up to. She got down on her hands and knees and wriggled after Philip through the hedge.

Priya walked along the servants' passage, holding the needle and thread she had gone downstairs for. She had an odd feeling she was being followed. She glanced behind her, but there was no one there.

It was Sunday afternoon, and with much of the family in London, the house felt very quiet. She would never get to like it, she thought. It was too cold and too big and too . . . too English. She longed for something, some smell or color or sound that would be like home. But there was nothing. Even the post hadn't brought a letter from her mother, and she was worried. Her father was ill, they had written in the last letter—nothing serious, but she knew they were trying to keep her from worrying.

She glanced to the side again and thought that she saw a shadow move outside the window. Surely it had just been a branch blowing in the wind.

She heard voices from the kitchen as she approached. Hushed whispers, as if the speakers were being careful not to be overheard.

Priya hesitated. The voices were Martha, the scullery maid, and Tobias, the stable boy. She drew near to the kitchen door and looked in. The two were by the fire, a steaming copper kettle was on the range, and they were huddling over something.

Feeling suddenly suspicious, Priya tiptoed forward.

"Not like that, you fool. You'll soak it." Tobias leaned over Martha.

"Well, you do it if you're such an expert!"

She was close now enough to see over their shoulders. Martha held a letter. Tobias was holding the copper underneath it, and the flap of the envelope was crinkling up.

"It looks like a man's hand, don't it?" Martha said gleefully.

"I'd say so. Not as innocent as she looks! I reckon Miss Ward will pay a good deal to know about her fancy man."

"Out on her ear without a reference. I like it." Martha grinned.

Priya realized what was going on, in a split second of shock.

"That's not yours!" she exclaimed.

Tobias spun around. Martha jumped and sent the pan of water flying. The fire hissed and steamed.

Priya snatched the letter out of Martha's hand. At a glance she could see it was addressed to Rose.

"Give that back, or I'll—" Tobias shouted.

"Don't you dare threaten me. Or I'll let Mr. Cooper know what you've done."

Tobias turned pale and glanced at Martha.

"I'm going to take this to Mrs. Cliffe, and you'll be lucky if I don't tell her everything." Priya turned and swept off toward the door, the letter clutched tightly in her hands.

She found Mrs. Cliffe in her parlor.

"This came for Rose, if you please." She bobbed a curtsy and held out the letter.

Mrs. Cliffe gave the letter a curious glance. Her expression serious, she put it away.

"Thank you, Priya."

Priya hesitated, wondering if she should mention what she had seen and heard. But it had been so little, and so perplexing. Why should Miss Ward care if Rose had a fancy man? And the last thing Priya wanted was to make enemies of the Somerton servants. She decided to say nothing.

"Ah, Mrs. Cliffe—and Priya."

Priya whirled round. Her heart beat fast. It was William. He was standing at the door, an unpleasant smile on his face as he looked at her. Priya dropped her eyes at once, feeling sick. William frightened her. He acted jolly, but his manner could change to cruelty in a second. She just did not feel safe around him. It was something in the way he looked at her—there was something very cold and greedy in his eyes.

"Can I help you, sir?" Mrs. Cliffe moved to block his view of Priya. Priya was grateful. She guessed that Mrs. Cliffe did not like William either.

"I simply came down to give some directions to Cooper about the wine for this evening. I'm expecting a few friends to play bridge. But since Priya is here, perhaps she can help me find Cooper. I wouldn't want to bother you."

"It's no bother at all, sir, and Priya must be getting back to the nursery." Mrs. Cliffe turned a meaningful gaze on her, and Priya, grateful for the rescue, blurted out, "Yes, Mrs. Cliffe."

She fled to the door. William stood back, but not quite enough, so she had to squeeze past him to get out. She shuddered at his hot breath on her neck and half walked, half ran down the corridor. She was trembling and her heart was beating fast. On impulse she went out the side door. She needed fresh air, and she couldn't stand the feeling that he was watching her.

She glanced behind her as she walked through the kitchen garden, just to check that William was not following her. She turned round and almost bumped into Michael Templeton. She started.

"Oh! Sir—I'm sorry—"

"No, it was my fault." He sounded confused and flustered. "I just—"

He had a bunch of roses in his hand. Priya hardly glanced at them in her haste to put distance between herself and William.

"Excuse me, sir." She quickly curtsied and hurried on.

She didn't feel truly calm until she was back in the nursery. Only then did she spare a moment to puzzle over the roses in Michael Templeton's hand, and the way he had been gazing at her.

Chapter Twenty-Four

Michael swore and thumped the roses against his leg angrily. Petals flew. He'd been following her for ages, trying to get up the courage to speak to her, and the roses had seemed like a good idea at the time. But then he had bumped into her, like an idiot, and of course she had been startled, and there had been no chance to give her the flowers. She was so beautiful. So naturally graceful and elegant—

"Michael!"

He looked up. Georgiana was standing before him, beaming, twigs in her hair, smudges on her face and a large grass stain down her dress.

"Georgiana! You're up." He looked her up and down. "But what have you been doing? You look as if you've been dragged through a hedge backward."

Her smile faltered, and she glanced down at the grass-stained dress as if she had only just seen it.

"Oh dear. Does it look that bad?"

"Pretty bad. Good job Mother's not here; she'd give you a scolding."

"I just wondered what you were doing here?"

"Here?" Michael looked around. "Oh, just . . . exploring." He remembered the roses he was still holding. Well, since he'd missed his chance to give them to Priya. "Want some roses?" he said glumly, thrusting them at her.

"Oh!" Her smile lit up, and he was pleased despite himself. Good old Georgie. She might be a bit of a scatterbrain but she was full of pluck and good humor. It was nice to be able to make her smile. And . . . the thought struck him suddenly. Of course. That was the other good thing about her. She was a *girl*. Easy to forget it, she was such a tomboy, but she was an actual girl. Didn't girls have some kind of shared bond? Wouldn't she be the best way of getting to Priya?

He beamed at her. "Come on, let's have a game of cricket. It's been ages—I've missed you!"

He clapped the delighted Georgiana on the shoulder, and they went out of the kitchen garden toward the lawns.

Sebastian walked back toward his room after a tedious lunch with the dean, along cobbled streets and past the sun-dappled stone of the ancient colleges. He was thinking of Oliver. His conscience twinged as he thought of the way he had acted the other day. Of course Oliver would have been upset; anyone would. It must have looked as if he were flirting with Ravi, when in fact he simply found him interesting and a challenge. It was provoking not to be admired, and he knew that Ravi did not admire him. But Oliver must have had a boring day of it, handing out champagne without being able to taste a drop himself, of course. Sebastian had been a little drunk, or he would have been more sensitive. He would have to make it up to Oliver. Perhaps, he thought as he climbed the stairs to his rooms, they could go for a picnic, or something similar. The devil of it was, it was hard to find an excuse to go gallivanting with one's valet without exciting suspicion. Perhaps if he could get invited to a country house party this weekend . . . He opened the door and went into his rooms.

"Oliver," he began, and then stopped dead. The letter lay on the mantelpiece, insolent as an intruder. Even from here he could see the handwriting was Simon's.

He crossed and picked it up, his hands shaking. There *was* no more money. Simon had to be sensible, he had to understand. But he tore it open and read what was inside it, and his heart sank in despair.

Mr. Sebastian,
I think you must be making a mockery of me. I know you are a rich gentleman and can pay whatever I ask. I think it is not too much to ask two thousand pounds to keep your name out of the papers. I have met a very pleasant gentleman from The Illustrated Reporter who is very interested to hear about you and I. Of course I wouldn't tell him a thing before hearing from you. I am sure you will see sense and let me have it for old times' sake. If not, the story will run this weekend.
*   Your humble servant,*
*   Simon Croker*

"Two thousand pounds!" Sebastian burst out furiously. The man had to be mad. He could never get such a sum. His mother held the purse strings too tightly and he could not ask her for such an amount with no explanation. And before the weekend!

It was impossible to approach Lord Westlake again. He had made it clear that the so-called investments should show a profit before he would put more money into it. And to threaten him with the papers . . . some American rag, no doubt, but the story would be picked up in London too. Unfortunately, there was enough evidence to support it. He had been seen and photographed frequenting too many parties with the Set to hope to pass anonymously.

"Sebastian?" Oliver came in. Sebastian could not answer his timid smile. Oliver stood there in his valet's uniform, and that reminded him of Simon. He'd trusted Simon. He'd been a fool. Perhaps no one could be trusted.

"When did that letter come?"

"Yesterday. It was pushed under the door—"

"Yesterday! Why the hell didn't you tell me before?"

Oliver looked startled and didn't answer. Sebastian swore.

"Pack my things. I'm going to London, alone."

If he had expected Oliver to make a scene, he was disappointed. Oliver hesitated, then turned away, his face impassive. *The perfect servant*, Sebastian thought bitterly. Perfect at hiding his feelings, and no doubt talking behind his back. It was unbearable. He shouted after him. "And be quick about it—I mean to have fun tonight!" It was childish but he didn't care. If only Oliver had showed some emotion, some flicker of feeling. But he was as cold as Simon, as able to turn his emotions on and off.

Sebastian snatched up the suitcase without looking at Oliver and stormed out. If he was quick he would be able to catch the last train to London.

Chapter Twenty-Five

"Here." Sebastian spoke to the cab driver, who clicked his tongue and whoa-ed his horse to a standstill. Sebastian paid him with his last coins and stepped out of the cab into the darkening evening, where the men were lighting the gas lamps. The old horse tossed its head and trotted off, and Sebastian was left staring at Featherstonehaugh House, iceberg-like in front of him.

He realized at once that he had not thought this through. There was a motorcar in front of the house and servants in livery were standing at the open door. Clearly Simon's employer was on his way out for the evening. How had he imagined he would get to speak to Simon, anyway? One could hardly call at a gentleman's house and ask to speak to his valet. The back door was a possibility, but there would be questions asked . . .

As he stood, irresolute, a tall young man in evening dress, top hat and cane came out of the front door, and with a nod to the butler, hurried down the steps toward the motorcar. Behind him came Simon.

Sebastian gasped sharply and headed across the road before he thought of what he was doing. As he drew close to the motorcar the man looked up at him with a curious expression. Sebastian realized he knew him. It was Lord Fintan. He had been there at the shooting party—of course, Sebastian realized. He really had seen Simon there, he hadn't imagined it. He faltered in his pace—damn, this was going to be difficult to explain—and lifted his hat with an awkward smile.

Lord Fintan tipped his own hat and smiled with an enquiring look.

"My dear Sebastian—it is Sebastian, isn't it? Were you looking for me?" he said. He sounded uncertain, and Sebastian could hardly blame him. He must have presented a very odd appearance, hesitating as if he were afraid of being seen. Behind Lord Fintan, Simon's face registered wary surprise; then the mask of the professional servant froze over it. He stared right through Sebastian.

"I . . ." Sebastian had no idea what to say. If he said not, he would have to walk on and miss the chance of speaking to Simon. If he said he was, he would have to produce some excuse. And since he had only the smallest of acquaintances with Lord Fintan, and no reason to speak to him, that would be difficult.

"Only I am rather late, for an engagement with the Wellingboroughs . . ." Lord Fintan gestured to his pocket watch. "My mother is inside and I am sure she would be delighted to see you."

That settled it. "No, I thank you. I was just . . . taking an early evening walk." Sebastian replied. He was angry at the shameful need to lie. Simon's face remained impassive. Sebastian, with an abrupt bow to Lord Fintan, walked past.

"Odd chap," he heard Lord Fintan say to Simon as he stepped into the motorcar.

"Quite, my lord." Simon replied. Sebastian heard him closing the door close behind his master.

Damn, damn, damn, thought Sebastian as he walked along the road, swinging his cane. It was clear there was no talking to Simon. Fear was like a knotted rope around his throat. He had to do something, and fast. But he was almost out of money, and nothing else would make an impression on Simon. He paused and opened his pocketbook under a lamppost, careless of the pickpockets who swarmed the streets of London. It was empty, practically moth-eaten, save for his return ticket to Oxford—and two other small slips of paper.

Sebastian opened them, wondering if they were pawnbrokers' bills. But they were not. He remembered them as he looked at them: earlier this year, just after receiving his allowance, he had bought two tickets for Vronsky's solo performance at the Albert Hall, when he would be premiering a piano arrangement of *The Firebird*, composed by Stravinsky. It was the most hotly anticipated musical performance of the year. The new Russian music had influenced everything from interior décor to clothes. It was a mark of how worried Sebastian had been that he had forgotten all about the tickets.

Still, he was in no mood for music. He was about to tear them up when he paused. Fight fire with fire, they said. It was a good scandal story, that Sebastian Templeton, the urbane man about town, committed the unspeakable vice of the Greeks, as his don called it. But there could be a better story. For months the gutter press had been trying to fix him with a woman, one of the Set. He had laughed at the time. But what he needed now was exactly that: a woman. A woman to escort to the concert, a woman who would help him prompt a story for the papers that would make

Simon's look ridiculous, unpublishable. Better, a mysterious woman. A beautiful woman. A woman who had never before been in the papers . . .

"Ada," he said, and snapped his fingers. "Cab!"

Chapter Twenty-Six

The sun came in through the large Georgian windows of Milborough House, and shimmered on the three dresses that lay in clouds of tissue paper across Ada's bed. Ada herself, still in her tea gown, paced back and forth across the room.

"Lady Ada, do stay still for a moment and decide which you're going to wear tonight to the Wellingboroughs'," Rose pleaded.

Ada reluctantly stopped pacing and looked at the dresses that lay on the bed. Beside La Vague, she had acquired two others. Her favorite was a long, shimmering, intricately ruched gown from Fortuny called Delphos. It was said to have been inspired by the moonlight on Grecian marble ruins, and it shimmered with a mysterious color that seemed somewhere between blue and silver.

"This is such an elegant shape," Rose said, as if echoing her thoughts. "You'd need to wear the new straight-line corset, my lady, but I'm sure it would suit you."

"I'm not sure . . ." Ada hesitated. It was a beautiful dress, perhaps even more beautiful than La Vague, but she couldn't concentrate on dresses now. She was feeling oddly nervous about seeing Ravi. It had been such a long time since their last communication.

"Or what about this lovely kimono style?" Rose went on,

smoothing the vivid silk of the third dress. "It's daring, I know, but the colors—"

"They're truly beautiful," Ada agreed. Bright, Eastern-inspired colors, lavish embroidery and exotic shapes were so much of the moment, with the fashion for Russian music and dance.

"Won't you try it on, my lady?" Rose suggested, holding the dress out to her.

Ada hesitated. "Perhaps later." She simply had too much on her mind. She went toward the door. "I must have a walk before I decide, to—to clear my mind."

She opened the door to the startled face of a maid, who had been just about to knock.

"Oh!" She searched for the maid's name; the Milborough staff were still strangers to her. "What is it, Polly?"

"Oh, I—" The girl blushed, clearly not accustomed to speaking directly to a lady. "There's a visitor for your ladyship. Mr. Sebastian Templeton is in the drawing room."

"Sebastian? Here, to see me?" Ada was surprised; she had thought him in Oxford. "I will be down instantly."

She hurried down the stairs and across the marble floors to the drawing room. Not for the first time, she thought how smart and fashionable Milborough House was—yet it felt somehow unlived in, not like Somerton. Perhaps she had finally come to think of Somerton Court as her home.

Sebastian turned toward her as she opened the drawing room door. Ada thought he looked tense; his face was pale and red spots burned in his cheeks.

"Sebastian!" she exclaimed with a smile. "What a pleasant surprise."

Sebastian looked at her with relief. "I'm glad to find you alone. I must have a word with you."

Ada, startled, nodded. "Of course." She looked enquiringly into Sebastian's face. "What's the matter? You look quite pale."

Sebastian forced a laugh. "Do I? It's just the cold. Ada, how would you like to see the artistic event of the year?"

She frowned, and Sebastian brought the tickets out of his pocketbook. "Vronsky's folk ballads recital. I quite forgot that I had tickets, but it seemed a shame to waste them."

Ada laughed in amused astonishment. "So you came down from Oxford today? Sebastian, you are extraordinary!"

Sebastian laughed, but it sounded forced. "Yes, another one of my freaks. But what do you say? You are so fond of music, I thought that it might amuse you to go."

Ada's face fell. "I can't, Sebastian. I'm very sorry, but we're all engaged for dinner at the Wellingboroughs."

"That will be a political thing, won't it? It sounds like a terrible bore. Can't you throw them over?"

There was something desperate in Sebastian's voice. Ada looked at him in surprise. "No, impossible."

"But if your father and my mother and Charlotte are all going—"

Ada shook her head. She was thinking of Ravi. "I'm terribly sorry, Sebastian. It was very good of you to think of me . . ." She hesitated, and a thought suddenly came into her head that made her flush with excitement.

"I may have a solution!" she burst out. "Sebastian—would you consider taking someone else instead of me?"

"Who do you have in mind?"

She beckoned him forward and whispered. "How about Rose?"

Sebastian stared at her in astonishment.

"Rose? You don't mean your maid?"

Ada nodded and blushed. She dropped her voice even lower. "Sebastian, you mustn't tell anyone, but that isn't me practicing the piano, it's her. You have no idea what a talent she has, but she's never had the chance to cultivate it. If she could go to this performance it would mean so much to her."

"I—but—" Sebastian was left speechless. He had thought he was up for anything, but it seemed his perfect lady of a stepsister was beyond him in audacity. Still, a maid is a woman, isn't she? Rose had grace and elegance, and she was very attractive even in a maid's uniform. And certainly no one would know who she was. The more he thought about it, the more it appealed to him. A smile spread across his face. Stake everything on one throw of the dice, that was his style.

"I'll ring for her at once." Ada had been watching his face, and now she swiftly rang the bell.

Rose was startled to find both Lady Ada and Master Sebastian waiting for her. She bobbed a curtsy, wondering why they looked so embarrassed and excited.

"Rose," Lady Ada burst out. "You would like to go to a concert, wouldn't you?"

"A—a—?" Rose tried to imagine what a concert could be like. She had heard of such a thing, of course, but never imagined going to one.

"Sebastian would like me to go to hear Mr. Vronsky tonight, but I can't, of course, as you well know. But I thought of you. I know you would enjoy it. The music is said to be exceptional—and exactly the kind of thing that would inspire you."

Rose had understood barely one word in ten of Ada's speech, but one objection stood out clearly.

"I couldn't, my lady. I wouldn't know what to do or how to behave—"

181

"I would take the greatest care of you," Mr. Sebastian said at once. "You needn't worry, Rose. No one would suspect that you are not—not—used to attending concerts."

"But I don't have anything to wear to such a thing." Rose was thinking of her wardrobe. Her one smart dress was sober and respectable, but she knew that it wasn't the thing to wear to a proper concert, with ladies and gentlemen there.

"Well, that is no problem!" Ada said triumphantly. "We're about the same height and the same size. You can wear something of mine—in fact, of course! You can wear one of my new dresses!" She clapped her hands. "Perfect!"

Rose opened and closed her mouth, but no words came out. Wear Lady Ada's new dress? Go to a concert? The one idea filled her with horror, the other with longing. She looked from Lady Ada to Master Sebastian.

"I—I—I'm not sure. I—"

"Oh, Rose, please, please don't argue! This is the most wonderful chance for you." Ada ran forward and took her hand. "Come with me and we'll arrange it all. Sebastian," she flung over her shoulder, "be ready to keep the coast clear."

Sebastian went after them and caught Rose's arm. He pulled her back and said, softly and seriously, "Rose, I must tell you, this is not a favor I am bestowing upon you. I am begging you—quite honestly—to be my companion for this evening. If you only knew it, you are my last hope."

Rose only had time to stare at him in astonishment before Ada came back to get her.

"I don't feel right about doing this." Rose looked nervously in the mirror as Ada helped her dress. "Your beautiful new gown . . ."

"Nonsense, Rose, it's a wonderful opportunity." Ada's cheeks were pink as she helped Rose undress. She was so pleased at the idea of Rose seeing the man who had praised her composition that she was determined to overrule any objections. "If you can bring yourself to introduce yourself as the composer of that tune he enjoyed so much at Lady Fairfax's—"

"I couldn't, my lady!" Rose blushed bright red.

"I understand—but you're really too modest." Ada sighed. She turned back to the dresses. "Now which one would you like to wear?"

Rose shrank back.

"Then I will choose for you." Rose held up the three dresses one by one, her head cocked to one side as she considered them.

"Oh yes!" she exclaimed as she looked at the Poiret kimono. "Rose, the rich blue makes your eyes simply sing."

"But it was so expensive—"

"All the more reason to get as much wear as possible out of it, then! Now, here we have an extraordinary object." She held up what looked like a very short bodice. "The sales girl called it a *brassiere*. It is to be worn beneath the kimono instead of a corset, in order to preserve the shape."

Rose made a face. "It doesn't look very decent." She managed to get it on. "I don't know what my mother would say."

"She won't know; no one will." Ada laughed.

She helped Rose dress, and turned her to the mirror to see herself. Rose's eyes widened and a smile broke through her worried expression. She looked like an exotic orchid, her dark hair piled delicately upon her head.

Ada twirled Rose around gently. The silk swung and

swished while still seeming elegant, and it suited Rose's slim, young figure perfectly. Her neck seemed long and white, and her large blue eyes were set off to perfection by the shimmering colors. Ada gazed in the glass and laughed as the resemblance between them struck her.

"Why, we could be sisters!" she exclaimed. "No one would ever guess you did not wear dresses like this every day of your life, Rose."

"You—you don't think I'm getting above my station?"

"I think your station is music," said Ada firmly. "I think nothing can be wrong that allows you to follow your dreams. And I think you deserve a beautiful dress for once in your life."

Rose nodded. "I love it, my lady," she said happily.

Ada squeezed her hand. "Come along, then—let's not keep Sebastian waiting."

Chapter Twenty-Seven

Featherstonehaugh House, the Foreign Secretary's mansion, stood at the most select end of Park Lane, imposing at the top of its flight of marble steps. Torches burned to mark the way up the staircase, and footmen in the Wellingborough livery of green and gold stood as motionless as statues to mark the way.

Ada stepped down from the carriage, the silvery sheen of her dress swishing around her. She had chosen the Delphos gown in the end. She snuggled a little deeper into her mink. The fabric was thin and it was still winter. For jewelry she had chosen a strand of pearls, so long that it reached her hips and accentuated the graceful, Grecian column-like silhouette of the dress. She also wore a curious, heavy bracelet of Indian silver that had belonged to her mother. Rose had suggested it, and Ada had seen at once that it would balance the dress perfectly, giving strength to its fragile elegance. She hoped that Ravi would notice that it was Indian, and take it as a compliment.

"You look wonderful, my dear," said her father, with a proud smile. He took her arm and led her up the stairs, followed by Fiona and Charlotte. "Don't worry," he added in her ear, "I have arranged everything with Lady Wellingborough."

What did that mean? Ada wondered. But she barely had

time to give her father a puzzled smile before the footman had sprung to open the doors for them and they were inside the imposing hall of Featherstonehaugh House. Ada blinked in the dazzling electric light. Before them, the butler threw open the doors and announced, "Lord Westlake, Lady Westlake, Lady Ada Averley, Miss Charlotte Templeton."

As she stepped into the crowded drawing room, Ada barely noticed the admiring glances that the gentlemen turned toward her. She was searching the room for Ravi. He was nowhere to be seen.

"My dear Fiona. Lord Westlake. What a true pleasure to welcome you to our home." A clear, imperious woman's voice cut through the chatter of the drawing room, and Ada saw Lady Wellingborough coming toward them, making her way through the Chinese vases and occasional tables upon which small, exquisite antique curiosities gleamed. The bright electric light from the chandeliers made the jewels around her neck and the jet beading on her dress sparkle. In one hand she carried a massive fan of ostrich feathers and ivory. At the same time, her husband, a serious, elderly man, approached Lord Westlake and shook his hand warmly. Lady Wellingborough and Fiona exchanged greetings, and Lady Wellingborough smiled at Ada and Charlotte.

"How lovely to see you both." Though she spoke warmly, she had an air of great dignity, and Ada felt she would never be able to relax around her. She outclassed even Fiona, who seemed positively girlish beside her.

Lady Wellingborough led them through the crowd. "You know Lady Emily Maddox, do you not?" she said, pausing by a group of women who stood exchanging pleasantries under a huge Burne-Jones tapestry.

Emily smiled as she turned to them. "How delightful to see you!"

Charlotte did not look at all pleased, but Ada did not have time to notice, for Lady Wellingborough was gently guiding her away from the group.

"And Ada, there is someone I am sure you would like to meet again."

Ada looked around as she followed Lady Wellingborough. There were about twenty people in the drawing room, and the chatter and laughter echoed from the high ceilings, but she could see Ravi nowhere. Her heart fell. Perhaps he had been prevented from coming, and this was all for nothing . . .

"Ada!" A man's voice brought her back to herself. She looked up to see Lord Fintan smiling at her. She hadn't remembered how handsome he was. He bowed over her hand, and she thought what a perfect gentleman he was.

"Now, you two know each other very well," said Lady Wellingborough. "I will leave you together to talk."

She glanced to the side as she turned away, and Ada followed her gaze to see her father smiling at her. She blushed. So that was what he had meant. He had arranged with Lady Wellingborough to set her up with Lord Fintan for the evening. She hardly dared glance toward Charlotte and Fiona. This would not make their relationship any easier. But she had given her father to understand that she was interested in Lord Fintan romantically, and she had to keep up the illusion or risk the truth being suspected. She tried to imagine how Charlotte would have handled the situation. There had to be something witty, flirtatious, that she could say—

"Old women always have matchmaking on their minds," said Lord Fintan in a low voice. His eyes twinkled. "But we need not let that stop us having a pleasant conversation, need we?"

Ada looked up in surprise. She hadn't expected him to be so aware of what was going on. The laugh that rose to her lips was natural and unforced, and she said, without even having to think about it, "It would be impossible to have anything other than a pleasant conversation with you."

The look of pleasure on his face made her blush and lower her eyelids. When she looked up, her heart almost stopped. Ravi was standing close behind Lord Fintan, near the fireplace. And from the look on his face, she knew he had seen and heard her flirt with Lord Fintan.

"I hear you have made friends with my sister," Lord Fintan was saying. "She is mischievous, but she means well."

Ada followed his glance over to where Emily was standing, still in conversation with Charlotte and Fiona. Emily smiled and raised her fan in a small gesture of greeting or approval, Ada was not sure which. She could not smile back. It seemed the whole room was expecting her to flirt with Lord Fintan, and she could hardly complain since she had given the impression that that was her intention. She could not back out now. Questions would be asked if she did. And yet Ravi was watching everything.

"Yes—Emily is delightful," she managed.

"Has she talked to you about Oxford?" Lord Fintan lowered his voice and leaned closer to speak to her. Ada knew it was just so that her father would not overhear, but she also knew it must look intimate. Ravi's frown deepened, and he abruptly walked away, heading toward the nearest group of men who were talking.

"Yes . . . but my father doesn't approve." Ada did not have to fake the despair in her voice.

"Ah," Lord Fintan said in understanding. "Well, perhaps he can be persuaded."

"Perhaps." Ada felt, at that moment, that she would have given up every dream of Oxford just to be able to explain things to Ravi. She desperately wanted to escape from this conversation. Then the butler entered and murmured something to Lady Wellingborough. Lady Wellingborough nodded, and he announced: "Dinner is served, ladies and gentlemen." Footmen flung open the big doors at one end of the room to reveal a beautifully dressed mahogany table with a gigantic ice sculpture of an elephant with a howdah on its back. The room was hung with Indian silks, and the chairs were decorated in the same way.

A collective murmur of gratification went up from the room. Lady Wellingborough took Lord Westlake's arm, and the others in the room paired up, each with their nearest equal in rank, as they prepared to proceed to the dining room.

"May I?" Lord Fintan offered his arm to Ada. She had no choice but to accept.

As they walked through into the dining room, she glanced behind her. She wished she had not. Ravi and Charlotte walked behind her, and both had faces like thunder.

Rose started to her feet with the rest of the audience. She did not hear herself applauding; she hardly heard the thunderous applause of the others. She had forgotten all about Sebastian, until he placed a hand on her shoulder.

She turned to him. "Oh, sir—I mean," she stumbled, remembering that she was supposed to be pretending not to be a maid. "Mr. Templeton. Wasn't it the most wonderful thing? I've never heard music like that."

189

"Yes, it was magnificent." Sebastian smiled at her. "Perhaps he'll give us an encore."

Rose wasn't sure what an encore was, but she kept on applauding. The music had been so simple and yet so rich, it had brought back to her the folk tales that her grandmother had told her when she was a child. Full of magic and wonder, little people, and enchanted stone rings—she had never dreamed that they could be turned into music like this. She clapped harder and harder as she remembered the way Mr. Vronsky's long, nimble fingers had flown across the keyboard as if they too were enchanted.

The applause increased as the Russian came back onto the stage, smiling and bowing. He strode to the piano, seated himself, and gestured for silence. As Rose and the rest of the audience sat down obediently, he said, "Zank you. Zank you. I am very appreciative." He ran a finger thoughtfully across the keyboard, then spoke to the audience. "I have been lucky to visit your English country houses recently. There I was played an enchanting little tune and I would like to share it with you. I do not have the permission of the composer, but I believe she would not object. It shows astonishing promise for one so young."

He turned to the piano, raised his hands, and began to play.

For the first few seconds, Rose did not believe what she was hearing. Then a deep blush came over her face. She glanced to either side, sure that people would somehow notice how she felt. But nobody looked at her. They were rapt by the music. They were entranced—by her "Eastern Dance."

Rose pressed her hands to her cheeks, trying to keep back tears of excitement and joy. Mr. Vronsky played so differently from Georgiana—there was a pathos in his interpretation, a skill that brought out meanings and feelings that she had never even suspected were there. Under his hands, her tune changed from the sweet but familiar song of an English blackbird to a mournful lament. When he at last ceased playing, there was an awed silence, and then the audience erupted in applause.

Rose, too, was stunned and moved to clap. She did not even know where she was until Sebastian touched her arm.

"Rose? It's time to go." He smiled at her kindly.

"Oh—yes—" she managed. Like a sleepwalker, she followed him from the box out onto the staircase.

"Are you quite all right?" Sebastian sounded concerned.

She nodded. "Yes. I—I'm just overcome . . ."

"Sit down here. I will fetch you a drink." Sebastian steered her to a chair and disappeared into the crowd. Rose sat clutching the edge of the chair. What had just happened? Her wildest dream had come true, and yet no one knew that she was the composer. She couldn't help wishing that they did. Suddenly Ada's words—*You must be proud of the flame within you*—made sense to her. She was frightened and exhilarated. It was as if she had touched the world of the gods for an instant—and now she had to return to earth.

Sebastian returned, holding a glass. It looked like soda water, and Rose took a grateful sip. She almost choked. It fizzed in her mouth like icicles melting, and it was certainly alcoholic. Her mother was entirely against alcohol; drunkenness, she always said, was the worst sin a servant could commit.

"Don't look so shocked, it's only champagne," said Sebastian with a smile. "Have you never tasted—? Oh, I daresay you haven't."

Rose shook her head. A good servant would have put the glass down and refused to touch another drop. But tonight was different. Tonight she was a composer. She put the glass to her lips again and finished it.

To her horror, Ada found herself seated between Douglas Varley and Lord Fintan. Opposite her was Charlotte, and opposite Lord Fintan was Ravi. She dropped her eyes as the footmen came around with the first course.

Lord Wellingborough, clearly thinking she was shy, leaned kindly toward her from the end of the table.

"Lady Ada, I don't think you know Mr. Varley? He is of the same party as me."

Ada managed to stutter out a few words without really looking into Douglas Varley's face or hearing his response. Lord Wellingborough then introduced Ravi, who said simply, "We have met."

"Oh?" Lord Fintan's eyebrows rose.

"At—at my father's wedding. Both Mr. Varley and Mr. Sundaresan were our guests." Ada was able to answer calmly now. She even dared to look into Ravi's eyes as he greeted her. His face was tense, and a small muscle in his jaw clenched and unclenched. Ada gave him a pleading glance, but she did not dare follow it up. Too many eyes were looking at her—not least Charlotte's, whose gaze seemed to burn into her like acid.

The next few minutes were torture. Ada could not believe the ease with which glib small talk came from her mouth, while every element of her was tuned to Ravi's smallest movement, the slightest glance of his eyes. *Do I live my life so unconsciously?* she thought in horror. If she could have divided herself in two, it seemed, one Ada could, ghostlike, have gone about her normal life with no one noticing a thing, while the other could have been with Ravi.

She tried to gather her senses. She had to remember what she was here for—to warn Ravi away from the dangerous path he was taking. Luckily, the ice sculpture and the decoration of the rooms had already turned the conversation toward India.

"What do you think, Mr. Sundaresan?" Lord Wellingborough inquired, dissecting lobster tails as he spoke. "Have our decorations conjured up an accurate vision of India?"

Ravi's lip curled. "It is certainly a vision, sir. But you must be aware that most people in India do not live in something like the Arabian Nights."

Ada jumped in: "But it is such a beautiful, enchanted country." She didn't know if what she was saying was sensible or not; she just knew that she wanted Ravi to speak to her.

"To an outsider, perhaps." He regarded her coolly, and she blushed. "But our problems are quite practical, as practical as those of the United States before the revolution there."

There was an awkward, embarrassed silence. Ada shrank inside. How could he say something so provocative in such company? Beside her, Mr. Varley stiffened and sent a warning look at his protégé.

"I hope you don't have privileged information, Mr. Sundaresan," said Lord Fintan with a smile. "Is there trouble in store for the Foreign Secretary?"

Ravi shrugged and returned Lord Fintan's smile, though it didn't reach his eyes. He had hardly touched his food. "I wouldn't know anything about that, sir."

"Lord Fintan," Charlotte broke in, her cheeks pink, "I wondered if you had returned to Gravelley Park since last season?"

193

"I cannot say I have," he replied, the hint of a frown crossing his face.

"There were so many memories there—so many intimate connections made—" She leaned across the table, her diamonds dangling in her bosom, the candlelight sparkling from the intricate beading around the neckline.

Lord Fintan did not take the bait. He looked directly into her eyes and said, "How true."

Charlotte pressed her lips together and drew back. It was hard to see in the candlelight, but Ada thought she was blushing.

"I think it is a shame," Ada said, her voice sounding high and nervous, "that so many Indians jump to conclusions about the intentions of the English."

"Ada is terribly political," Charlotte said in a voice of repressed rage.

"Then she's sitting next to just the person to appreciate her," Emily said with a wicked smile and a glance toward Lord Fintan. Charlotte breathed out hard and stabbed at the lobster on her plate as if she wished it were Emily's head. Lord Fintan cast Emily an amused, warning glance. Ada watched Ravi's gaze flick between the three of them, and knew from the expression in his golden-flecked eyes that he was taking everything in.

"I would not call it jumping to conclusions. I would call it coming to an . . . understanding of the situation based on the very good evidence before my own eyes," he said to Ada, his voice still cool.

Ada felt her face grow warm. The remark was pointed. She knew he meant that he had observed her behavior with Lord Fintan. She was upset, but she was also angry. How could he judge her without hearing her side of the story?

"It's true that we are not in India, and cannot judge these things," Lady Wellingborough said, her intelligent gaze passing over the table. Ada had the sense that she knew something was going on, but was not able to tell exactly what.

"But I have spent several years in India," Lord Westlake said. "And I cannot approve of the way that certain bodies— this hot faction of the INC, for example—recklessly cast the British as their enemies. True, some situations have been . . . poorly handled, but you cannot deny we have brought many benefits to the country—schools, a railway system . . ."

Ravi gazed back at him steadily, his eyes cold. "And would you call the Partition of Bengal and the famines benefits?"

Lord Westlake frowned. "Of course not. I was vocally opposed to the Partition and assisted in the famine relief myself." He shifted in his seat. "You are young," he said stiffly. "Of course you feel passionately about these things."

"I am young, sir, but I am not blind." Ravi's voice was mild, but Ada sensed the fervor behind it. "I, too, have spent several years in India—my entire life, as it happens—and more than this, I *am* Indian. You must allow me a different perspective on its government by the English than you might have."

"But my dear boy," Lord Wellingborough said, seriously, "do you really think the poor masses of your country fit to rule themselves? They are so divided."

"So was Britain, until late in its history, and if we consider the Irish question . . . But I think that is irrelevant, if you will forgive me. The question is whether it is just for a people to have no voice in the government that rules them. I cannot think that it is."

Lord Fintan laughed uncomfortably. "Steady on, old chap. You're beginning to sound like quite a rebel."

Ravi cleared his throat, glancing at Mr. Varley. "I could certainly not betray a country that has given me so many opportunities. But I'm sure we can agree that little treacheries have been committed by both sides, can we not?" He met Ada's eyes.

Ada bit her lip angrily. "There is no question of treachery where no allegiance is owed," she said. How dare he imply such a thing? They had agreed to be just friends. She owed him nothing. She could flirt with whomever she wanted.

She was rewarded with an unmistakable flash of pain in his eyes. She was briefly triumphant, and then miserable.

Lord Fintan raised an eyebrow as he glanced between her and Ravi. As the third course came around, he said, as if to no one in particular, "Well, I confess I'm not up on India. But I see it has its fascinations—for the ladies especially."

Rose shivered in her cloak as they went out into the frosty street, where cabs and cars were jostling for space to collect the patrons. It had begun to snow, and flakes whirled down, dizzying as the bubbles in the champagne, polka-dotting the gentlemen's top hats for a moment before they melted. Rose turned her face up to them, remembering how she had spun and danced in the snow as a child, trying to catch snowflakes on her tongue. She was aware of some admiring glances, and smiled, flushed with sudden confidence in her own beauty. Then, as she looked down, she saw Mr. Vronsky.

He was coming out of the stage door, surrounded by a knot of admirers. His lanky shape stood head and shoulders above the top hats and fox furs, and there was a benign smile on his face.

Rose stared at him. She would never have another chance to speak to him. It was out of the question to tell him who she was, but she could thank him, at least, from the bottom of her heart, even if he didn't understand why she was doing it. "Mr. Sebastian—please—could we speak to him?" she burst out.

Sebastian looked around. "Why, of course." He tucked her arm into his own and led her toward the crowd. Rose would never have been able to make her way through the press of people alone, but Sebastian's confidence seemed to part them like a sword.

"Excuse me, please. This young lady is anxious to speak to you, Mr. Vronsky—she enjoyed the concert very much."

Rose found herself looking up into Mr. Vronsky's face as the crowd surged behind her. "It was magical," she blurted out. "Oh, sir, it was the most beautiful thing I've ever heard."

Some of the fashionably dressed ladies next to her tittered behind their hands, and the gentlemen in their silky top hats covered their mouths to hide smiles. Rose faltered. She had been too enthusiastic—oh, and she should never have called him sir. What could make her look more like a housemaid?

She became suddenly aware of herself, frightened and awkward in a beautiful, borrowed dress, aware of her work-hardened hands inside the kid gloves. She had tried so hard to behave well. She barely spoke; she did exactly what Sebastian told her . . . and now she had ruined everything.

She backed away. The spell was broken.

But before she could escape the crowd, a commotion behind Mr. Vronsky arose. One of the gentlemen had brought out a camera.

"Mr. Vronsky—the press, if you please. A photograph? Perhaps Mr. and Mrs. Churchill would care to be in the frame?

Oh! And Mr. Sebastian Templeton and his lovely companion, of course."

"Very well." Mr. Vronsky smiled and stepped back to give the photographers better room.

"Oh no—" Rose shrank back, but Sebastian urged her forward. "I don't want to—"

"Please, Rose. For me."

She was startled by the desperation in Sebastian's whisper. She allowed him to maneuver her into the photographer's frame, although all the time her heart was beating with terror. She had never been photographed before.

She tried to duck her head, but Sebastian was pulling her around to face him. She saw his face, set as if he were about to do some dreadful act of heroic courage.

Then he kissed her, just as the flashbulb popped.

Rose had never been kissed before. It seemed to whirl over her, like a blizzard. For a few seconds she had no idea what was going on. Sebastian's lips pressed hard against hers. She heard Mr. Vronsky exclaim something in Russian, and laugh. Other people gasped. More lights flashed and popped. Then Sebastian released her and, his arm around her protectively, hurried down the steps to the waiting cab.

Rose, too shocked and confused even to be angry, found herself bundled into the cab. It was only then that the idea of screaming came to her. She managed a small, very quiet shriek.

"Oh please don't!" Sebastian said in anguish, leaning forward to her. "I'm sorry, Rose. I shouldn't have done it, I know. But I had to."

Rose gasped at him. The cab rumbled across the cobblestones. The thought came to her that she might be being kidnapped for terrible purposes. But if so, it was not a very discreet kidnap—everyone had seen them leave. Everyone had seen the kiss. The thought made her blush bright red in horror.

"Mr. Sebastian—sir!" She burst into tears of shock.

Sebastian groaned. "I truly apologize. I had no intention of upsetting you."

"No intention—no intention—I thought you were a gentleman, sir! Where are you taking me?" She lunged for the door handle, but Sebastian grabbed her hand.

"No, no, Rose, you've got it all wrong. We're just going home. I—" He ran a despairing hand through his hair. "I know what I did just then must seem, well, insane."

"I never thought you that kind of man, sir," Rose sobbed. "I *liked* you!"

"I'm not. I promise I'm not. I have no dishonorable intentions toward you." He added wryly, "Or honorable ones, for that matter. I'm very sorry, Rose. Call it one of my freaks, call me insane, call me anything, but please forgive me."

Rose slowly wiped away her tears. There was no mistaking the honesty in his tone.

"Then what did you do it for? Was it to make a mockery of me?" She was angry now. "I never thought you would do such a thing, sir."

"I would never mock you, I promise. Please don't think that." Sebastian dropped his head in his hands. "I had no choice," he repeated miserably.

Rose gazed out the window, unable to think of a word to say. She had to believe him, she realized. He was too clearly upset by what he had done. But what did he mean, he had no choice? Was he insane? There didn't seem to be another explanation. If her mother were here, she would say *I told you so*. This was what came of getting above your station.

199

As soon as the cab pulled up at Milborough House, she jumped out and fled to the door, ignoring Sebastian's anxious calls. She slipped in, using the key Ada had given her, and tiptoed up the stairs, shoes in hand. She was far too tired to notice that Stella's door was ajar, and that light still shone out through the crack of it. She managed to undress and then fell into bed, forgetting completely that she was meant to wait up for her mistress.

Chapter Twenty-Eight

Dinner was finally over, and Ada rose to retire with the ladies. As soon as she reached the drawing room she went to the window, gazing out at the falling snow, trying to cool her cheeks and calm her miserable thoughts.

Emily touched her on the shoulder. "Are you quite well, Ada?"

"Yes—yes. I'm just so terribly hot." Ada looked out across the garden of Featherstonehaugh House. Dark box hedges loomed in front of her, and the snow made the steps down between them gleam. She was furious with herself, and furious with Ravi. How could the evening have gone so wrong?

"You think me cruel to Charlotte, I'm sure." Emily was speaking in a low voice, and Ada had to bring her thoughts back to the moment. "But if you knew what happened at Gravelley Park last season, you would understand."

"You won't tell me?" Ada was curious despite herself.

"No, I can't. That would be too indiscreet even for me. Suffice it to say that it was a very eventful Saturday to Monday." She smiled without humor. "And that Charlotte ensured that certain things happened that made me very unhappy."

"I'm sorry," said Ada, touched. Emily always seemed so

lively and cheerful, Ada had not imagined she had a tragedy in her past.

"No matter. I make a point of never dwelling on seasons past." Emily smiled. "Tell me, did you get the book I sent?"

"I did. I liked it very much."

"So you will come to Oxford, then?"

"If I can." Ada answered absently. She had seen a figure cross the path, walking between the gardens. It was impossible to tell, in the darkness, who it was, but then a match flared, illuminating his face as he lit a cheroot. It was Ravi. His face was set and moody. She moved instinctively closer to the window. If only he would look up, look through the glass and see her.

Emily moved forward too, curiously following her gaze. "Oh . . . and of course there may be more than one good reason to visit Oxford," she said meaningfully.

Ada drew back, her heart thumping at the knowledge that Emily suspected something. Emily met her frightened look with a smile.

"Don't worry. I didn't see a thing," she said under her breath, and moved away.

Ada stood, indecisive for a moment, by the window. When she turned back, Ravi had gone.

The rest of the evening passed in a haze. She only came to life when the gentlemen joined them, starting as if she were about to get up, when Ravi entered the room. But there was no chance of speaking to him. He kept his distance, and she was too nervous to approach him. Instead, she smiled at compliments and laughed at jokes. Lord Fintan also stayed away, and she wondered if he too suspected something. She could not bring herself to be miserable about it if he did. Her mind was in too much turmoil. One moment she determined she had to speak to him, they could not part like this; the next she was angry and felt that she never wanted to speak to him again. And then it was time to go home.

Unhappily, she followed her father and Fiona out into the hall. Lord Fintan paused before getting into his motor, to bow over her hand.

"It was a pleasure, as always," he said. Ada managed a smile.

Emily kissed her warmly on the cheek. "I hope to see you before too long," she said meaningfully. She exchanged frosty smiles with Charlotte, and went out to her carriage.

Ada, wrapped in her furs, stood close by the doors. Her family was in conversation with the Wellingboroughs, and no one was looking in her direction. On a whim, she stepped out into the flurries of snow—and felt her arm caught tightly.

She barely had time to gasp before she was pulled into the shadows beside the door. She knew at once it was Ravi who held her. "Let me go!" Furiously, she shook herself loose.

"With pleasure," he said coldly. "I thought—but never mind; I was clearly mistaken."

"You *are* mistaken." Her anger cooled as she remembered how she had behaved. A note of pleading crept into her voice. "It is not fair to accuse me of treachery. You don't know—"

"What is there to know? I saw everything. I suppose you have known Lord Fintan long?"

"Not particularly, no." She held her head high. "But it should be no concern of yours whether I have or not."

"Of course. My apologies," he said ironically. "As you said, you owe me no allegiance."

"I didn't mean—"She stopped, trying to control her frustration and anger. It did not help that she longed to kiss him as much as ever. The lingering scent of his cheroot took her back to the *Moldavia*. "We agreed we would just be friends."

"Again, you're quite right. I have no right to feel this way."

"You don't understand, I feel it too, but—"

"But what?" he flashed out. "But I am not quite the kind of man you could see yourself marrying. Lord Fintan, on the other hand—"

"That is not fair!"

His eyes flashed fiercely, and he stepped closer, drawing breath for a retort. The next thing she knew, she was in his arms, and his lips were pressed passionately onto hers. She gasped, her head whirling, feeling out of control again. The falling snow bit into her bare skin as her furs slid from her shoulders. She felt his warm, smooth hands caressing her arms, and pressed her body closer, every care of the evening wiped clean from her head. She could go on kissing him forever. But they were right by the door, and at any moment her father could step outside, or the car could draw up. It was intolerable that he was risking her exposure like this, and terrifying that he had such a power over her, power to make her forget herself, her family, her station in life, her ambitions—everything except the terrible joy of kissing him. It could not go on.

She managed to pull herself free. "We must never meet again," she said, her voice shaking. Then, before she could change her mind, she hurried down the steps just as their carriage pulled up. She followed her family into the carriage in a daze, her eyes blurred with tears as if by snowflakes. In the carriage, she sat back and closed her eyes, murmuring something about a headache.

Stella dozed in the chair before the fire, waking with a start now and then. Waiting up for Miss Charlotte was her least favorite duty. When the door finally slammed downstairs, and she heard the voices of the family in the hall, the clock showed three o'clock in the morning.

Stella jumped to her feet and wiped the sleep from her eyes just in time as Miss Charlotte opened the door and flounced in. Stella could see at once, from her expression, that the night had not been a success.

"Stella," Charlotte began without hesitation, as she stood before the mirror, "I want you to find anything you can against Ada. I don't care what it is. She must have done something to be ashamed of at some point; no one could be so horribly innocent as she seems to be. I want to know what it is. I want to know her secrets."

Stella hurried to undo her mistress's buttons and help her with her jewelry. She was startled but not surprised. It was clear that Miss Templeton was jealous of Lady Ada, but for her to come directly out and instruct her like this, instead of dropping hints, the hatred must run very deep.

"I'll do whatever I can, miss," she said. She hesitated, wondering if she should tell Charlotte about the near miss with the letter. If it had not been for the interfering nursemaid, they might have had solid evidence to get Rose sacked by now. "And against the maid, too—I'm hopeful of getting information very soon." She finished undressing her and held out the peignoir for her to step into.

Charlotte made a gesture of angry dismissal and shrugged on the silken dressing gown.

"I don't care about the maid. But I want Ada ruined." She barely troubled to conceal the venom in her voice. "Just see to it, will you?"

"My dear Fiona," were Mrs. Verulam's first words as she entered the drawing room of Milborough House the next morning. "Who on earth is this mysterious lady at the center of Sebastian's latest scandal? As his mother, surely you must know."

Ada looked up in surprise from the thank you note she was writing to the Wellingboroughs. Charlotte, who was leafing through the latest *Bon Ton* magazine, looked as startled. The parlormaid, who was laying out the tea things, started and chinked a porcelain cup against a saucer.

Fiona raised her eyebrows as Mrs. Verulam placed a decidedly gaudy-looking piece of newsprint in front of her. Ada could see at a glance it was not one of the more reputable papers.

"What on earth is this? Something from the servants' hall?"

"Yes. Baines, my butler, is kind enough to keep it for me."

Charlotte walked across the room and looked over her mother's shoulder.

"*The Illustrated*?" she said with a shocked laugh. "Oh, Mrs. Verulam, you don't read that dreadful rag, I'm sure."

"Oh, are you?" Mrs. Verulam turned a piercing eye on her. "I most certainly do. How else is one supposed to know what one's friends are up to?"

The parlormaid stifled what seemed to be a cough and hurried from the room, her shoulders shaking. Ada put her own hand to her mouth to cover a smile.

Fiona sighed and picked up the newspaper. "What has the

wretch done now?" she said indulgently, although there was a note of concern that she could not quite hide.

"Turn to page nine, that's where the society news usually is," said Mrs. Verulam.

Ada watched nervously, aware of the unwritten law that a lady should have her name in the papers only three times: at her birth, marriage, and death. She hoped Sebastian had not done anything that would reflect poorly on the Averleys. And for the first time that day she thought of Rose. Knowing Rose would be tired, Ada had not woken her when she got in, or in the morning. She had contrived to dress herself. It had given her a delightful feeling of independence.

Fiona gasped as she looked at the newspaper. "Well!"

"Isn't it exciting?" Mrs. Verulam whisked the paper from her hands and showed it to Charlotte. Ada could no longer control her curiosity and hurried over. "At least he was caught *in flagrante* with a *woman*—"

"Mrs. Verulam!" Fiona's voice was icy.

"—who is both well-dressed and beautiful, I was going to say," Mrs. Verulam finished calmly.

Ada stared in horror at the photograph. There was no mistaking it. From the center beamed the tall figure of the Russian pianist, on either side of him stood the Churchills, and to one side—unmistakably—were Sebastian and Rose, caught in the moment of kissing.

"Oh my goodness," she said faintly. What had happened? Why had Sebastian done this? She looked up and saw from Charlotte's and Fiona's faces that they had recognized Rose instantly, too.

Mrs. Verulam took a piece of cake and nibbled on it daintily. "Now people are saying she must be a Russian princess of some kind. She doesn't look Russian to me, but then what can one tell from these pictures?"

Charlotte found her tongue. "I wouldn't have thought she was any kind of princess. More likely some woman of the town he paid to accompany him."

"No, no, impossible. I know people who were really there, and they said she was a perfect lady. That kind of thing, you know, cannot be faked." She picked up the paper again and surveyed it closely.

Ada swallowed. She did not want Lady Verulam's clever nose sniffing out more than it should. If she gained so much as an inkling of the truth, friend of Fiona's or no, it would be all over town by lunchtime. Her fingers itched to whisk the paper out of her hands and into the fire.

To her horror, Lady Verulam said, "Ada, if it's not too much trouble, I would like to speak to your lady's maid. I understand that she trimmed that hat of yours I liked so much at the reception, and I would very much like Dobbs to do something the same with my blue silk. Would you mind?"

"N-no," Ada managed. Charlotte and Fiona were looking at her in horror, but there was nothing else she could say. "Of course not. I'll . . . ring for her at once."

As she crossed to the bell, Charlotte and Fiona burst out together, "Really, is it necessary?"

"Perhaps Ada could send over the instructions later on, or—"

"Oh nonsense, why should I put Ada to so much trouble? It will only take a moment," Lady Verulam replied.

Ada rang the bell, feeling as if she were summoning Rose to her execution.

* * *

Rose hurried down the stairs, feeling sick with nervousness. She was still exhausted from the night before, and she had almost begun to think—to hope—the kiss had all been a dream. She was just glad that she had not had to see Lady Ada since the kiss. She did not know how she could face her—but now she had to.

She paused to catch her breath and smooth down her skirts, then knocked and entered the drawing room. She saw Ada looking at her in what seemed like terror and pity, Charlotte and Fiona fairly glaring at her from the sofa, and Mrs. Verulam beaming encouragingly from her chair. Rose dropped to a curtsy.

"Come here, dear, no need to be frightened. I just want to speak to you about the trimming you made on your mistress's ivory cloche." Mrs. Verulam beckoned her over. "Goodness, she is young, isn't she," she added to Ada. "Well, she always makes you look perfectly turned out, and that is the important thing."

Rose walked over obligingly. "Well, ma'am, I"—and at that instant she caught sight of the newspaper on the table. Her stomach turned over as she spotted the photograph. The paper lay directly in front of Mrs. Verulam; there was no way she could fail to see that the real version stood before her.

"It was the stitch I wanted to ascertain," Mrs. Verulam went on, as Rose failed to answer. "The beads are very pretty but I think I would prefer jet . . ." She looked encouragingly at Rose.

"I . . ." Rose's voice seemed to have taken a leave of absence. She hoped she was not going to faint. There was a terrible silence.

"Come along, dear, don't be shy." Mrs. Verulam sounded impatient.

Rose managed to stammer out an explanation of the stitch. Mrs. Verulam listened, nodding. It began to dawn on Rose that Mrs. Verulam was *not* trying to lead her around to admit she was the girl in the picture. Incredibly, it seemed she had not made the connection. After all, it was not surprising, Rose thought. Ladies and gentlemen hardly looked at servants; to see them outside their usual employment was not merely shocking—it was inconceivable.

But as for the ladies in her own family—that was another story.

"Thank you so much, Rose." Mrs. Verulam smiled as she came to the end of her explanation. "Now, I must be taking my leave. Fiona, if you have any light to shed on this mystery"—she gestured to the paper—"you will let me know, won't you? The whole of London is talking about it."

As Fiona escorted Mrs. Verulam to the door, Rose dared lift her head and look around. The expression on Miss Charlotte's face extinguished all hope. Lady Ada was quite pale.

As soon as the door was closed behind Mrs. Verulam, Charlotte burst out, "This is the last straw!"

"It's quite horrible," said Fiona through white lips. She strode over to the table, picked up the paper without looking at Rose, glanced at it and threw it down again. "I cannot believe Sebastian would be such a fool. Kissing—actually kissing—her! She must have made a play for him. Nothing else explains it. The manipulative, shameless . . . and I do believe she is actually wearing Ada's new dress."

"My lady, I didn't make a play for him!" Rose burst out.

At the same moment, Ada exclaimed, "I can explain the dress. And I'm sure there must be some explanation"—her eyes pleaded with Rose to say there was—"for the other thing. Isn't there, Rose?"

"Please do not encourage that fallen creature to address you," Fiona said icily. "It is a matter of disgust to me that such a person remains in this room. Given the insult to your dignity and ours, I am sure you will not have the slightest objection to dismissing her without notice or a reference, this instant." She rang the bell.

Rose turned white. The room seemed to spin. "Oh, my lady—please, no!" She felt sick. How could it have come to this? She had never wanted Mr. Templeton to kiss her. "Please, if you only ask Mr. Templeton—I'm sure he will explain it wasn't my doing—"

"Hold your tongue, hussy!" Charlotte snapped. Rose flinched.

Fiona continued to ignore Rose.

"I don't consider Sebastian blameless; however, he should know better than to be caught by a scheming little minx like that. She must have been planning this for months."

"It's not true! I didn't—" Rose knew she was making things worse for herself by speaking, but she could not help it. It was too unjust.

"Will you hold your tongue!" Charlotte repeated. She looked at Ada. "You can explain the dress? How, pray?"

Ada blushed and stammered. "I—I—lent it to her."

Charlotte snapped out a disbelieving laugh, and Fiona raised her eyes to the heavens. "Ada, I have no idea why you are so keen to defend your maid, but please do not expect us to believe something so outrageous. Not even you could be so blind to every sense of propriety—"

"Well, it's true!" Ada's temper was roused at Fiona's scornful tone. "Rose is a very talented composer, and she deserved to go as much as any society woman."

"A talented . . ." Charlotte shook her head. "Ada, she is

211

your *maid*. How could she possibly be a talented composer? You have no idea how ridiculous you sound."

"I knew it would come to this when you said you read books," Fiona said coldly. "Clearly there is no talking sense to you. I order you to dismiss your maid. As your stepmother, I can do so."

"No!" Ada cried out.

"I expect her to be gone from this house in an hour or less," Fiona said. "Come along, Charlotte. Ada, you know your duty."

She turned and swept out of the room. Charlotte followed.

Rose, from pure shock, burst into tears as soon as the door had shut behind them. Through her sobs, she became aware of Ada's comforting arm around her shoulders. Guilt twisted her heart—how could she have let Lady Ada down like this?

"Oh, Lady Ada," she sobbed. "I'm sorry. I had no idea he was going to do it, I truly didn't. I don't know what I did to lead him on. I didn't know how to tell you, and he said he didn't know what came over him—I had no idea this horrible photograph would appear."

Ada patted her shoulder. "Don't worry, Rose. I believe you. I don't think you would ever have done something like this on purpose, and Sebastian is a thoughtless fool—though this does seem shocking, even for him. He must have known the photographers would be there." She sighed. "You shan't lose your place. I don't know how, but I'll make sure it doesn't happen. Now dry your eyes and I will see what I can do to soothe Fiona's and Charlotte's wounded pride."

Chapter Twenty-Nine

Ada was shaking inside as she went out of the drawing room after her stepmother and stepsister. She had disgraced herself, in their eyes, and she knew that perhaps nothing she could say in Rose's defense would be good enough. But she had to try.

As she reached the bottom of the stairs she saw a familiar, tall, fair-haired figure pacing in the hall.

"Sebastian!" She ran toward him. "What were you thinking?" she demanded in a hissed whisper, aware of the footmen stationed at the door. "How could you do such a thing? Have you no decency?"

"I know, I know," Sebastian groaned. "I came as soon as I saw the papers." He was in an odd mood, Ada realized, both penitent and in high spirits. She frowned. Had he not yet realized what a disaster this could be for Rose? When she spoke again, her voice was cold.

"Well, you had better explain exactly what your part in all of this was to your mother and sister. They are determined that Rose should lose her place, with no notice and no character. They think she snared you. I think that's as likely as a rabbit snaring a poacher."

"Lose her place?" Sebastian sounded genuinely shocked. "No, that mustn't happen. Let me explain to them."

They found Fiona and Charlotte in the conservatory, talking in low, furious voices.

"Mother, I've come to explain," Sebastian began at once. "You've got the wrong end of the stick. It was my idea to take the girl out, and it was my idea entirely to kiss her. She was taken completely by surprise and cried all the way home. I won't see her lose her place—she was not at fault, it was me."

No one spoke for several seconds.

"Well!" Charlotte broke the stunned silence. "I must say, Sebastian, this surpasses even your low standards."

Sebastian flushed, but answered with forced good humor. "I deserve that, I'm sure. I'm sorry that it ended up in the papers. But if you must punish someone, punish me. I deserve it, not Rose."

"You are quite sure you have not compromised yourself?" Fiona said in measured tones. "You understand, don't you, that that photograph could easily be used in a court of law to support a breach of promise case."

"Rose would never do such a thing," Ada said, scandalized.

"Don't be naïve, Ada. She's a poor girl, and there is plenty of money in breach of promise." Fiona steepled her fingers and looked at Sebastian. "If you have compromised yourself with this girl, I will publicly disown you."

Sebastian swallowed, a look of hurt crossing his face. "There won't be any need for that. I can assure you, she is as embarrassed by my ungentlemanly behavior as you are," he said quietly.

Charlotte gave a disbelieving sniff.

"You won't force her to go, will you, Lady Westlake?" Ada pleaded. "Not when you've heard her defense from Sebastian himself."

"Be quiet, Ada!" Fiona rapped out. Ada, shocked, was silent. "I do not think you have any idea of just how shockingly *you* have behaved. I am thoroughly ashamed of you, and so would your father be if he knew."

Ada opened her mouth to protest, but Fiona surged on. "By encouraging your maid in her ridiculous pretensions, you have shown that you have no respect for the consequence of your family or mine. You have made us a laughing stock today. If you have no thought for your own reputation, will you not think of your father's good name? He has barely recovered from the unfortunate slanders that surrounded his Indian career. If any hint of your part in this scandal gets beyond the family, it could do great damage to your chances this season, and thereby to his standing."

Ada felt tears start to her eyes. She tried to speak, but no words came out. Fiona was right, she knew that. It had been thoughtless of her to allow Rose to be exposed in that way, and by encouraging her she had harmed more people than Rose herself.

"Sebastian, you are greatly at fault, but the maid is more so. She has passed the boundaries of decency for a woman and gone beyond her station. That simply cannot go unpunished. I would be failing in my duty as a parent if I allowed a woman who had become so exposed, so fallen, to remain in this house with my daughters."

Ada stood silently, tears in her eyes. She had never felt so guilty in her life. Rose had become so important to her—such a friend. She could not bear the thought of losing her, much less in such a way.

There was only one hope left—her father. She quailed inside at the thought of his knowing about her foolishness, but there was no help for it. She had to save Rose. She turned and ran from the conservatory.

Ada found her father in the library, poring over the newspapers.

"Papa?" she said, seeing his frowning expression. "Is everything all right?"

"Ada?" He looked up with a tired smile. "The situation on the Continent gets ever more troubling—but what did you want to see me about?"

Ada took a deep breath.

"I've been foolish," she blurted out. "Very, very foolish—and it has hurt someone who doesn't deserve to be hurt. Please, Father—I need you to help her."

Quickly, she told her father the story, wincing as she saw the expression of shock and anger in his eyes.

"Rose would never have been there if it were not for me," she finished miserably. "She is innocent. It was all my fault."

"And Sebastian's!" her father exploded. He was furious, she could see that. He got up and paced back and forth. "Fiona is acting exactly as a responsible mother should. Such an incident, so public, cannot be let slide, especially on the eve of your first season. If the merest breath of scandal touches you . . . What were you *thinking*, Ada?" He turned on her. "Could you not see how vulnerable Rose would be, alone with a rake like Sebastian?"

Tears of humiliation rose to Ada's eyes. He was even angrier than she had expected him to be. "I'm sorry, Papa. I just meant—I only wanted to help her."

"The road to hell is paved with good intentions," he muttered. He looked as if he were thinking deeply, or remembering something that she did not know about.

"Please, Father," Ada said. "Rose doesn't deserve this. You can't let Lady Westlake turn her out without a penny in London."

"No indeed!" Her father looked very serious, more serious than she had ever seen him. "It would mean ruin for her. I should have done something before, something to ensure her safety."

Ada looked puzzled. Her father caught her eye and cleared his throat, looking embarrassed.

"I shall not let Fiona dismiss her until we have arrived back at Somerton and she has the support of her mother," he said firmly. "But Ada, I don't know if I can keep her in service with us. The damage has been done."

Rose packed her clothes through a haze of tears. She could hardly believe this was happening to her. It all seemed like a horrible nightmare. She could not stop thinking about what her mother would say when she heard. Would she believe that it was not her fault? She shuddered at the thought of how angry and disappointed she would be.

She had few possessions; her uniforms belonged to the family. The belongings in her suitcase looked small and pitiful. She turned to the door, and started. Stella Ward stood there, watching her.

Rose dashed away the tears with the back of her hand.

"I suppose you've come to gloat," she said. Stella had never liked her, that was clear.

"I did say that those who ride on high horses have a long way to fall." Stella's smirk made Rose tingle with the desire to slap her. She controlled herself. "But you do me wrong, Rose. I am here to help. I have an idea that could save your position."

Rose's laugh was a mixture of surprise and disbelief.

Stella looked wounded. "Don't say you don't believe me. I feel sorry for you, Rose. You were so clearly out of your depth as a lady's maid. I gave you good advice that first day, don't you remember?"

Rose shook her head. She was too tired and confused by the events of the day to know what Stella was speaking about. "You will have to remind me."

"I told you that lady's maids often hear things that have a certain . . . value to them." She watched Rose's face, a faint smile hovering on her face. "Now is the time to cash in that valuable knowledge. I'm sure you have some. I'm just not quite sure what it is."

"You mean I should threaten to reveal Lady Ada's secrets in order to keep my position?" Rose said bluntly.

"No need for you to do anything so crude. Simply tell *me* the secrets. If they're juicy enough—and I'm sure they are—I promise that your situation will be saved."

"And Lady Ada's will be lost," said Rose. She thought how it would be for her if the story of her relationship with Ravi got out. It would mean the end of all her chances that season, at the very least.

"What does that matter to you? She doesn't care about you. She got you into this trouble in the first place. She'll weep crocodile tears as she cuts you loose without a penny or a character. Do you know what happens to girls without money or character in London, Rose?" Her voice was hard.

"Yes," whispered Rose. She was terrified, though she fought to hide it. Where would she go? What would she do? Somerton—her home—would be closed to her. It was so far away; how would she ever reach her mother again? If she was turned out onto the street that very afternoon, how

218

would she survive? London was huge, and she knew no one. If she pawned her few possessions, they would bring in hardly anything. There was only one way of making enough money to survive. She knew that many girls resorted to it. She also knew that she would rather die—but then, she had not been truly tested yet.

"So you see, no one could blame you for what you are going to do," Stella went on. "You are simply doing what you can to escape a worse stain on your soul and character."

"You are mistaken," said Rose. She was speaking automatically, her lips felt numb. "I am not going to do what you suggest."

A flash of anger crossed Stella's face. "Think, Rose! What do you owe Lady Ada? Nothing."

Rose shook her head. "It isn't about what I owe to Lady Ada. It's about what I owe to myself. I could never respect myself if I betrayed Lady Ada's confidence. My answer is no."

Stella seemed about to answer, when there was a knock at the door.

"Yes?" Rose called, glad of the interruption.

Her eyes widened in shock as the door opened and she saw Lord Westlake.

"My lord!" She jumped almost to attention, smoothing down her dress. Stella looked as startled as Rose felt.

"Good afternoon, Rose." He looked and sounded ill at ease. "I am sorry to intrude. May I have a word?"

Rose nodded blankly. "Of course, sir . . ."

"In private," he added to Stella.

Stella backed to the door. As she stepped out, she gave Rose a last, meaningful glance. Rose met her eyes proudly.

I have nothing to be ashamed of, she told herself. *And I won't sink to your level, no matter how much you want me to.*

She dropped her eyes as Lord Westlake approached her. He had surely come to give her formal dismissal. Well, she would take her tongue-lashing bravely.

"I'm very sorry about what has happened, Rose." His voice was surprisingly soft, and she was startled enough to raise her eyes. The look she had seen once before on his face—tenderness—was there again. "I don't deny that you were foolish, but I believe that you never meant to do wrong. And Ada should never have encouraged you. She should have known better."

Rose hung her head.

"I want you to know that you will not be dismissed until we return to Somerton," he went on. "I would not turn a vulnerable young girl out onto the streets without money, friends, or character. You cannot continue to serve as Lady Ada's personal maid, but I will not be the cause of your ruin, be sure of that."

Rose looked up at him in disbelief and gratitude. "Sir, I don't deserve your kindness—"

"And I don't deserve yours, if you only knew it," he replied quickly.

It was such a strange thing for him to say that she was struck silent. She simply bowed her head. She had been saved from a fate worse than death—but her future was still insecure. What would become of her once they were back at Somerton?

Stella hesitated outside Rose's door, but she could hear nothing from inside but the low rumble of Lord Westlake's voice. Angry and frustrated, she turned away. The little hussy managed to act superior even when she was so clearly disgraced.

She stalked away down the corridor, her mind working fast. Stella's conscience had hardened over the years, but it still had raw spots, and these twinged now, and that made her even more angry. And an angry Stella was a dangerous Stella.

She paused by Lady Ada's room. It was a risk, but she had begun her career this way—snooping in rooms she had no right to be in, looking through dustbins for discarded notes that their authors might have preferred not to be seen. She was not proud of it. But with a fallen sister and a drunkard father to support, she could not be picky either. That was what Rose would have to learn, sooner or later.

She pushed open the door of Lady Ada's room and slipped in. No one saw her. No one saw her look into the waste-paper basket and take out all the paper that had been thrown there. No one saw her sorting through it, reading quickly, now and then glancing at the door nervously. And no one saw her when she paused at certain scraps of mauve paper, covered in neat, ladylike handwriting.

She placed the pieces on the dressing table and jigsawed them into place. A smile came over her face as she looked at the message written on the paper.

"Not such a waste of a day after all," she said to herself. She swept the paper back into the bin and went to find Miss Charlotte.

Chapter Thirty

It was the first real day of spring, and Oxford students were punting along the river, looking smart in their boaters and striped jackets. Their shouts and laughter echoed up the tree-clad banks, and the clatter of carriages and motorcars echoed from the bridges they passed under. The spires of the city were faintly hazy in the mist of the afternoon sunshine.

As Ada walked along the bank of the river, her folded parasol in her hand, many of the Oxford students turned to look at her. They were not used to seeing women in the university precincts, except for the occasional visit by their sisters and mothers, and the few women students who had braved the walls of the academic fortress. And they were certainly not used to seeing such an elegantly dressed, pretty and seemingly well-bred girl walking alone in the shade of the willows.

Ada did not notice the admiring and inquisitive glances that followed her. She was too nervous, her mind too caught up in other things. The meeting she had just had with Miss Gorman, the mistress of Somerville, had gone better than she could have hoped. But as soon as she allowed herself to become exhilarated by that thought, she was brought crashing down again by the thought of the obstacles that stood in her way. Now that she was in disgrace for getting Rose dismissed, it was even less likely that she could persuade her father to let her go to Oxford. It hardly mattered if the mistress of Somerville was encouraging if she had really no chance of coming here.

And then there was Ravi. Ever since she had met Emily at the station, she had been looking around for him, nervous and anxious lest they should bump into each other. Half of her ached to see him, the other half scolded her for her weakness. It could only complicate matters. She had said they must never meet again, and she should stick to her words.

And then there he was, coming toward her along the path, handsome in his white linen suit.

If she had had a moment to think about it, she might have been able to walk past, pretending she hadn't seen him, but he registered her at the very same second that she saw him. His face lit up with startled pleasure, and she couldn't stop the smile breaking over her own face. The eye contact was enough. It felt as if a sheet of ice covering her heart, which she hadn't even known was there, had cracked and melted at the soft touch of his gaze.

He came to a halt as he reached her, his smile uncertain, both joyful and anxious. They stood on the path while around them the world went on without their notice. "I somehow thought we might meet like this," he said softly. "I knew that could not be the last time we saw each other. Life could not be so cruel."

She lowered her eyes, remembering the last time they had kissed, the passion, the bite of the snowflakes on her bare arms.

"I want to apologize for the way I behaved," he went on. "I was a jealous fool."

She looked up quickly. "And I never meant to provoke you," she said. "I have no feelings for Lord Fintan. There had to be some excuse for me to be able to attend the dinner and see you, and he was it."

"I believe you. I'm ashamed that I let my insecurity get the better of me."

"And I'm ashamed that I let my temper get the better of me."

They smiled at each other. Ada thought she had never felt so happy.

"May I accompany you?" he asked. "Are you here alone?"

She nodded. "That is, I came to see Lady Emily Maddox. She was kind enough to arrange a meeting with Miss Gorman." She continued walking, and he paced beside her. Their arms were close but not quite touching. Ada tried to drive the memory of his embrace from her mind.

"And?"

"It went well. She was very encouraging, but it all depends on my father . . ." She sighed.

"You don't think he can be persuaded?"

"I don't know. I can only try. And I will try. Being here has strengthened my resolve to come and study here. For so long I've thought of Oxford as a dreamland, and now it's real and solid. I can hardly believe it."

"In some ways it is a dreamland," he said.

Ada thought he did not sound entirely happy, and hurried on, not wanting anything to spoil the moment. "The process sounds dreadfully complicated. It seems I can take one of two exams, the Oxford Seniors or the Scholarship. I suppose I shouldn't try for the Scholarship. It's only for the most promising candidates."

"Why on earth shouldn't you try? I got a scholarship. And

you are just as intelligent as I am, so I don't see why you shouldn't."

Ada blushed. "I wouldn't want to risk it. If I failed, it would be all over."

"Sometimes one has to take risks," said Ravi.

Ada, noticing something in his tone, said, "But what about you? Tell me what you have been doing since we last saw each other."

"Studying. That, and attending a lot of meetings."

"Political meetings?"

"Yes. A chapter of the INC meets in London." He glanced at her. "I know you don't approve—"

"I was frightened for you," she broke in. "Such awful things are said about the hot faction. I don't want you to come to harm."

He placed a hand comfortingly on her arm.

She stopped walking and looked up at him pleadingly. "Please, Ravi. Are you sure you are doing the right thing, getting mixed up in this business of Indian independence? Can't you be happy as you are?"

"Can you?" he asked.

She dropped her eyes. She knew he was comparing her own desire for independence with his own, and it hurt to acknowledge he was right. She reached into her reticule and drew out a folded magazine. "My article came out," she said, holding the copy of *The Spectator* out to him. "My first published work, and the first work I've been paid for."

"Ada! Congratulations!" He smiled proudly as he skimmed through the article.

"What I mean to say is . . ." She hesitated. "It was the earnings from that publication that paid for my train ticket to come here. And somehow I feel I've earned it, the right to be here—now, with you—more than if I were squirreling away money from my dress allowance. So I do understand. Yes. I understand how you need independence."

He looked down at her, his eyes soft. "I want to kiss you very much now," he said gently.

She blushed. They were in public. Students in their gowns strolled past on the bridges; tramcars and motorcars rattled by.

"We'd better not," she said quietly.

They walked on together, a new sense of closeness between them.

He cleared his throat. "Maybe this is a good moment to tell you something I have discovered. Well—something I set out to find out. I knew it mattered to you."

"What is that?"

"Your father. I know—forgive me, but it is impossible not to know—that his reputation was badly tainted by his actions in India. I asked around to find out the truth of the matter."

She clenched the handle of her parasol tightly. "Go on."

"It's not what you think. He refused to conceal the deaths of Indians in British custody, men who had protested the Partition of Bengal. Certain people did not like that, and forced his hand. Smeared his good name to protect their own foul ones. He *is* a just man, Ada. You should be proud of him."

Ada smiled. "I am," she said. Her heart swelled. At last she could hold her head up again. Her father wasn't a coward, wasn't a traitor, wasn't any of the things they had called him.

"I was too harsh in what I said at dinner. Your father believes in something greater than himself. He believes in the British Empire, in everything good about that. And I—I believe in India." He hesitated, then went on. "I think we all have to believe in something greater than ourselves. Something as distant and magnificent as the stars."

They had reached the street on which Emily's rooms were. Ada paused, her heart heavy at the thought of parting from Ravi. It was too soon; they had so much more to speak about.

She turned to him to ask when they might see each other again, and was aware as she did so of a growing, roaring noise in the air. It seemed to come from all around her, to sweep her up like a gigantic wave or a hand. It trembled in the old stones of Oxford, it shivered the spring leaves on the trees. Confused, she stepped back and looked around. Others in the street were doing the same, some looking excited, others frightened. The noise was so loud now that she could barely hear herself think. She looked up—and above her, in the gap of blue sky between the buildings, came something as huge and bright and terrible and smoky as a dragon. She gasped.

"An aeroplane!" she heard Ravi exclaim through the shuddering roar of its engine.

She looked up, following his gaze. He was right. She had only heard of such things, never seen them. Her mouth opened in awe. Sunlight glinted from the aeroplane's fuselage, and she thought she glimpsed the pilot looking down, tiny and goggled as an insect. The pigeons took flight in panic from the stone ledges of the ancient buildings. People called to each other in excitement, rushing out of houses and cafés to point up as it flew on.

"An aeroplane!" she echoed, her fear giving way to excitement. Looking upward and turning to follow it, she felt dizzy, exhilarated, and frightened too.

"But how can it fly? It must be heavier than air—" She

tailed off. It didn't matter how it was happening: it *was* happening, right before her eyes. The impossible was possible.

"It's the future," Ravi murmured. His eyes shone. "I told you, didn't I, Ada? Everything is possible. We only have to aim high enough."

She looked at him, her eyes shining. But as she did so, she saw something that made her heart sink faster than an aeroplane crashing into the ground. Parked opposite them was her father's motorcar.

Ada ran, breathless, up the stairs to Emily's rooms. Her heart beat out an agonized tattoo. Her father couldn't have seen her with Ravi. *Please, no.*

She opened the door, ready to face the worst. Her father rose from an armchair, a thunderous scowl on his face. Emily stood with her back to the window. Her face was streaked with tears.

"So there you are," said her father ominously.

Ada had no words. She looked at Emily, but Emily just shook her head despairingly.

"Please do not distress me by lying. Charlotte told me where you were going and why."

Charlotte? Ada was shocked. How could Charlotte have found out?

"I am sick at heart to think that you set out to deliberately deceive me—to see Miss Gorman behind my back."

He could not possibly have seen her with Ravi, she realized, or he would have spoken of that at once. Horrible as the situation was, she was relieved. Her real secret was safe. It gave her courage to speak.

"Papa—I'm sorry. But I *want* to go to Oxford. I—"

"We'll speak of this in the car. Good morning, Lady Emily." Her father's voice was icy. Ada gave a last despairing glance back to Emily as she was pushed out of the room. Emily mouthed, *I am so sorry.* That was the last Ada saw before her father slammed the door shut behind her.

He marched her down the stairs in silence and pointed to the motorcar. Miserably, Ada got in. He followed her.

"Back to London, James," he commanded the chauffeur.

As the car pulled away, Ada looked through the window, hoping for a last glimpse of Ravi, but he was nowhere to be seen.

"I cannot understand your behavior!" her father burst out. "First the incident with Rose and now this? I would never have thought it of you—Georgiana, perhaps, but not you! Ada, I am ashamed."

"Well, I'm not!" Ada found herself retorting. Part of her was horrified at herself, but she knew she could not stay silent. She was in enough trouble as it was—and it would be dishonest to betray her own principles. "I am doing what I believe in, Father. It's only what you did in India."

Her father pressed a hand to his forehead as if he were in pain. "Yes, and my reputation suffered untold harm as a result—as will yours if this gets out. Do you not understand that your only hope is to make a decent marriage? And you are destroying your chances before you are even formally out."

"Why is my only hope marriage?" Ada protested. "Papa, some women go to university and practice as doctors and solicitors. Some are journalists. Some are—"

"And some are washerwomen and some scrub floors, but *you* are an Averley!" her father snapped back. "Your employment is to find a good husband this season."

"I don't care for the season! I don't want to spend three years dancing meaningless dances with mindless men. I want to be independent, I want to earn my own money. If I go to university, I can—"

"Stuff and nonsense. You have no idea how difficult the life of a working woman would be."

Ada bit her lip, hurt by the scorn in his voice. He softened his tone, seeing her face.

"I don't wish you to be unhappy, far from it. But you are not Lady Emily Maddox, who has an independent fortune and an indulgent brother." He paused, then went on. "The truth is, William has been profligate. More than profligate. If I had not married Fiona, the estate would now be bankrupt. He has been running an illegal gambling den from the Marquess of Carlton's house in Grosvenor Square. He has lost hundreds of thousands."

Ada stared at him in wordless shock.

"Yes. You see now why it is so essential that you marry well? You talk of independence. How much independence do you think you will have as an old maid, dependent on William for every penny? How much do you think Georgiana will have?"

In a gesture of frustration and anger, he slapped his glove against the window. Looking out, he added, "And if you do not marry well, Somerton could be lost to the creditors. Do you want people to say that was your fault? The loss of an estate that has been in the family for over five hundred years?"

There were tears in his eyes, Ada was shocked to see. She could think of no reply. The world, that had seemed full of limitless possibilities a moment before, now seemed to have shrunk to a prison of glass and steel. And yet Ravi's words came back to her: *We all have to believe in something greater than ourselves*. Those words gave her strength, and she knew that she would never give up her dream of independence. Somehow, despite all the obstacles, she would find a way.

Chapter Thirty-One

"Georgiana," said Michael, as he looked around the door of the music room, "may I talk to you?"

Georgiana, who was looking through some sheet music, jumped and the papers slid to the floor.

"Why, of course!" she said eagerly. She glanced toward the windowsill, where the roses he had given her stood in a vase, lovingly, if not very artistically, arranged by herself. "And thank you again for the flowers—they've lasted so well."

Michael gave them a cursory glance. "So they have."

He led the way from the music room down the stairs. Georgiana as good as skipped along behind him, with a quick glance in the mirror to check that her hair was becomingly arranged.

"So what is all this mystery about?" she asked as she followed him out of the side door and into the gardens.

"You'll see." He sounded awkward, and her curiosity deepened. He was leading her into the maze—no, into the rose garden. How romantic! She trembled with anticipation.

Once they were deep within the rose garden, he stopped and turned to her abruptly. He looked self-conscious. "Georgiana, I have something to tell you." He was blushing.

Georgiana's heart skipped a beat. Surely, surely, this was it. He had led her into a rose garden, after all. He had given her a bunch of roses. And now he was shuffling from foot to foot and clearing his throat. Nothing could look more like love.

"I wonder if you can guess what it is," he went on.

"Is it—is it about love?" she managed.

His blush deepened. "Well, yes. As a matter of fact, it is. How did you guess?" He shrugged. "I suppose it was obvious from my behavior the other day."

Georgiana almost swooned.

"I want to ask you something," he went on. "I hope you'll say yes."

This was moving too fast even for Georgiana. *Am I too young to get married?* shot through her head. Michael was so very handsome—and yet she had been looking forward to her first season so much. Besides, what about Ada? It would look bad for the younger sister to marry before the older.

"I—I don't think I can," she blurted. "Not yet, at least. I don't think it would be fair to Ada."

"Ada?" he stared at her in surprise. "What does she have to do with Priya?"

Georgiana stared at him with her mouth open. The world, which before had been spinning deliciously, ground to an abrupt halt. "P—Priya?" she managed. "You love Priya?"

"She's the most beautiful, most elegant, most ladylike—" A dreamy expression had come over his face, one she had never seen before.

"O-o-o-oh . . ." Georgiana tried desperately to hide her disappointment. "So the roses—"

"Yes, I meant to give them to her, but like a fool I ruined the moment. That's what I wanted to ask you, you see. Every time I come near her I can't think of a word to say. So I thought maybe you—" He looked at her pleadingly. "I mean, you're a girl, aren't you? You know what to say to girls. If you could just let her know how I feel, maybe find out how she feels—"

Georgiana took a deep breath. Her insides felt like a sand castle that had just been hit by the biggest wave on the beach. But she could not let him see that. It was not his fault that she had been mistaken. And besides, she had Averley pride.

One thing stood out clearly to her. "Michael—she's the nursemaid," she said as gently as she could.

"So? She's beautiful!"

"I know, but . . ." She searched for words. Being the calm counselor of reason did not come easily to her, but she sensed that she had to warn him. "Michael, you'd never be allowed to be together, don't you see?"

He kicked angrily at the gravel. "I didn't think *you* would be so snobbish about it—"

"I'm not being snobbish. I'm being practical. Can you imagine what your mother would say?" From the expression on his face, she gathered that he could. "Is it really fair to Priya, to put her under such pressure?"

Michael hung his head. "Maybe not," he muttered. "But then what am I to do?"

"Wait," said Georgiana instantly. "I don't think you should give up loving her, but I think you should wait a while before speaking to her. I think it would be easier for both of you."

The look of unhappiness on Michael's face caught her heart. She came close to him and put a hand gently on his arm.

"Don't despair, Michael. I promise that if you still feel like this in a year's time, I'll do everything I can to help you be together. But it's got to be above board, don't you see? For everyone's sake."

The lamplight flickered in the darkness of the servants' passage. It threw eerie shadows across Martha's face as she glanced behind her.

"Hurry up, Tobias. I don't like this."

"Getting cold feet?" Tobias grunted. He was working away at the door of the housekeeper's parlor with a small metal instrument.

"You know what'll happen if we're caught." Martha shivered.

"Don't fuss. I've used this trick a thousand times. They won't know what's happened unless we're clumsy." The lock clicked open as he spoke. "See?"

They hurried into the parlor. Martha exclaimed as she bumped into something, but it was only the rocking chair. The room was silent and dark; Mrs. Cliffe had retired hours ago.

"Just look for Rose's letter. Miss Ward will pay us well for it," Tobias said. He scowled. "I'll never forgive that nursemaid for putting me to all this trouble."

Martha hurried to the secretary desk in the corner. Setting the lamp on it, she opened the desk and began looking through the various papers that were filed neatly away.

"Look out, you idiot, don't put them out of order or she'll guess."

"Here, you sort through this lot." Martha handed him a wedge of papers tied with ribbon.

"These are no good," said Tobias, after a moment. "They're just old bills—"

He stopped speaking abruptly. Martha, still looking for

Rose's letter, did not notice. Tobias read on, his sly face intent. After several minutes, Martha noticed the silence and looked up.

"This ain't a library," she began.

"Shut it," Tobias interrupted. A grin spread slowly across his face.

"What's up? You found it?" Martha snatched the paper from his hand. She frowned. "This is just old payments to Mrs. Cliffe from Lord Westlake."

"Nothing strike you as strange about it?"

"No. He pays her wages, so what?"

"Look at the dates, Martha." Tobias pointed. "Mrs. Cliffe wasn't employed here then. I was here and I know, she only came in 1904. And I do remember she knew the house very well, and she said she'd been a housemaid here before she left to get married."

Martha shook her head. "You've lost me."

"Lord Westlake was paying money to a housemaid who left his employ years ago. And who came back as housekeeper with a daughter? A daughter who thinks herself a cut above the rest of us and gives herself airs? Come on, Martha. You're not *that* innocent."

Martha's mouth fell open. "Now you say that," she said slowly, "I do remember that he came down to see her the night he got back from India. I wondered at the time what they were up to—he was in her parlor at midnight."

"So it's still going on." Tobias grinned. "Forget Rose's letter. If Stella Ward doesn't pay for *this* information, I'm a Dutchman."

Chapter Thirty-Two

The trains whistled and hooted, filling the air with steam. Porters hurried here and there, pushing trolleys full of trunks. Ada, on the platform, watched the crowds of people moving about; rich and poor, young and old. Ada felt as if she were looking for someone, but she did not know who she expected to see. Her father had insisted they leave London as soon as possible. She had barely had time to scribble a note to Ravi. Even if he had received it, he would have lectures to attend—

And there he was. The clouds of steam cleared and blew away, revealing him standing by the ticket offices, looking small and isolated. He was looking around him. Ada's heart gave a leap. She turned to Rose, who was guarding her trunks.

"Rose . . ." She gestured toward him with a glance. Rose's expression showed she had seen him. "I have to speak to him. Will you make some excuse for me to Charlotte and Fiona?" They were farther up the platform, harassing a guard about the time the train was due to leave.

"Of course, my lady, but be careful," Rose answered. "This is a very public place."

Ada nodded. She did not need to be told of the danger, not since the shock of meeting her father at Oxford. As she walked back toward the booking offices, she glanced around.

No one seemed to be paying attention to her. She caught Ravi's eye, and saw the flash of recognition. Instead of stopping to talk to him, she walked straight past, hoping he would know to follow.

Not daring to look behind her, she moved through the crowd toward the dark and dusty end of the station, where the lost luggage office was. A chocolate vending machine and a trolley full of stacked trunks made a corner of shadows. She paused at the vending machine as if she were contemplating buying a Fry's chocolate bar, and sensed him walk up behind her. He stood very close but did not touch her.

"You got my letter," she said quietly, her finger tracing the prices on the machine.

"I have to talk to you." The urgency in his voice startled her, and she half turned before remembering where she was.

"Is something wrong?"

"Not—exactly." He hesitated. "Step behind those trunks when I tell you the coast is clear."

She nodded. A few moments later, during which time she felt she had memorized the price of every chocolate bar in the machine, he said, "Now."

Ada stepped to the side, around the corner of the machine, and found herself in the shadow of the trunks on one side. A moment later, Ravi followed her.

"I'm so glad to see you," she began, her voice trembling because she could see from his face that all was not well.

He took her hand and pressed it. "I—I don't know how to begin."

His voice was so serious that she was frightened. "What is it? Has something happened?"

"Yes—but nothing bad."

"That's a relief." She smiled.

He did not answer the smile. "You know I have been communicating with the Indian National Congress."

Ada blinked. The rush of relief was quickly replaced with fear. "Have you done something wrong?"

"On the contrary, it seems I have impressed some very important men here in Britain, sympathizers with our cause. They have asked me to act as a bridge between them and the Congress in India."

Ada gazed at him, eyes wide. "That's . . . wonderful," she said hesitantly. Was it? Her father, she knew, would consider it verging on treason.

"It is. It is work that I want to do, that I know I can do well, and that I would respect myself for doing." He frowned as he spoke.

"So . . ."

"The post is in Bombay."

There was a long silence.

"I see," said Ada faintly. Bombay! It was so far away. "But—won't you finish at Oxford first?"

He shook his head. "It is a dreamland, I see that now. For you, it's the right place to be. But I must return to India. I feel it is my duty to do so."

He was speaking again, and through the roaring in her ears she made out the rest of his words.

". . . I wanted to say something to you at Oxford, but I could not find the words to express it. I have to try, though, so that you understand." He took her hand. "I believe in India, and the other thing I believe in, Ada—is you."

She looked at him in confusion.

"Ever since I met you on the *Moldavia*, and saw how determined you were to go to Oxford, to break out of the crystal prison that holds you trapped in society, I have admired you so much. You have the power to achieve anything you want to. I don't want to take that away from you. I don't want to be responsible for clipping your wings before you have even taken flight."

"I don't understand," she said. "How would you do that?"

"By giving in to my dearest wish—and asking you to marry me."

Ada's breath hitched. The noisy train station suddenly seemed to fall silent as she stepped closer to Ravi, trembling. He hurried on.

"I have thought about it since I received news of this post. I dreamed that we could be married, that we could go to India together, that we would be poor but happy. And then I saw how selfish I was being."

"But I will marry you," she blurted out, realizing that this was what she had wanted all along. She had never wanted anything more in her life "I will. How can you doubt it?"

"I don't doubt it. But I will not ask you."

She pulled her hands from his grasp. "I don't understand what you're saying."

"I am saying that as much as I want us to be together, I know it is impossible. I have come to say good-bye."

"But I love you," she exclaimed.

"And I love you. Very much. Too much to shackle you to a marriage you will without doubt regret, to steal your chance of independence from you."

"Ravi, what nonsense." She was half laughing and half crying. "You have given me every kind of freedom. I have never felt as free as I have with you. You have made me determined to go to Oxford, and—"

"And how would you attend Oxford if you were in India, the wife of a low-paid clerk working for an organization that the British government considers bordering on treasonous?"

Ada opened her mouth, then closed it again. The shock must have showed on her face, because he put his arms around her and hugged her fiercely. She pressed her face into his chest, every ounce of her longing to be held like this forever.

"Ada, you will thank me for this. Not next year, perhaps, nor the year after that, but in ten years, when you have achieved all your dreams and are happy, you will know that I did the right thing."

"You can't leave me this way," she choked out, her voice muffled by his white linen shirt.

"I have to. I have to, for your sake."

Nothing in her life had prepared Ada for this terrible sense of loss. How could it have come to this? Even as Ravi spoke, she was thinking, *Something will happen. Some thunderclap, some miracle will happen to change things.*

But they remained standing where they were. The station clock struck twelve.

"The train—" Ada exclaimed. The time had gone so quickly.

Ravi looked pale. He caught her in his arms and kissed her. Ada let herself melt into the kiss, her head swimming as he ran his hands through her hair then wrapped a protective arm around her waist, tugging her closer still. Through her head ran the thoughts, *This can't be the last time. This can't be. It's impossible.*

A beam of light flashed across her face, and instinctively they let go of each other. A porter was pulling the trolley away. Ravi backed into the shadows. The porter started as he saw Ada.

"Beg pardon, miss. Didn't see you there. Hope I didn't catch your dress?"

She managed to say, "No—no, I'm perfectly all right, thank you."

"You shouldn't stand there, really, miss—it's dangerous, could get crushed." The porter went on, but Ada hardly heard him.

Charlotte was standing at the end of the platform, looking directly at Ada. The expression on her face was unreadable. Ada's heart almost stopped. Had she seen them kiss?

Slowly, reluctantly, she walked over to Charlotte. If she had seen, her reputation—her future—any chance of going to Oxford—were entirely in Charlotte's power.

"So there you are," Charlotte greeted her.

Ada did not reply. Was there some meaning behind that? Charlotte's face was completely closed, but there was a spark in her eye—at least Ada thought there was.

"Do come along. The train is about to depart and the guard is getting most impatient with us." Charlotte turned and marched off up the platform. Ada followed. She could see Fiona's hat as she leaned from the window to beckon to them, and the guard waved peevishly.

She hurried onto the train, and the whistle blew almost at once. At least she had an excuse for her breathlessness and red face. Fiona was alone in the first-class carriage; Rose and Stella had already been exiled to the second-class one.

"Really, Ada, you do dawdle," said Fiona with some annoyance.

"I'm sorry," Ada murmured as she took her seat.

"I should think so," Charlotte said, and Ada looked up sharply. Charlotte met her eyes for a fraction of a second,

242

then turned to the window. The train began chuffing out of the station, the engines churning and the steam drifting back past the window in veils. Ada gazed through them, desperate for a last sight of Ravi. But hard as she looked, he was nowhere to be found. The train picked up speed, and then she could see nothing, not even the smoke, for the tears in her eyes.

CHAPTER NINE

ACT THREE

SOMERTON

Chapter Thirty-Three

Rose stood in her mother's parlor, nervously twisting her fingers together as she waited for her mother to come in. She had known from the moment she stepped down from the pony trap that everyone at Somerton knew about her disgrace. It was in the sympathetic way that James's eyes followed her as she walked into the house; in Priya's startled, pitying look; in Cook's silence and Martha's malicious giggle. It was Stella's doing, she was sure of it. And now the only person she had yet to face—the only person she was truly afraid of facing—was her mother.

The clock ticked steadily on, like water dripping away at stone. She had hardly noticed it before, but now it nagged at her. She found herself wishing there was a way to stop it—and then the door opened and her mother came in.

She looked exhausted. Deep shadows were under her eyes, and her face had lost its color. They gazed at each other silently. Then Rose gave a sob and rushed into her mother's arms.

She felt her mother's strong arms go around her and her rough hands stroking her hair. Rose sobbed on her shoulder. "Mother . . . Mother, I'm so sorry."

"Hush, hush." Her mother guided her to a chair and sat

her down. She stood in front of her. Rose could not meet her eyes.

"Rose, what came over you?" The sorrow in her voice was worse than anger. "How could you do such a thing? Did you not imagine the consequences?"

Rose dried her eyes. She had to set matters straight. "I was foolish but I wasn't wicked, I promise you. I know it was wrong of me to go to the concert. I know I was getting above my station. But I never enticed Mr. Templeton to kiss me. That I would never do."

Her mother looked at her steadily, and then drew out an envelope from her pocket. Rose looked at it for a moment before realizing what it was. It was Ravi's last reply to Miss Ada, directed to her. It must have missed her and arrived at Somerton in her absence. She turned pale.

"I see by your expression that you know something about this." Her mother's voice trembled.

"Have you opened it?"

"No. I wanted to give you the chance to explain." She went on. "I want to believe you did not lead Mr. Templeton on. But then there is this: Rose, can you swear to me this letter is not from a man?"

There was silence. Rose could not reply. She could not bring herself to swear that it was not from a man when she knew very well it was.

"I thought as much. Oh, Rose!" Her mother's voice broke, pained. "After all I have said to you about the importance of keeping a perfect reputation. If you only knew—" She broke off, and said instead, "Open it now, please. In front of me."

Rose did not take the letter.

"I—I can't." If she let her mother know what was in it, Lady Ada's secret would be out. How could she do that to her when she knew how it could destroy her life? Perhaps her mother would not tell, but Rose could not betray Lady Ada like that.

"You understand that if you refuse, I have to think the very worst of you." Her mother's voice was cold. Rose hung her head.

Her mother flung the letter down on the table and paced back and forth.

"I cannot stay here when you have been dismissed. But what are we to do? Where are we to go? Everyone in the village will know your shame, Miss Ward will see to that. I don't think you understand the trouble you have plunged us into."

"I do, Mother." Rose dashed away tears. "But I promise you, I will work at any honest job to support you. I can scrub floors, I can work in a factory or a field. I won't let us starve."

Her mother was hardly listening. "Perhaps it was my fault." She gazed into the mirror above the fireplace. "Perhaps I should have told you the truth."

Rose frowned. "What do you mean, Mother?"

Her mother turned quickly. "Rose, I—your father—" But before she could go on, there was a sharp rap at the door, and without waiting for an answer, Stella Ward walked in. After the first moment's astonishment, Mrs. Cliffe drew herself up. "Ward, how dare you burst in here?"

Rose was looking at Stella's face. The look of sheer triumph on it made her feel sick.

"You're wanted in the drawing room, Cliffe." Stella's grin widened. "And you too, Rose."

Rose was shocked by the casual insolence with which she spoke.

"Are you drunk?" her mother demanded.

"No need for your cheek. You should get up there at once. Her ladyship's waiting."

She flounced out, head high. Rose looked at her mother in astonishment and fear.

"What can she be after?" Mrs. Cliffe murmured. She hurried after Stella, and Rose followed.

As Ada left the breakfast room, Cooper came up to her. Ada was startled to see that he looked worried.

"I beg your pardon, miss. But Lord Fintan is here."

"Lord Fintan?" Ada was surprised but pleased. "Well . . . show him into the library, Cooper, and let my father know. You surely know what to do with a gentleman visitor better than I do!" She laughed, but her laughter died away as she saw his concern deepen.

"I'm afraid, miss, that your father is . . . engaged, in the drawing room, with Lady Westlake and Miss Templeton. There is no one else to receive his lordship."

"Is everything quite all right, Cooper?" Ada asked.

"I would not venture to say, my lady," Cooper said mournfully. "Shall I show his lordship into the library?"

"Y–yes. Please do, and I will be there presently." Ada glanced into the mirror that hung in the hallway, and unconsciously smoothed her hair. Lord Fintan here at this time of the morning, and her father too busy to see him? It seemed extraordinary. But it was against the rules of hospitality to keep a guest waiting. She hurried to the library.

She found Lord Fintan standing in the light that came

through the great arched windows, hands behind his back. On the desk beside him were a couple of books, half open.

"Lord Fintan! What a pleasant surprise." She came forward, and he turned, smiling, to greet her.

"I'm so terribly sorry that my father isn't available at once. Perhaps you can be persuaded to make do with me for a time?"

"I need no persuasion," he said, bowing over her hand. "Really, it was you I came to see."

Ada heard him, but she paid little attention. Her thoughts were on her father in the drawing room. What on earth could he busy with? A sense of foreboding settled over her heart. There was one explanation, of course. If Charlotte truly had seen that kiss, and if she had told him . . .

"Shall we walk in the gardens?" Lord Fintan suggested. "It is such a fine morning."

"With pleasure," Ada managed, though at the thought of what might be happening in the drawing room, she had turned dizzy.

Lord Fintan unfastened the French windows and they stepped out onto the terrace. She took a deep breath of the fresh air and felt better. The sun glinted on the lake, and the horizon of rolling hills made her relax at once.

They strolled down toward the ha-ha. Ada kept up with Lord Fintan's conversation mechanically. Had Charlotte seen anything? And if she had, would she tell?

". . . must have wondered why I came here to see you."

Ada became aware that Lord Fintan was looking into her face with a particularly serious expression.

"I—" She remembered, then, that Charlotte saw her as a rival for Lord Fintan's affections. Could Charlotte have told him about the kiss? She flushed red and could not look him in the eye.

251

"I see you have some suspicion," Lord Fintan went on.

Ada could not manage a single word in answer.

"I will take your evident confusion as a hopeful sign," he went on, more gently. "With all your strength of mind, your nobility of soul, you have never done anything that could cause a true lady to blush. That is why I feel so strongly that I am doing the right thing. Ada, will you marry me?"

Ada gaped at him. She realized that her expression was the opposite of a lady's, and hastily closed her mouth.

"But—but what about Charlotte?" she found herself saying. At once, she wished she could sink through the ground.

Lord Fintan's expression changed just a fraction. "Ah. I understand." He nodded. "No, no"—he waved a hand as she began stumblingly to apologize—"there is no need to say anything. I certainly do owe you an explanation. You are rightly sensitive." He cleared his throat, looking a little embarrassed. "I hardly like to say this, as of course she is your relative now, but Miss Templeton and I—well, our connection at Gravelley Park was not of the kind likely to lead to marriage. I will say no more."

Ada nodded, shocked and astonished. So Charlotte had behaved . . . indiscreetly with Lord Fintan. She would never have thought it of such a calculating person. Perhaps she had misjudged Charlotte. Perhaps Charlotte felt about Lord Fintan the way she felt about Ravi.

"I understand you may feel some repulsion at the idea of my connection with your stepsister." Lord Fintan kicked at a clod of grass with his shoe. Ada realized, to her amazement, that he was embarrassed. "I want you to know that I never meant for her to misunderstand my intentions."

Poor Charlotte, thought Ada.

She hesitated. Lord Fintan looked up the slope toward

the house. "Isn't that your sister?" he said in quite a different tone of voice. "Should she run like that in her state of health?"

Ada whirled around. Georgiana was running down the slope toward them—really running, with no thought for her dress or the thin indoor shoes, which slipped on the dewy grass. As Georgiana reached them, Ada saw that her face was streaked with tears. Her breath came in great rasping gasps.

"Georgie! What is it?" Ada ran to meet her. Georgiana flung herself into her arms, just as she had done when she was a little girl and she had scraped her knee or fallen in the mud.

"You must come at once—please come at once," she sobbed. Her legs seemed about to give way.

Ada slipped one arm under her. Lord Fintan instantly took her other arm, and together they supported her.

"The drawing room—oh, it's too terrible—"

"But what has happened?" Ada's thoughts jumped to her father. Perhaps he had been taken ill. Terror caught her and gave her new energy. Together, she and Lord Fintan, not needing to exchange a word, helped Georgiana up to the house. Georgiana collapsed on a chair and Ada knelt before her, trying to calm her with words, while Lord Fintan rang the bell vigorously.

"I must go—"Ada was convinced that her father had been taken seriously ill or was dying. She jumped up as a startled housemaid came in. "Please see that Lady Georgiana is taken care of, and call the doctor!"

"Yes miss!" The housemaid took Ada's place and Ada went to the door. Lord Fintan followed.

"Can I help? I don't wish to intrude but—"

"Yes, yes, please come!" Ada clutched his sleeve. If her father were sick or dying, she did not know if she could be of use. Lord Fintan would help; he was the kind of man to take charge.

They ran to the drawing room, and Ada burst through the door. The first person she saw was Rose. She stood in the center of the room, one arm around her mother. Her face was white. Mrs. Cliffe was sobbing into her hands. Her father sat on the sofa, his head in his hands as well. In front of Mrs. Cliffe stood Fiona, her face twisted with rage. She was shouting, for reasons Ada did not understand, at Mrs. Cliffe.

". . . shall leave this house this instant!"

Ada ran to her father. "Papa, dear, what's happened? Are you unwell? Georgiana came to find me—"

Her father groaned, and as he raised his head Ada was shocked to see his face was wet with tears. "Calm yourself, Ada. I'm well. I should shoot myself, no doubt, but I'm in the best of health," he answered bitterly.

Ada shook her head in confusion. "Shoot yourself? Papa, what do you mean? Don't say anything so terrible!"

"There, there. I'm sorry to have frightened you." Her father's voice softened and he placed a hand on her shoulder.

"Very touching indeed!" exclaimed a bitter, furious voice. Ada looked up, startled. She had not seen Charlotte, but now she did, and saw—to her shock—that Stella was also standing by the door. Something about the self-satisfied grin on the lady's maid's face made her blood boil. She jumped to her feet.

"Will someone kindly explain what is going on here?" she demanded, looking around the room.

Fiona turned on her. "I think your father is the one who owes us all an explanation," she said coldly.

Ada turned to her father in shock. "Papa? What does she mean?"

Her father pinched the bridge of his nose and then stood up, slowly, as if every muscle ached. For the first time, Ada thought of him as an old man. The wrinkles on his face seemed to have deepened.

"Fiona is correct," he said in a low voice. "I do owe you an explanation. All of you. But I want to correct one impression. Our relationship was over when Rosaline left the house."

"As if I could believe that, when Ward tells us that you visited her in her room the very night you arrived back at Somerton! This explains why you were so anxious to defend her brat."

Ada's mouth was open with shock. Behind her, Lord Fintan coughed discreetly. She had forgotten he was there, and turned around in dismay.

"I think that I had better wait in the library," he murmured.

Ada nodded, grateful for his tact. If this scandal—and she was beginning to realize what had happened—was to be heard by anyone outside the family, it was best for it to be Lord Fintan. She knew he was a gentleman and would not spread the story.

"I—I don't think I quite understand," she began faintly.

"Really, Ada, is it so hard to comprehend?" Fiona said fiercely. "Your father has kept a mistress under his roof for more than seventeen years. He has dared to bring me as his bride to a house where this hussy and their illegitimate child were actually in residence. I have associated, unknowingly, with this shameless creature—"

"One moment, please—"Ada put a hand to her head, which was beginning to thud with a headache. "You cannot possibly mean Mrs. Cliffe?"

"But I do," Fiona said. "And she doesn't deserve the title of *Mrs.*"

Ada looked at Mrs. Cliffe in disbelief. The housekeeper was no longer sobbing. She wore a look of complete resignation. She looked so respectable in her black dress, it was impossible to connect her with the words Fiona had used.

"Ada," said her father heavily, "the truth is that Rosaline and I were young, and we had a—a—connection—"

"A very elegant way of describing it," said Fiona scornfully. Lord Westlake winced.

"—that resulted in a child."

Ada looked around the group, her mouth open. Her gaze lit upon Rose. Rose stood, her face pale with shock, silent tears streaking her face.

"*Rose?*" she said, finally understanding. "You mean to tell me, Father, that Rose is your daughter?" The last piece of the puzzle finally fell into place in her mind: "And that Rose . . . is my sister?"

Chapter Thirty-Four

The rest of the day passed like a horrible nightmare. Ada stayed with Georgiana until she had recovered, and then put her to bed with the help of Priya. The nursemaid's eyes were sympathetic, and Ada knew that the truth must be all over the house already. She could hardly bear the shame.

It was not until Georgiana was sleeping soundly that she had time to think of Rose and her mother. She hesitated, not knowing what she should do. Then she made up her mind. She could not face Mrs. Cliffe now, but Rose was another matter. It was not Rose's fault.

She climbed the stairs to Rose's room and tapped at the door. She had never been in her room before, there had never been need, and now she felt strangely like an intruder. She did not know what she was going to say, but she did know that she had to say something. She could not ignore what had just happened.

"Come in," called a faint voice.

Ada pushed the door open. Rose, looking exhausted and still in shock, was placing her clothes into a small, battered trunk that lay on the bed. Beside her stood Annie, her eyes red with weeping.

"Oh my lady, I'm so glad you've come," Annie burst out.

"Please, can't you help Rose? It isn't her fault—whatever Mrs. Cliffe has done, it isn't her fault."

Looking down, Rose said, "Lady Westlake demands it. Either my mother and I leave the house today or she does."

Ada shuddered at the thought of the scandal that would follow if Fiona did leave. Then she pulled herself together. "Annie is right. It isn't your fault," she said gently.

"I can't let my mother go alone, my lady," Rose said stubbornly. "Besides, I have already been dismissed."

Ada fell silent. Rose was right, there was no answer to that. "I simply don't know what to think," Ada began hesitantly. "I suppose it must be true, but it seems so unbelievable, so . . . And how was it discovered after all this time?"

"It was Stella Ward who told Lady Westlake," Annie said scornfully. "Just like her."

Tears were running down Rose's face. "We can't show our faces in the servants' hall now," she whispered. "It's better that we go."

Ada and Annie went forward as one to put their arms around her. Ada couldn't help but wonder how Stella Ward had weaseled this information.

"I didn't know," Rose sobbed. "I had no idea, you must please believe me."

"We do, Rose, of course we do." Ada stroked her hair. She felt terrible. This was all her father's fault, there was no escaping it. Rose was the same age as she, which meant that he had been intimate with Mrs. Cliffe even while he was married to her mother. How could he have done it? She felt tears squeezing between her own eyelids. She summoned up courage.

"Rose, at the least, promise me you will not go far. Stay

in the village. I don't believe my father would think it fair for you both to be thrown out like this."

Cook started when she saw Lady Ada at the door of the kitchen. The house was in such a muddle. She could hardly believe the rumors that were coming down from above stairs. But Martha and Tobias were in unbearably high spirits, and it was true that Mrs. Cliffe and Rose were nowhere to be seen. Cook was shocked to her core. "I couldn't believe it of her," was all she could say, over and over again. If Mrs. Cliffe could fall, then the best of them were doomed.

"My lady!" She struggled to her feet. The day was turning more and more pear-shaped, what with the gentry in the servants' passage.

"Please don't get up, Cook. I just would like to take a tray to my father." Ada looked pale and fragile. It was clear she was taking the news very much to heart.

"Of course, my lady. I never heard a bell, I'm very sorry. I'll get Annie to take one up at once—"

"No, please let me do it." There was real anguish in Lady Ada's voice. Cook looked at her in surprise. "I would just like to—to do something for him myself. You understand?"

Cook nodded. She had had an ailing parent once, and she remembered the comfort that came from bringing her soup and toast. Lady Ada was a kind soul, she thought.

"I do, my lady." She brought out some cold meat and bread. "If you'll wait a moment, I'll make some hot soup—the ranges are still warm—"

"There's no need. Perhaps just one of those apples. Thank you." Lady Ada smiled gratefully at her and took the tray.

Cook watched her go, her heart heavy. It was a terrible thing that had happened to the household, and it was a shame it had rebounded on Lady Ada this way. She had said it from the beginning: Stella had brought trouble.

Chapter Thirty-Five

Ada set the tray on a dresser and tapped at the door of the library. She was trembling inside at the thought of this interview with her father. It would be hard even to look him in the face. She felt so sorry for him, not the least because she knew he was conscious that he had done wrong. But she could not ignore him and abandon him, as the rest of the household seemed to have done. And besides, she had to speak up for Rose and Mrs. Cliffe.

"Come in," came the voice, finally.

Ada went in, carrying the tray before her. Her father was sitting alone at the big reading desk. The reading light was on, but he was not reading—he was staring into the darkness.

"I—I brought you something to eat," she said quietly, setting the tray down.

"Ada." He started. "Thank you."

Ada hesitated. "Mrs. Cliffe and Rose have gone," she said.

"Gone?" He sat forward, sounding shocked. "Where to?"

"I persuaded them to stay in the village, at the Averley Arms. Lady Westlake demanded that they leave the area. But I couldn't think you would be happy to have them driven away completely."

"Good God, no." He sounded miserable. "Ada, I have done

261

the most foolish, terrible thing. I owe everyone in this household the most abject apologies. But I swear to you I had no idea the consequences would be so bad."

Ada bowed her head. She was thinking of her relationship with Ravi.

Her father went on, almost as if he were reading her mind. "Sometimes, feelings are so strong . . . they can override any sense of duty and responsibility."

Ada swallowed. "And love? I mean my mother, Papa."

Her father was silent, then he said in a low, painful voice, "You see, I grew up with Rosaline . . . She and I were friends always, when she was a maid and I was a schoolboy. But I knew that I must marry well, my parents always said so. I had the greatest respect for your mother. The very greatest respect."

"But no love," Ada said quietly.

"No. I am so sorry, Ada."

There was a long silence.

"I have done the most shameful, ungentlemanly thing," her father said, almost to himself. "There is no excuse."

"Don't say that, Papa."

"Oh, I did my best to put it right. I supported Rose throughout her childhood, and as soon as I knew we would be going to India I arranged for them to come back here, where they would be secure. But my life has been a lie."

"It seems incredible," Ada said. That her father had kept this secret all this time, that they had known nothing about it. But she could find no anger against him. She understood, all too well, what it was to be carried away by passion. The only thing now was to make sure that the innocent were protected.

"Papa, you will not let Rose and Mrs. Cliffe be thrown out, will you? It isn't fair. Mrs. Cliffe has been loyal to you, and if you would forgive one of us for an indiscretion, then you should do the same for Rose. She is your daughter too, and you know the fault was mostly mine."

Her father sighed. "Most certainly, they will want for nothing as long as I can provide for them. But returning to Somerton . . . I don't know."

The sun was setting, and the wood pigeons cooed from the chestnut trees around the Averley Arms. Mrs. Cliffe sat in her chair by the window, reading by the last light—or pretending to. She could not slip into her familiar novels as she always had done before.

They had asked questions at the public house. She had not answered, and Rose had made some excuse, but she could see the questions still, in their eyes, hear them in their silences. Sooner or later they would discover the truth. It was almost a relief. She had waited so long for this day, fearing it, that it was almost as if her own death had arrived. It had, in a sense—or at least, the end of her life. Before her stretched the unknown.

There was a gentle tap at the door. "Come in, Rose," she said, knowing it was her daughter.

Rose pushed the door open and came in. One glance at her face made Mrs. Cliffe put down her book. "What is it? What has happened?"

"He's here."

Rose's face was pale, with just spots of color in her cheeks. She had grown thinner over the past few days; she was hardly eating. It wrung Mrs. Cliffe's heart to see her this way. *He.* It could only be one person: Lord Westlake. "Tell him to come up," she said quietly. She stood up, smoothing down her skirts. Her heart was beating fast; it was impossible to know what was in his mind.

Rose disappeared onto the landing. A few moments later, there was a hesitant knock at the door, and Lord Westlake came in.

Mrs. Cliffe faced him with her head held high. It was strange to see him in this homely room, outside the halls of Somerton. He looked awkward and unhappy.

"Rosaline . . ."

"Edward." There seemed no need for pretence anymore.

He looked around. "Are you comfortable here? I was sorry that you left. I did not want you to."

"There was no choice," she said.

He sighed. "I suppose not."

There was a brief silence. Mrs. Cliffe broke it. "You knew this day would come. So did I. It makes it no easier, but let us not pretend that we did not know the consequences of our actions would be bad."

"If I could have prevented this in any way . . ."

"I know. I did my best. I don't know where Stella got her information from, but I can guess." She thought of Martha and Tobias. Yet she did not even have the energy to be angry with them.

"I have been thinking," Lord Westlake went on. "This situation is all my fault."

"Not all."

"Yes it is. All. We were both young, but I should have known better. I should have remembered my duties, the responsibilities of an Earl of Westlake."

She bowed her head.

"I want to do the right thing, Rosaline."

"And what is the right thing?"

"I don't know." He stepped forward, almost pleading. "You have always been my moral compass, though you may not have known it. You understood, better than anyone, that we were mere stewards in charge of Somerton. I have always thought of you as the model of selfless duty. What should I do, Rosaline? How can I make this better?"

"I don't think I can tell you that."

"It isn't right that you should lose your character, your position, because of me."

"I do not care about myself. I knew at the time that what I was doing was wrong. But Rose—"

Lord Westlake looked at her, a question in his eyes.

"She deserves better than this, and you know it, Edward," Mrs. Cliffe said. "You must do right by her."

"I will. I promise you that. I have seen what she is like, and I—I care about her. So do my daughters."

Mrs. Cliffe nodded. "That is all I will ever ask of you."

Chapter Thirty-Six

"Somerton!" exclaimed Sebastian as he drove round the corner of the lane and, through a dip in the hedgerows, saw the familiar honey-colored stone of Somerton Court rising before him. "At last."

Oliver did not reply. Sebastian cast him an anxious glance. He had done everything he could to make up for his behavior now that the fear of exposure was lifted from him. But Oliver remained distant and cold.

He made up his mind. They had to have it out, there and then.

He pulled the motorcar over into the lee of the hedges. As the engine sputtered to a halt, he looked over at Oliver. They were quite alone, only the distant bleating of spring lambs and the close birdsong in the hedges disturbed them.

Oliver stared straight ahead, his face expressionless as only a professional valet's could be. Sebastian sighed. "I know you are angry with me, and I'm sorry," he began. "I was thoughtless and unkind, but I—I didn't mean to be. There were reasons. I have had a lot on my mind."

"Really, sir?" Oliver did not look at him. "Can you tell me what?"

Sebastian hesitated. He was ashamed of his relationship with Simon. He was ashamed he had allowed himself to be fooled, and more, to be seduced by someone so vulgar. It had been a passionate but brief affair, for he had soon realized that they had nothing in common. He did not want Oliver to think him a fool, and he did not want him to think that he made a habit of his valets.

"I can't," he said, aware of a strange hot sensation in his face. To his shock and almost amusement, he was blushing. Surely that had not happened since he was sixteen. "But please believe me. Things will be different from now on."

"Very different, if the picture in *The Illustrated* is anything to go by," said Oliver dryly.

Sebastian wilted inside. Of course. Of course Oliver would have seen the wretched picture. It was the talk of Oxford, why had he imagined his valet would be the only person not to have seen it?

"There was a reason for that," he said. "I had to kiss that girl."

"But you can't explain why."

"I—well—no."

Oliver nodded, and looked at him for the first time. There was something steely in his blue eyes. Sebastian found himself not just abashed but a little frightened. He began to realize that Oliver was strong inside, stronger than he was, perhaps.

"You don't have to apologize, sir. We all make mistakes."

Sebastian sighed in relief, but Oliver went on.

"I understand that gentlemen sometimes like to . . . experiment with their valets, before realizing that is not their nature. But I am not accustomed to being treated as an experiment." A muscle jumped in his jaw, the only sign of the intensity of his anger. "In the circumstances, I feel it would be inappropriate to continue in your service."

267

Sebastian stared at him for a moment before realizing what he meant.

"Oliver, no! You can't leave me!" It tore out of him before he could stop it.

"I will stay until you are suited with another valet, of course, sir." Oliver looked away. The conversation was clearly closed.

"Please think this over," Sebastian begged.

"Thank you sir, but my mind is quite made up. I regret that I can have no further conversation on this topic."

Sebastian bit his lip. How had it come to this?

Ada walked across the lawn, her parasol held loosely in her hand. She had hoped to distract herself, but it had not worked. She could think of nothing but Rose and Mrs. Cliffe, and the cloud of sadness and shame that once again hung over the house. Her father's name had just been cleared in her mind, but she didn't see a way to get around these new accusations. He had gone out walking very early and was not yet back. Fiona had not appeared in the dining room since the scene the other day, nor had Charlotte. Georgiana seemed to be taking it particularly badly, poor thing. This morning at breakfast Ada had noticed that she was tired and her eyes were red with weeping. Even Michael was subdued. Not sulky, but more serious than she had ever known him before.

"May I speak to you?"

Ada started and looked up. Lord Fintan was coming toward her. She managed a smile, though her heart sank. With everything that had happened, she had almost forgotten about his proposal.

"Of course." She smiled politely. He looked at her with serious, genuine concern.

"I feel, that to be perfectly discreet, I should have left at once. But I did not like to leave you here, knowing how you must feel."

Ada's smile was warmer this time. Whatever her own feelings toward him, he did care for her. Of that she was sure.

"You're very kind."

"I also did not wish to leave abruptly and leave you to fear I would spread the story."

"I never feared that," Ada said with complete honesty. "I know you are too much of a gentleman."

"I hoped you would say that." He hesitated. "I want you to know that I do not regret my words the other day."

"Oh . . ." Ada felt she should show more enthusiasm. It seemed almost unreasonable of her not to. Lord Fintan was handsome, a gentleman, and he believed in women's education just as she did. In every way, he was a perfect husband, and she knew that many men would have run in horror at the breath of scandal that had touched their household. But he had stayed.

And yet he was not Ravi.

"I feel that Lady Westlake is perhaps making more of this than need be," he went on. "I understand the outrage to her feelings, of course. But I do not think it should come between her and her husband."

"I can understand it must be painful for her," Ada said, thinking of her own mother. Had she known, or guessed, that her husband did not love her?

"Certainly. But it seems the connection was over long before he wed Fiona—"

"You believe that then?" She was so relieved that she interrupted him.

"Yes, I do. I think your father acted unwisely in the eyes of the world in choosing such an indiscreet way to support Mrs. Cliffe and their child, but I understand why he did it. Old affections are not so easily put aside."

"No," said Ada, thinking of Ravi.

"And a gentleman has certain moral responsibilities, even if the law does not acknowledge them."

"I am glad you see it that way." She looked at him in relief, wishing that they could continue their friendship without the awkward question of marriage coming between them.

"The truth is that I understand your father's actions," he said thoughtfully.

"You understand that he took a mistress while married to my mother?"

"Don't mistake me. I don't think it was right. But marriages, in our class, are rarely entered into purely out of love. And that is as it should be, for too much is at stake"—he gestured around to indicate Somerton Court and the Averley lands— "for love to be the only consideration. But a marriage without love is a very hard thing to live through. And men are easily tempted."

Ada sighed. Again, she was thinking of Ravi. Would he be tempted to forget her? She could not imagine that he would stay single all his life. There would come a time when she would be forgotten. The thought tore at her heart. Surely she would never forget him.

"In my case, the temptation has already happened," he went on. "I understand that you must be offended by my connection with Miss Templeton, but it is over entirely, the illusion is gone. I now know that I do love you. And in all other respects it would be such a desirable marriage—"

But I do not love you, thought Ada. She was sure of it. He did not make her heart beat as Ravi did. She was not overcome by passion when she was near him. And he was right, a loveless marriage was a prison sentence. And prisoners such as her father did desperate things to survive, things that hurt other people. She could see, in the example of Rose and her mother, how the innocent were hurt when people gave into temptation. Was she strong enough to resist temptation? No, because she had fallen for Ravi. Would she be more likely to resist it when she was Lady Fintan? No. And the result would be—again—the innocent hurt, and the guilty left with remorse for the rest of their lives.

"Lord Fintan, I have thought about your proposal," she began. "It truly is a great honor. I—well, I wish that my answer could have been different. But I must—"

He touched a finger to her lips. Startled by the sudden connection, she fell silent. "Please," he said, gently. "I understand that you are very upset because of what has happened. May I beg you not to speak too hastily? I am more than prepared to wait for an answer."

Ada hesitated. It was true that she was not in complete control of her emotions. It was too soon after breaking with Ravi. And if the choice were between Lord Fintan and a man such as Douglas Varley . . .

"I . . ."

"There is really no need to say more. I understand that your feelings are confused, and that you have many other things to concern you now. It was an unfortunate moment to propose."

She managed a smile. "Yes, sadly."

"I will await your answer," he said. "But for now, I think you would prefer it if I left."

Ada sighed. "I don't wish you to feel driven away, but the household is in such confusion . . ."

"I understand perfectly. I am happy now that I have some hope." He smiled at her and she returned the smile, though not without the niggles of a guilty conscience. Was it fair to let him hope when her heart was still given to Ravi?

There was the sound of a motorcar coming up the drive. Ada turned in surprise and dismay.

"Oh dear, who can that be? We were not expecting visitors . . . oh, goodness, Sebastian!"

Lord Fintan turned back. "Sebastian Templeton?"

"Yes!" Ada put her hands to her face, unsure if she were glad or sorry that Sebastian was here. "What a time to pay a surprise visit. I expect his room is not ready—excuse me, I must give Cooper instructions."

She fled toward the house. As she went into the hall, she saw her father. He was entering the library. With him was a plump, black-clad man who at first she thought was a stranger. A second later she remembered who he was. It was her father's solicitor, Mr. Hobbes.

"But my lord," she heard him saying as they went into the library, "are you entirely sure—"

The closing door cut off the rest of his words and her father's reply.

At any other time Ada might not have paid much attention. But today, with the shocking news still ringing in her ears, she froze. What was her father planning?

But there was no time to wonder what was going on. Cooper was opening the door, and Sebastian, looking as elegant and debonair as ever, was smiling at her.

"Sebastian!" She went toward him, her hand out to greet her stepbrother. Her face was flushed and her smile felt forced. "I'm so sorry. We have had a slight difficulty—the housekeeper was . . . forced to leave for family reasons, and so nothing is in order, not even your room. We'll have it ready as soon as possible, but meanwhile won't you come into the drawing room?"

"Mrs. Cliffe? She left suddenly?" Sebastian raised an eyebrow. "It seems very unlike her."

"Yes . . ." Ada was blushing. Sebastian glanced at her sharply, and said no more. Ada was grateful for his tact.

Lord Fintan followed them into the house. Sebastian stopped dead as he saw him.

"Ah, Sebastian!" Lord Fintan gave him a friendly smile. "How are you? I was sorry not to be able to meet you that evening in London."

Ada wondered what was wrong with Sebastian. He seemed stunned. He shook Lord Fintan's outstretched hand, but she could tell from the tense look on his face that there was something very wrong. Sebastian hid it well, but he had been shocked to his core to see Lord Fintan there.

Oliver went down to the kitchen.

"Hello, what's all this I hear about Mrs. Cliffe leaving?" He greeted James, who was coming toward him down the corridor, carrying a tray of silver cutlery. "Is it some kind of joke?"

James didn't smile as he shouldered open the door of the butler's pantry. "No joking matter."

Oliver, startled, went on to the kitchen. Inside, he saw Cook at the range. Mary was plucking her way through a chicken at the open door, feathers flying, and Martha was flirting with a sulky-looking fellow in an unfamiliar livery, who sat at the table, doodling on a corner of last week's newspaper.

Oliver nodded to the stranger and greeted the others.

273

"Oh, Oliver!" Cook turned from the range, her face hot and flustered. "That means Master Sebastian's here, I suppose. One more room to get ready and one more for dinner." She groaned.

"Sorry, Cook." Oliver got out of the way by sitting down at the table. He decided the news of his resignation was best left until later. The household seemed in enough trouble already.

The strange man startled him by exclaiming: "Sebastian Templeton, here?"

Oliver looked at him with dislike. There was something too familiar in his voice.

"Mr. Templeton to you," he said. "Whoever you are."

The man stared at him and grinned slowly. "Name's Simon. Valet to Lord Fintan."

Oliver held out his hand, but the other ignored it and went on, eyes never breaking contact with Oliver: "And I think Mr. Templeton and I know each other well enough to be on first-name terms."

He shoved back his chair and went from the room. Oliver stared after him openmouthed. "What was that fellow up to?"

"No good, I'm sure." Cook scowled. "Lord Fintan's valet, he hangs around with a face like a week of wet Sundays."

Oliver glanced down at the doodles that the man had been drawing. He froze. The man had been practicing writing his name, Simon Croker, and the handwriting—it was the same as he had seen on the letters that Sebastian had received more than once, the letters that always put him into a dark mood.

Oliver pushed his chair back abruptly.

"Where you off to? You've just got here!" Cook exclaimed.

"I'm going upstairs," Oliver muttered. "I think Master Sebastian may need me."

He hurried up the stairs, and went quickly to Sebastian's room. He broke into a run, caught by a sudden fear, along the corridor. Outside the door he paused, listening.

Through the wood he heard subdued voices. Sebastian speaking quietly; another man's voice getting louder. Simon Croker. "Don't mock me . . . regret it . . ."

Oliver pressed his ear against the door.

"I haven't got it," he heard Sebastian say. "Two thousands pounds? You must be mad, where could I find it from?"

"You stand there in your fine clothes, your motorcar's in the stables and you expect me to believe that?"

"Not a penny of it is my own until I am twenty-five. My mother—"

"I don't care whose it is!"

There were more angry whispers, then: "Get it to me by the time we leave or I tell Lord Westlake everything!"

"You wouldn't dare!"

"Try me."

Oliver had heard enough. He burst through the door of Sebastian's room. The two men were so busy arguing that they did not see him come in.

"I tell you, I can't get it!" Sebastian was shouting.

Simon snarled. "And I tell you, you had better get it!"

"That's enough!" Oliver strode across the room, placing himself between them. "You." He addressed Simon. "If you know what's good for you, you'll get out of here and never come back"

Simon looked at him in astonishment, then in growing realization. To his surprise, Oliver saw tears of fury in his eyes.

"So this is my replacement," he said in a voice full of meaning.

"I'm nothing like you and don't you forget it," Oliver retorted.

"You're an idiot. These toffs are all alike. They'll use you and throw you away. Don't think you're so high and mighty!" Simon's voice rose. Oliver glanced at the door.

"Will you keep your voice down?"

"Like hell I will! I'm going to tell the whole family exactly what kind of a degenerate Sebastian Templeton is."

He flung himself toward the door. Sebastian was quicker. He darted past Oliver.

"No!" He caught Simon's shoulders and shoved him back. Simon, caught off-balance, smashed face-first into the bedpost. He gasped in pain and blood exploded on his lip. He turned a savage white face to Sebastian.

"You want to try me, you bastard?" He swung a punch at Sebastian. Sebastian managed to duck and it caught him a glancing blow. He grabbed for Simon's hands, trying to restrain him. Oliver watched them struggle, terror overwhelming him. Simon could not be allowed to tell. Sebastian would be utterly ruined. His chest tightened at the thought of his handsome, high-spirited master being disowned by his family, turned away at the door of every respectable establishment.

"Look out!" Oliver cried. Sebastian tripped over the open portmanteau and fell heavily against Simon, who staggered backward. There was a crash of breaking glass as the two men toppled. Oliver rushed forward and saw Sebastian grasping for the window frame, pain spreading across his face, as Simon stumbled farther backward. Oliver's and Simon's eyes met for a split second. Simon's expression was shocked. Then he overbalanced and fell through the broken window, toward the conservatory below.

Chapter Thirty-Seven

Ada stood on the front steps of Somerton Court, waiting to bid goodbye to Lord Fintan. There seemed to be some confusion. His car was waiting, but his luggage stood by the side and neither he nor his valet were anywhere to be seen.

She was about to walk down to speak to the chauffeur when the front door opened behind her and Lord Fintan came out with Cooper and James, frowning and looking annoyed. "I can't think what has happened to him," he was saying to Cooper. James began loading the luggage into the motorcar.

"I'm very sorry, sir. If we hear anything we will of course send word at once."

"Yes, do. I haven't found anything missing, but it's very odd."

"Is there something the matter?" Ada asked.

"Yes, rather a bother. We can't find Croker anywhere—that's my valet."

"Oh, how strange," Ada exclaimed. "Does he make a habit of disappearing?"

"Hardly. He's very professional, though you never know when a valet may decide to pocket your cuff links and slip off." He looked around and shrugged. "I don't like to leave without him."

"No indeed. It would be very inconvenient for you." Ada looked around at the gravel drive and the distant lawns, then up at the stone front of the house. It was a big place, Croker could be anywhere.

"A sacking offense, really, and I don't like to do that unless I really must." He checked his pocket watch. "But I have to go. Otherwise I shall miss the train." He took Ada's hand with a warm smile, and opened his mouth as if to bid her farewell. But before he could speak, there was a huge, deafening crash, as if a thousand chandeliers had collapsed all at once.

Ada and Lord Fintan started.

"What on earth was that?" Lord Fintan looked up in astonishment.

"It sounded like the glasshouses . . ." Ada was already hurrying toward the source of the noise, Cooper at her heels. "If this is Georgiana's fault *again* . . ."

But as soon as she rounded the corner of the house, she could see that it was not. The conservatory roof was smashed through, and in the center of the marble floor lay a motionless figure.

Lord Fintan exclaimed sharply, "Croker!"

Oliver hauled Sebastian back from the window.

"Sebastian! Breathe. Sebastian." He was shaking his shoulders. Sebastian took a desperate gasp of air. Oliver pushed him back into the chair and went to the window. He looked out. When he looked back again, he saw his shock mirrored in Sebastian's face.

"He's dead—isn't he?" Sebastian was trembling. Sweat had formed on his upper lip, and he wiped it away with his sleeve.

"Don't see how he can't be," Oliver managed. The sight of Simon's staring eyes and the blood spreading from the back of his head would stay with him forever, he thought.

Sebastian put his head in his hands. "Oh God. What have I done?"

"He was blackmailing you, wasn't he?"

Sebastian nodded. "I've been a cad, Oliver. I swore I'd never trust anyone again, not after he betrayed me. I've treated you badly. Can you forgive me?"

"Of course, you fool," said Oliver. Sebastian took his hand. He was still shaking. Simon felt an overwhelming urge to brush the strand of blond hair from his master's eyes, to hold him until he stopped trembling.

"He threatened to put it in the papers. That was why I kissed Rose. That poor girl! I know it was wrong of me. I have regretted it ever since." He looked up, his face anguished. "I thought you would despise me if you knew the truth."

"There's no fear of that."

Outside along the terrace, there were running footsteps. Someone screamed.

Sebastian half rose, but Oliver pushed him back down. His mind was working fast.

"Don't move. What are we going to tell them?"

"The truth?" Sebastian looked at him, not understanding.

"Impossible, unless you want your secret to come out anyway. No, there's no way. We've got to think of something else." He pressed his fingers to his lips. Outside in the corridor, there were terrified, shocked voices. He looked at Sebastian, his beautiful, beloved friend. He made up his mind. "Stay there," he told Sebastian.

"But—"

"Just do it!"

Oliver ran to the door and down the stairs. He ran to the conservatory and slowed as he saw that a crowd already surrounded it. Lord Westlake was there, and so were many of the servants and family.

James looked toward him as he came along the terrace.

"Oliver! Dear God—Simon's dead—"

"I give myself up," Oliver heard himself say.

"What? What happened?"

"We had a fight. He . . . owed me some money." Oliver could not bring himself to meet James's eye. "I pushed him and he fell. It was my fault. Mr. Templeton tried to part us but it was impossible."

James stared at him. "Oliver . . . You . . . I can't believe it."

Oliver flinched at the tone of his voice. But that note of disapproval was nothing to him. He had lived the worst shame a man could face before, and anything that came now could not be as bad.

"Call the police," he said, in a voice that did not seem to be his own.

Sebastian paced back and forth across his room, gnawing his nails. The silence from downstairs was as terrifying as the earlier commotion had been. He had heard the voices of policemen downstairs, but they had not come up to arrest him. And where was Oliver?

He could bear it no longer. He went to the door and marched out. If he were to be arrested, he would take it bravely. He could not cower like a fox in a hole any longer.

As he reached the bottom of the stairs, he heard strange voices coming from the blue sitting room. He glanced in and at once recognized the uniforms of the local police. They were questioning someone—Oliver! He put a hand on the door, ready to march in and confront them. But a hand closed on his own arm with a tight grip.

He turned round. "Mother!"

"Sebastian." Her face was white. She moved so that she was between him and the doors. "You must leave."

"I can't. You don't understand. I have to explain—"

"You will do nothing of the kind!" she spat. She was not just angry, he realized. She was afraid. She pushed the doors closed and put her back against them.

"But I can't let them accuse Oliver! It was me, I—"

"Be silent!" She was shaking. "I will not allow you to disgrace your family like this. Oliver has confessed. You are safe. Leave it at that."

Horrified, Sebastian moved to the door, but she raised her arms to bar the way.

"You will have to physically strike me to move past," she said. There were tears in her eyes. "My son, don't you think I knew about you and Croker? I did everything I could to hush it up then. I will not allow you to expose your family to disgrace now. It has ended the best way it could."

"You knew?" He was shocked.

"I *am* your mother, Sebastian," she said quietly.

Sebastian felt as if a blow had been struck against his heart. He had never felt close to his mother, and in recent days had come to feel contempt for her. But she loved him. He realized that at this moment. And he could not possibly strike her.

"Mother, I can't let Oliver take the blame, they'll hang him!"

"He knew what he was doing when he confessed."

Sebastian gritted his teeth. "I can't let Oliver take my punishment, Mother. I can't!"

He turned away and broke into a run. He pounded through

the corridors, looking for a way into the room from the other side. Two of the doors he tried were locked. In desperation he burst into the servants' stairs, running past a shocked maid, who flattened herself and her pile of towels against the wall. He ran down the kitchen passage, ignoring the exclamations of Cook, and burst out of the back door. He ran across the cobbles, and round the house to the front. The Black Maria was there, and just as he saw it, it was pulling away.

Sebastian redoubled his pace. He ran to the motorcar. A face inside turned and looked back at him through the rear window. A face that he loved, he now realized.

"Oliver!" he shouted. He grasped the edge of the window. The policeman looked at him in shock.

"Sir, please release the vehicle—"

Sebastian ignored him. He had eyes for nothing but Oliver, his pale, desperate face. "I'll get you out," he gasped. "I'll do it, if it's the last thing I do."

He clutched for Oliver's hand. Oliver was cuffed, but he managed to squeeze his fingers back. Then the vehicle accelerated, and Sebastian was flung aside. He stumbled to a halt, gasping for breath, gazing after the motorcar as it disappeared into the distance.

Chapter Thirty-Eight

It was a fine spring day, and Ada had walked out with Georgiana for their morning's exercise. Birds sang in the hedgerows, and everything was calm and peaceful.

"It seems things are finally back to normal," Georgiana said as they made their way back toward the house.

"Hardly," said Ada. She thought of the defense she was helping Sebastian prepare for Oliver, and the continuing absence of Rose and Mrs. Cliffe.

"No, of course you're right," Georgiana agreed. "Things aren't exactly normal, not without Rose and Mrs. Cliffe, and with that terrible accident. I simply can't believe that Oliver meant to kill him. All I meant is that things seem quiet again."

"Yes, let's hope they stay that way." Ada paused and looked toward the house. Men from the village were working on the conservatory roof, rebuilding it. Soon it would look as if nothing had ever happened. "Perhaps we are just getting used to how things are now."

"I suppose we have no choice," Georgiana said. "But don't you remember walking here the first day we were back from India? How little we guessed what would happen!"

Ada didn't have a chance to reply. Cooper was coming toward them from the terrace, and he looked anxious. She speeded up her pace.

"Excuse me, my ladies. Your father requests your presence in the library," Cooper greeted her.

"Both of us?" Ada exchanged a look with Georgiana. "Oh dear, I wonder what we have done now."

They hurried into the house and along to the library. As they approached, Ada saw Sebastian and Michael coming the other way.

"You were summoned too?" Sebastian asked Ada.

"Yes. What is it about, do you know?"

He shook his head. "The solicitor was here," Michael ventured. "He and Lord Westlake have been shut in the study for ages."

"Might it be something to do with Oliver's case?"

Sebastian looked puzzled. "I should know, if it is."

They opened the door and went in. The first person Ada saw was her stepmother, sitting bolt upright with a sour look on her face. Charlotte stood by her. William and Edith sat on the sofa, William with a glass of wine in his hand and a sulky expression on his face, Edith trying to keep hold of Augustus, who was wriggling out of her grasp. Ada's father stood by at his walnut desk, and the solicitor, pen in hand and spectacles on nose, stood next to him.

Her father cleared his throat. "Are we ready, Mr. Hobbes?" he asked.

"Yes, sir. You simply need to sign here." He indicated the place and offered his pen. Lord Westlake took it and signed. Then he looked up.

"I have an announcement to make," he said. "There is to be a happy event in the family."

There was a puzzled silence. William looked worried. Lord Westlake turned aside. Ada realized there was a figure standing there, in the shadows—a girl.

"Come, dear," he said into the shadows.

The girl stepped forward.

"Rose!" exclaimed Ada in delight.

She looked tired and anxious, and she had lost weight, but she was as pretty as ever. She looked down, blushing as all eyes turned to her.

Fiona jumped to her feet.

"What is the meaning of this?"

"I hope you will understand, Fiona, as a mother yourself," Lord Westlake said gently. "I have thought very hard about my decision, and I am sure I have done the right thing."

"That does not answer my question. What is she doing here?" Fiona drew herself up, furious.

"What Rosaline and I did was wrong," Lord Westlake said in reply. "But Rose is innocent. Rose has done nothing to be ashamed of."

Charlotte made a disbelieving sound.

Lord Westlake ignored her. "I know that what I have done is not orthodox. But I believe it to be the only just, the only honorable thing to do. I have adopted Rose as my daughter."

There was total, shocked silence. Rose hung her head, looking on the brink of tears.

Ada put a hand to the table to steady herself. Adopt Rose! Could he mean it?

"From now on, she will be Lady Rose Averley," Lord Westlake said.

"What?" Charlotte shrieked.

"This is . . . outrageous!" Fiona exploded.

"I do not see why," Lord Westlake retorted. "As I said, Rose has done nothing wrong. And she is my daughter."

"But the girl's a maid—a servant—a vulgar skivvy!" Charlotte's voice rose higher with every word.

285

"She's no such thing!" Georgiana rounded on Charlotte, who looked as astonished as if a goldfish had barked. "She's always acted like a perfect lady. We've always said so." She turned to Rose. "I'm glad you're my sister, Rose," she said impetuously. "But I hope you will still do my hair, just in a sisterly way, I mean. No one else gets it as nice as you do."

Rose, who looked on the brink of tears, managed a laugh.

"This is a disgrace. I shall contact my solicitors!" Fiona's voice rose to a screech. She turned on Sebastian. "Do you, my son, intend to stand there and let this go unchallenged?"

Sebastian looked nervous. "Mother, I don't really see what I can do about it—"

"Oh, you are useless!" Fiona spat. She leaped up from her chair and slammed out of the door. Charlotte hurried after her.

"I didn't mean to cause trouble," Rose managed. "Please believe me, this was Lord Westlake's idea, not mine."

Her frightened voice jerked Ada out of her shock. At once she knew exactly what she had to do. She crossed the room and took Rose's hands. "Welcome to the family," she said, with a smile of happiness that she felt from the bottom of her heart.

Ada woke early, just as the dawn light was filtering in though the shutters of Milborough House. She lay there sleepily, remembering this day was important but at first not recollecting why. Then her heart gave a huge thump as it occurred to her. Today was the day she, Rose, and Charlotte were to be presented to the sovereign. Today, she was officially coming out.

She hastily got up and opened her wardrobe. Her court dress still took her breath away with its beauty. The ivory crepe de chine was smooth and light, folded into deep, rich pleats like the petals of a rose. The net train was sprinkled with pink silk rose petals and diamond dewdrops. Her mother's pearls were all that she would wear as jewelry.

Ada turned to the dressing table and opened her jewel case. Among the pearls lay some small, folded notes, fragile from having been read over and over again. As she gazed at the pearls and strung them through her fingers, her thoughts were far away. She was remembering another time she had worn those pearls, and the boy who had kissed her. Where was Ravi now? Was he happy? Did he ever think of her? Or had he already forgotten?

There was a knock at the door.

"May I come in, my lady?" Rose's nervous face peered around the door.

"Of course you may, *my lady*," Ada said laughingly. "And you really must learn to call me Ada."

Rose laughed too, and looked embarrassed. She scurried in on bare feet.

"Have you no slippers?" Ada asked. "You must be cold."

"I do, only I keep forgetting." Rose sighed.

"You don't seem happy." Ada looked at her in concern. She so wanted today to be perfect for Rose.

"Oh no! Of course I am. How could I not be, after Lord Westlake's generosity?"

"You don't have to pretend to me, Rose," said Ada. "You and I have always had an understanding, I think."

"It's just that . . . it's so strange. I didn't realize. I didn't think it would be easy, but I didn't know it would be this difficult, either." Rose's voice trembled.

"If you mean mastering the etiquette, I don't think you have anything to worry about on that score. You are doing very well."

"It isn't really that. I learned a lot when I was a maid, from watching how others did it. No, it's more that I feel so lost. So out of place. I don't know how to fill my days, now. It is a joy to be able to play the piano whenever I wish, but—but—I am used to working, and now I can't." She hung her head. "I miss my mother. And I miss the servants' hall. I know I shouldn't. Perhaps it is vulgar of me. But I used to have friends, my lady . . . Ada, and now all my friends are my servants. I can't talk to Annie as I used to. They all look on me differently now. And after today, when our season begins, there will be even more of a gap between us."

"Oh, poor Rose!" Ada put a hand on her sister's arm. She realized how lonely she must be. "I have been so insensitive. Of course you feel like this."

Rose managed a smile. "I shouldn't be so ungrateful."

"It isn't ungrateful, it is simply natural." She pressed Rose's hand warmly. "But Georgiana and I will continue to do everything we can to make you feel truly one of the family. Time will do the rest."

"You are kind," Rose said. She looked searchingly into Ada's eyes. "I feel I can ask you this, now that we are sisters. Have you heard nothing from Mr. Sundaresan?"

Ada swallowed. "No. I do not expect to. We parted the best of friends, but it is all over." She thought of their last kiss, and hesitated.

"You don't seem certain."

Ada glanced around to be sure no one was watching. "I'm frightened, Rose," she said under her breath. "I believe that Charlotte saw us together, that last time at the station. I fear she may have seen us . . . kiss."

Rose drew in her breath. Ada knew that she realized the

severity of the danger. "But surely she would have said something."

"I can't be sure. Charlotte is capable of a lot. She may have seen nothing, of course. But if she has . . ."

"Try not to worry," Rose replied. "Charlotte does not want scandal to touch your family either. It would compromise her own prospects."

"I hope you're right."

Their voices had dropped low. The gentle knock at the door startled both of them.

"Come in!" Ada cried.

The door opened, and the startled French maid looked in.

"Oh—my lady, I did not realize you were already awake. I am sorry. I must be late—"

"Not at all. We are early." Ada smiled at her.

"I must go back, or my own maid will think I have run away." Rose got up and went to the door. Ada smiled her goodbye.

"Nervous, mademoiselle?" The French maid smiled sympathetically as she pressed waves into Rose's thick dark hair.

"Horribly." Rose managed a smile. She could hardly restrain herself from helping the maid as she pinned her hair up, hardly stop herself from protesting: "I can do it myself!" It was so hard to learn to be a lady. There was so much one had to forget: how to light a fire, how to dress oneself . . .

"I am sure you will be a great success," the maid went on. "Your dress is so beautiful, the Brussels lace is most simple and elegant."

If only my mother were here to see it, Rose thought, and tears came to her eyes. But her mother would be proud of her whatever happened, she knew.

She stood and allowed her maid to sew her into her

corset. She breathed in deeply and obediently, the bones pressing her into shape. Then the petticoats were skillfully arranged.

From outside, she heard the strains of a barrel organ. Her maid frowned.

"Excuse me, my lady, I will shut the window against that vulgar noise."

"Oh no, Céline—leave it." As simple as the tune was, Rose clung to it. Music was a good omen. Perhaps one day her real dream could come true, to be a composer. But for now it seemed the demands of society were the most pressing. First she had to become a lady.

She looked in awe at the dress that her maid was carefully holding up for her to step into. It was white satin, with a lace-and-chiffon bodice and a train decorated with tulle and pearls so it looked like a cloud dusted with glittering raindrops. She had never seen anything so beautiful; it was still hard to believe that she was actually going to wear it.

The dress slipped over her shoulders and the train spread out behind her. Rose looked at herself in the mirror and could not avoid a gasp of simple admiration.

"Mademoiselle, you look like a princess," said Céline with a pleased smile. "What jewels will you wear?"

Rose thought hard. Lord Westlake had bought her a simple string of pearls. It was all a debutante was expected to wear. But even that seemed like too much. It didn't feel like her. Instead, she reached for the bouquet of white and pink roses that had been sent from Somerton. She plucked a single one and held it up to her hair. The shining petals reflected light onto her face and neck. It reminded her of Somerton—of her mother.

"Is this acceptable?" She glanced up anxiously at her maid.

Céline smiled. "*Bien sûr, mademoiselle*. That will be perfect."

Lord Westlake's face was fixed in a thoughtful frown as he studied the newspaper that lay on the hall table. But he smiled as he saw Rose and Ada coming down the staircase. The morning light shone through the stained glass and cast shimmering colors over their white dresses.

"My dears, you look wonderful," he said, as they reached him.

Ada smiled, and Rose blushed.

"Oh, look at all these flowers!" Ada exclaimed a moment later. The hall was crowded with bouquets from admirers and friends. Roses, carnations, and lilies filled the room with their scent and color. "So beautiful!"

Rose went eagerly to look at the flowers. Ada was about to follow, but her father held her back.

"Is everything all right, Papa?" she asked. "You look troubled."

"Oh, no—I mean, yes, everything is fine." He glanced at the newspaper again. "I'm a little concerned by events in Europe—nothing you need bother yourself over. But I . . . would like you to step into the study for a moment. There is someone there who would like to speak to you."

"Of course." Ada was surprised, but she went to the study door and pushed it open. Closing it behind her, her eyes took a moment to adjust to the light. A familiar face smiled at her.

"Lord Fintan!"

"Ada." He gazed at her in admiration "You look exquisite."

Ada blushed and curtsied.

He went on, "I hope you will forgive an old friend visiting you at such a time, but I wanted to remind you of a conversation we had not so long ago."

"Of course," said Ada slowly. It was not something she wanted to think about at once.

"I have spoken to your father. I hope you don't mind."

"It's quite proper," said Ada. But she could not help feeling that she disliked being discussed behind her back, as if she were property to be disposed of.

Lord Fintan cleared his throat. "I understand from my sister that you want to go to Oxford, and that this has put you off the idea of marriage."

Ada nodded. It was half the truth, at least.

"I told your father, therefore, that I would expect my wife to be educated. He agreed. He will let you go to Oxford if you become engaged to me."

Ada stared at him in silence.

"It is not something to be answered immediately," Lord Fintan said hastily. "But it is something I wished you to be aware of—before the start of the season."

"This is extraordinarily generous of you," Ada said, stumbling over the words.

"Nonsense. Our views on women's education have always coincided. In fact, I believe our views on every subject have always coincided—which is one reason I believe we would be well matched."

Well matched, thought Ada—but is that enough? She thought of Ravi. The memory of him was like a dagger to her heart.

"It will take some time to come to a decision—" she began.

"Of course," Lord Fintan replied at once. "I will wait as long as you wish."

He raised his hand, and she saw for the first time that he carried a small bouquet of roses and carnations. "I hope you will do me the honor of carrying these with you today."

"They're beautiful," said Ada sincerely. She took the flowers, thinking that, after all, she would have liked to choose her own blooms. But she could not refuse the gesture without offending him. She took a couple of the sprays and fixed them into her dress, smiling at him.

"The perfect touch," he said, and bowed over her hand. "I wish you a delightful presentation, and I will hope to have the pleasure of dancing with you at the state ball."

Ada smiled her farewell. Deep in thought, she walked into the hall. The flowers, massed by the stairs, overwhelmed her with their scent. She went to them, reading the cards that had come with them, her mind far away.

"Ada, are you ready?" Rose came toward her, flustered. "Mrs. Verulam is here and it is time to go."

Ada started and put down the cards. "Quite ready," she said, and followed Rose out of the door to the waiting carriages and motorcars.

As she followed Charlotte and Rose into Mrs. Verulam's carriage, a footman hurried breathlessly up to them.

"Special delivery, my lady. It came just now." He handed her a small, white box.

"For me?" Ada was surprised. She opened the box, and a rich, delicious scent was released, a scent which made her head spin with memories of India. Inside lay a small bouquet of white flowers, their blooms shaped like strange, exotic sculptures.

"How lovely," Mrs. Verulam said, leaning forward to see. "I think they are Indian orchids. Who sent them?"

"I don't know," said Ada, blushing as she caught Rose's eye. "There was no card."

And yet she knew. It was Ravi. It had to be. Ignoring Charlotte's cold stare, she pulled out Lord Fintan's flowers, and tucked the spray of orchids into her dress. These were the flowers she would wear, and no others.

The Court was hushed, and the queue of young girls waiting to make their curtsy waited nervously on the threshold as one by one they were called forward into the royal presence.

"Lady Ada Averley!" announced the footman. Their Majesties smiled graciously as the young woman walked toward them, her eyes cast down, and sank into a deep, unwavering curtsy.

Charlotte watched from the queue. Her mind was not on the ceremony. It had been ruined for her anyway. She was a laughing stock among her friends, having to make her curtsy alongside a housemaid. And almost worse than that, the news was out about Lord Fintan and Ada. One stepsister a common drudge, the other a shameless poacher.

"Lady Rose Averley!"

Charlotte pressed her lips together so that they were even whiter than her pearls, which had a faint but brazen pink blush. Rose looked nervous, but to Charlotte's great disappointment she did not trip. Her curtsy was a model of grace and elegance.

"Miss Charlotte Templeton!"

Oh, but she would have her revenge, Charlotte thought, as she glided forward and sank into a deep curtsy, her white satin skirts rustling on the blood-red carpet. She had seen Ada compromise herself with that filthy Indian boy. And she would pick her time to use that knowledge as a man forced to fight for his life would pick a weapon: very, very carefully.

Don't miss the next thrilling instalment
of the AT SOMERTON saga –

DIAMONDS & DECEIT

Coming early 2014

Leila Rasheed

Leila Rasheed was brought up in Libya and moved to England when she was thirteen. She has worked as a children's bookseller for Waterstone's in Brussels and for a national children's literacy charity, but now writes and teaches creative writing full time. She has two Masters degrees, one in children's literature and one in writing.

She currently lives in Birmingham with her husband, who is a Danish composer, and their baby son. She loves reading about history and archaeology and would like to be reincarnated as Indiana Jones.

SECRETS & SAPPHIRES is Leila's first novel for young adults.

Find out more about Leila at:

www.leilarasheed.com

Twitter @LeilaR

www.hotkeybooks.com